GOOD TIME CHARLIE

A Mafia Soldier's Story

CHARLES A. COZZUPOLI

DEDICATION

This book is dedicated to my wife Roseann. She has stuck by me for over forty years through thick and thin. In many ways, she has saved my life. She and she alone helped to make me a better person, better father, and now grandfather! I would also like to thank her for her involvement in the writing of my novel. Then…now…forever…I love you.

ACKNOWLEDGMENTS

A special thanks to Mark and Tracey along with Patrick and Rae for their support and believing in me and my first novel.

PROLOGUE

Keep your friends close, but your enemies closer.

--Michael Corleone

As Charlie lay in his raggedy bed in the disheveled hotel room he has been staying in for the past few months, he tried to make some sense of and get a grip on some reality that might be left in what to this point was a pathetic existence. He lay motionless and reflected while staring into space in between taking notice of his pitiful surroundings. The hotel room was now a filthy, cramped one-room with dingy filmed windows and walls of peeling paint, making Charlie wonder when the walls had last seen fresh paint. He thought the room fit in well since this hotel was located in a section of the Bronx where even bums wouldn't flock to live. That's how bad the neighborhood was. The hotel was so rundown that, even if it were condemned, no one would want it because of its unsavory location. Charlie looked at all the mismatched furniture as he pulled up his filthy stained sheets and blankets after feeling a slight chill from a brisk wind coming in through one of the broken windows. He turned to his side and looked at the dirty torn up carpet and watched as a spider began to crawl up the wall.

Charlie began to slip into deep thought searching his mind to find a reason to get out of bed, trying desperately to motivate himself and get himself back into the real world outside his door. In his efforts to do so, his body and heart were unable to respond, feeling all used up he felt unable to go on.

At forty-eight years of age, Charlie's lifestyle has taken its toll and it showed in his face, which was drained. The fast-paced life Charlie was accustomed to made him act and look older than his years. It had once taken him to the top, the pinnacle of what he always dreamed of, only to wind up alone in this hotel room, a place he wouldn't even have his pets stay in. What was the reason? Where did it go wrong? Why did it go bad? These were Charlie's thoughts as he looked for the answers. He thought that all he needed was that one break, that one score to get him out of his slump and get him going again and he wanted to start over someplace else, someplace far away from the environment that had consumed his energy for the past 28 years. Twenty-eight years chasing that elusive lifestyle for himself and to become his own person.

Charlie shifted in his squeaky bed and his attention was drawn to the old black and white television in his room, which he had left on. The news started and he half-heartedly paid attention to what was being said on the newscast as the picture flickered a bit. He thought about getting up to move around the bent antenna to get better reception, but he decided to live with the inconvenience of the antique TV set which probably had been in the hotel since the sixties. As the newscast went to commercial, first announcing the upcoming lotto drawing, Charlie's attention was drawn to a lotto ticket taped to the TV. Charlie was a habitual gambler among his other vices and liked the action, but was never one for taking chances on things he didn't have some control over, or so he thought.

Charlie reached over to one of the scratched and badly chipped nightstands and grabbed his cheap bottle of vodka. It wasn't the real good Finlandia vodka that he was used too, but for the time being this one served its purpose. Charlie opened the bottle and took a quick slug of the already half empty bottle. After a few more swallows, Charlie put the now one third full bottle of cheap vodka back on the night table and turned around facing the other night table where his .45 automatic pistol lay within reach.

Charlie reached and picked up the phone receiver that he had left on the bed and began to dial the old style telephone. The ringing began on the other end, as he stared at his gun on the night table. An answering machine on the other end clicked on, so he just hung up. He checked his wristwatch.

Charlie is seemingly at the end of his rope. The walls are closing in on him and he doesn't know if he can keep on going with the way his life is. For as long as he can remember now, the good times seem so far away and he just lies there thinking of how he can get back to those times, but Charlie is unable to move as his mind wanders and he dreams of yesterdays when he was a somebody!

CHAPTER 1

Harlem, 1951

It's a cold snowy March early morning. A woman named Mora is about to go into labor as she awaits her husband's return, a man named Sal, who could care less about any mundane home sweet home life as well as being there in her time of need. They live in a seedy apartment in a dilapidated neighborhood of Harlem. Mora is scared and alone as she feels the pains come upon her, so she reaches for the phone.

Mora is a petite woman, frail looking, sickly and her living conditions of the past three years haven't enhanced her health by any means. Sal is a local, small time wiseguy in the neighborhood who's trying to be somebody he is not and has always dreamed of becoming a big time wise guy in the ghetto. Mora weakly dials and waits until she hears a ring on the other end.

Sal is sitting at the edge of the bar eyeing a sexy blonde who is sitting at the other end of the bar. He is a good-looking man, five feet ten inches tall, and a muscular hundred and eighty-five pounds, with dark hair. He is trying to be an Al Capone type, but he's a little fish in a big pond. He talks like he's the Man, taking action on the horses and numbers while telling anyone who listens he's the number one man in

Harlem. Sal should watch his mouth though, because the real wise guy in Harlem, Tony (The Hammer) Squateri, might catch on to Sal's cutting in on his action. The bar phone continues ringing and the bartender finally answers it. After hearing Mora's request to speak to her husband, he covers the receiver and calls out to Sal. Sal, knowing its Mora, just shakes his head no as he speaks, "Tell her that I was here but left and that I said I'll return in a few hours." He then continues to try to impress the blonde bimbo with a few drinks at the bar as the bartender relays Sal's message to Mora and hangs up.

Mora hangs up the phone and just sits there looking at the door hoping Sal will walk in. She knows this is the day she will give birth to their first child. Hours go by and still no Sal as Mora feels more labor pain. She is in awful pain as she calls for a cab to take her to the hospital and, as quickly as her condition would allow, she packs a small bag and walks down four flights of steps to get to the cab waiting outside. She instructs the driver to take her to Saint Luke's Hospital as quickly as possible as her pains are coming closer together.

Twenty minutes later, Mora is being admitted to Saint Luke's where she is fielding a few questions from the nurse about her husband's insurance carrier among other questions she answers, through all her discomfort.

Back at the bar, Sal, now drunk, is trying to pick up a sexy redhead next to him who is also inebriated. Her name is Gloria and a new face at the bar. Gloria is a real looker, standing five feet-seven inches tall in heels with a voluptuous body, big breasts, a nice round rear, and a pretty face. She had it all, Sal thought as he stared at her and her cleavage. When she got up and walked over to the jukebox to play another tune, Sal was thinking about how much he wanted to fuck her. They began a conversation and Sal learned she had a very jealous and mean boyfriend, which Sal shrugged off because he was the Man and he let her know who he was and told her not to worry about it. Sal let her also know that this was his neighborhood and he wasn't scared of anyone, especially in his own domain where he was the boss.

Back at Saint Luke's, Mora is crying in her hospital room in the women's ward. It's been a few hours since she has arrived and she's having trouble with the delivery. With the lack of medical insurance, Sal warned her that the hospital would put her at the bottom of the list of important patients. The doctor finally shows up to tend to Mora, after finishing with his more important patients, only to discover that Mora has to be rushed into the delivery room.

At the bar, Sal was about to give up on Gloria and head home to Mora. But as Sal was readying himself to leave, Gloria uttered to him, "Okay Mr. Big Shot, we can go to my place."

With that invitation, they were out the door where Sal hails a cab for them. Once inside the cab, Gloria drunkenly barks out the address to the driver, "Eighty-first and Broadway," to which Sal looks at her.

"Nice fuckin' neighborhood," Sal said and then asked in his drunken wise-guy manner, "Why so far from home?"

"It's my boyfriend. He knows the bars to look for me there," Gloria replied. "And with a Big Shot like you Sal, I have nothing to worry about and you're bigger and younger than he is," Gloria added.

"You bet your sweet ass," Sal stated, running his hands over her body and up her skirt as they kissed and became a little friendlier. The cab pulled up to Gloria's building as Sal threw the driver the fare money and a nice tip, playing the Big Shot in front of Gloria. After they exited the cab, Sal followed Gloria into the building where Sal also tipped her doorman upon entering, making a point to tell the doorman his name thinking that he might know who he was. Sal and Gloria then step into the elevator where Gloria presses her floor number six. After the elevator door closes, they engage in a heated kiss, Sal grabbing her round ass. He pulls back and says, "You're going to get fucked real good tonight."

Meanwhile, after the elevator door closed, the doorman walked over to the phone in the hallway and made a call. The doorman is silent a moment and then speaks, "Hi sir, it's me, the doorman Eddie. She's home, but not alone." The doorman pauses a moment and speaks again, "Sal, his name is Sal, sir."

At Saint Luke's, Mora is in immeasurable pain and in trouble as the front desk nurse is trying to reach her husband by phone, but Sal is not home. The doctor was consoling Mora, saying not to worry as he administered an anesthetic to put her under so she would not experience any more pain. Once Mora went under, the doctor knew he had to get the baby out as soon as possible or the baby's life would be in danger.

It was four in the morning and Sal and Gloria were in bed kissing each other, but they were so drunk they were more close to passing out. Sal in his stupor never took notice of the picture of Gloria's boyfriend on the dresser or remembers that Mora might be close to having the baby this morning. As Sal and Gloria's kisses subsided, giving into their condition, they resolved themselves to screwing each other the following morning and just lay there.

All of a sudden the bedroom door flew open and in walks two tall and muscular men, each weighing over two hundred and forty pounds to the surprised look of Sal and Gloria. As they sit up in bed, another though older stocky man walks in, a five-eight, two hundred pound gorilla named Tony (The Hammer) Squateri, Gloria's boyfriend. Tony has a look on him that could kill and Sal, even in his wasted state, immediately recognizes who he is. Sal was going to speak, but nothing came out as Gloria spoke first.

"Hi baby! I guess I don't have to introduce you to big Sal here, your boss up in Harlem," she said coyly with a smile and thinking she had nothing to worry about.

Tony was furious, but he calmly walked over to Gloria and backhanded her square in the face, immediately drawing blood from her nose and mouth. "THROW HER IN THE SHOWER!" Tony commanded one of his men. After one of his men took a shaken and weeping Gloria to the bathroom, Tony approached Sal and spoke in a lower but more threatening tone of voice, "So, you're the big shot with the big mouth, taking book and other action at that bar in Harlem on 125th Street." Tony looked at him and Sal doesn't respond. Tony continued, "You say you're too big to pay me respect or anyone else. Well, you're wrong, asshole," Tony stated and then instructed his other man to take Sal to the roof so they could talk some more.

At Saint Luke's in the delivery room, Mora's doctor is working hard to save her baby who is coming out with the cord around his neck and the nurse also notices that Mora's breathing has become irregular. The doctor is finally successful in his attempt to free the baby of the cord and slaps him on his ass after freeing him. The baby boy cries out. The doctor unfortunately could not save Mora who died moments before the baby was born. The doctor looked at the nurse with a sad look on his face.

"You did what you could doctor," the nurse said and also informing him that they are still trying to reach the father.

Tony was on the roof with Sal as Tony's two men are holding Sal.

Sal is begging Tony, "Please Tony, maybe we can work out some sort of deal! Tony, please! My wife is going to have a baby soon!" Sal stated, looking at Tony.

"That's not my problem. I didn't fuck your wife," Tony said with a cold stare and then stating, "You have to learn respect." With that, Tony speaks while motioning to his two men with his thumb pointing over the roof, "Let's see if the big shot can fly."

Sal began struggling with the two big goons, but they were too strong for him. Sal again begging Tony, "Please Tony! NO! DON'T DO THIS!" Sal yelled, trying to escape the claws of his two men with Tony in true wise guy fashion, answering his plea.

"Hey big shot, look at it this way, you're finally going to be that big hit on Broadway you always bragged about!" Tony laughingly mocked Sal as his two men heaved Sal off the roof with Sal's screams heard until his body hits the pavement. Tony goes over to the edge of the roof and looks down. Tony observes Sal's dead body below and laughs and he then looks at his watch and looks at his two henchman. "I'm in the mood for some scrambled eggs. Let's go," Tony The Hammer said.

Back at Saint Luke's Hospital, the newborn baby boy is being attended to by a nurse, not knowing that within a span of ten minutes he had just lost his mother and father. And so it was that the baby to be known as Charles Anthony Luzzi, and Good Time Charlie was born.

CHAPTER 2

It was a cold January day in 1958 at St. Patrick's Orphanage in Harlem. Sister Teresa is looking for Charlie Luzzi, an eight-year-old terror of the orphanage. Charlie is a big boy and also mentally advanced for his age. He is wild in his ways, not willing to go along with the other boys as shown by the way he behaves and acts. Sister Teresa is the only one who has a special interest in Charlie and the only one who cares for his welfare ever since he arrived at the orphanage at six weeks old. She knew the whole story about Charlie—parents lost to him on the day he was born and no other relatives would claim him, so she was Charlie's mother and father throughout his early life. Charlie's boyish looks and charm coupled with his big brown eyes always seemed to win over Sister Teresa, no matter what he did wrong. With the other nuns, however, Charlie didn't have it as easy, especially with the Mother Superior who was a large woman with a hand that felt like iron. When she slapped you across the face with that steel mitt of hers, you knew it was something you didn't want to experience twice. She was the one who administered the discipline and punishment for all the problem boys. Charlie was one of her regular offenders.

Charlie had gone to several foster homes but always wound up back at St. Patrick's. Charlie didn't have much luck with foster homes; one couple that took him in treated him badly. The husband was a drunk and beat him often. One time, the husband came back home drunk and tried to hit Charlie. Charlie took a chair and smashed it against his head, causing him to get twenty stitches in his face. In another home, Charlie ran away three times saying that the people there didn't feed him enough and they only wanted him in order to work him in their store fourteen hours a day seven days a week.

Charlie was a tough kid at eight years old, the toughest in the orphanage even standing up to the twelve year olds. Charlie wasn't scared to take on anyone older than him. As tough as he was, however, Charlie wouldn't look to instigate any fights, just finish them and, once provoked, he could go crazy and do serious damage to anyone trying to fuck with him. This is also why Charlie was pretty much a loner and an outcast at the orphanage. His temper was what upset Sister Teresa the most and she tried very hard to work with him to control his anger and possibly lose it, but it was a tough order when Charlie was hurt and mad.

While all the boys at the orphanage would go into the yard and play ball, Charlie would go around the corner to some of the local bars and stores and shine shoes. Charlie would also run errands for anyone who wanted him to and do just about anything else to make a buck. Charlie was saving his money saying how one day he was going to leave the orphanage and be somebody special. He couldn't wait to become a man of respect, something like the wise guys he observed in the neighborhood and for whom he shined their shoes. Charlie would be a man of power and someone people would look up to.

On Saturdays, Charlie would be up at the break of dawn, go out and do his business and sometimes wouldn't return to the orphanage until late, which would drive the nuns nuts because they would have to go and find him and bring him back. Charlie would make ten or twelve dollars for the day and that was a pretty good day's pay for an 8- year old. For Charlie, though, it was just a start because when he got older he would be making the big bucks.

One Saturday, Charlie was shining shoes in a bar called the Top Hat on 125th Street off Broadway, not far from the orphanage in Harlem. It was a black bar where he would get a lot of business on Saturday morning. Charlie began buffing a pair of shoes for a pimp named Leon, a mean man. Leon had purposely let Charlie shine his shoes so he could make fun of a white boy on his knees shining a black man's shoes.

When Charlie was almost done, his buffing rag hit Leon's sock by accident smearing some polish on it. Leon got all pissed off screaming at Charlie calling him a dumb white fuck and he kicked Charlie in the mouth knocking him to the floor. As Charlie got up off the floor his mouth was bleeding. Leon then got off the bar stool ready to say or do something more to Charlie when all of a sudden a huge black man with red hair smacked Leon across his face saying, "Sit the fuck back down!" and Leon did just that, muttering.

The huge black man continued to say, "Nigger, leave the young brother alone. He's only trying to hustle a couple of bucks. He's not hurting anybody and he gives a real good shine." The huge redheaded black man then turned to Charlie and asked him if he was all right with Charlie nodding his head yes. The huge black man, whose name was Big Red, then apologized for the way Leon mistreated him and promised him no one would fuck with him again or they would have to answer to him. Big Red looked at Charlie and asked him, "How about a shine, son?"

Charlie shined Big Red's shoes and when he was done he said to Big Red, "No charge, sir."

To which Big Red replied, "Son, you do a good job, now you take this." Big Red handed Charlie a twenty dollar bill. "Now, you go home little brother and put some ice on that lip. It's getting late," Red suggested, sounding like a friend.

Charlie smiled and thanked Big Red and thought to himself as he left that things didn't turn out too bad. He wouldn't mind getting kicked every time if he could score a twenty spot every time. He would clean up making that kind of money. Charlie touched his lip to feel it hurting and swollen.

As Charlie stood outside, Big Red came out and passed by. Charlie became a little curious and asked the man next to him who the man with the red hair was. The man told him his name was Big Red, telling Charlie that he was a big man in Harlem, the real deal.

Charlie thought to himself as he started walking back to the orphanage that someday he would be a big man too and that he would pay Big Red for looking out for him this day. As Charlie turned the corner to go back to St. Patrick's orphanage, he said to himself, "Someday," and repeated, "Someday."

CHAPTER 3

The next few years, Charlie continued to shine shoes and run all sorts of errands to make money and he also kept getting into trouble at the orphanage for being out late or not attending Mass and not doing his chores. To cover himself, Charlie had hired some of the St. Patrick's boys to do his work at the orphanage and he paid them off with candy and dirty books. He received a lesson along with the strap from the Mother Superior for these actions plus punishment for lending money to some boys and charging them interest, which he learned on the streets of Harlem. Sister Teresa was always talking to Charlie trying to get him to straighten out and walk with God, as she would tell him. Charlie would tell her that he never ran into God when he was out walking around and that God must be walking too slowly 'cause he kept missing him. Sister Teresa would only say to him, "I'll pray for you, my child. I will pray a lot for you Charlie, because you are my boy."

At twelve years old, Charlie was very big for his age. He filled out like his father although he didn't know that because he never knew him.

A man named Anthony Fusco who said he was Charlie's Uncle came to the orphanage one day to claim him and take him home with him. Being Charlie's Uncle on his mother's side he had the right to claim him but Sister Teresa asked Mr. Fusco, "Why didn't you come sooner for Charlie, if you knew he was at the orphanage all this time, for twelve years?" Mr. Fusco replied, "It wasn't that we didn't want to, but a lot of years my wife was sick and unable to care for anyone, especially a baby at that time." Mr. Fusco went on and gave various explanations for the twelve years and said it was different now, and they wanted the twelve-year-old Charlie. Mother Superior got involved and said that Charlie should be with family, but all Mother Superior thought about is how much nicer it would be to not have Charlie around and that it was a blessing.

Charlie then said his goodbyes to the boys at the orphanage and the nuns. He only shed some tears with Sister Teresa in a private moment: "I love you, sister. I'll miss you always." Charlie blurted out to her.

Sister Teresa grabbed him by the shoulders and told him, "You come visit me you hear?" She went on, "You be a good boy, mister. I know people and I'll have them watching you so don't disappoint me, my son." Charlie and Sister Teresa hugged each other with Sister Teresa repeating, "Make me proud…make me proud."

A little later, Charlie left with his Uncle Anthony and arrived at his new home, where Aunt Carmella, Anthony's wife, was waiting. They lived in a modest apartment on West 106th Street and Amsterdam Avenue in Harlem just over a mile from the orphanage. Charlie felt happy; he wasn't too far away from the action he has known for the past few years and his uncle and aunt owned a small fruit and grocery store.

As Charlie entered the apartment, Carmella took a long look at him and remarked, "He looks just like that son of a bitch Sal," and immediately Charlie knew she was referring to his father and that he thought he was in trouble just for looking like him as Carmella went on, "look at the size of him! He's gonna eat us out of house and home." Charlie thinks to himself as he looks at his portly aunt and uncle that they must be doing a pretty good job of eating themselves. Charlie was also thinking about the days in the orphanage and the times he prayed to have a family and how bad his luck was that he would wind up with people like these two fat bastards.

In the next few months, Charlie woke up at six and helped his Uncle in the store until he had to go to school. After school he went back to the store and worked until seven at night. Then he would have dinner with his uncle and aunt, who it turned out, was a hell of a cook. Then, after dinner Charlie would sweep the store. Saturdays and Sundays, Charlie only worked in the store until noon. Then the rest of those days he had time to himself to do as he pleased. So Charlie would hike up to his old haunts and shine shoes and run errands to make extra money. Charlie built up a good following after working in this area for so long. When other boys tried to work his spots, Big Red would send them away, because he liked Charlie and the way he handled himself.

One Saturday, around six in the evening, Charlie was outside the Top Hat ready to call it quits. As he started back home, Charlie saw a man running as two men in suits chased him. Charlie knew that the man worked for Big Red, known to Charlie also as a bookmaker and loan shark, and the two men he recognized as plain-clothes cops. When the man turned into the alley way, he tossed a bag into a dumpster and kept on running with the two cops in pursuit. After a few minutes, Charlie looked down the alley and saw nothing so he went over and grabbed the bag the running man threw into the dumpster. Charlie took another look around and saw no one and ran off a few blocks to the river where he looked inside the bag. He removed some of the contents which consisted of slips with numbers on it, about five hundred dollars in cash and a .32 automatic pistol which Charlie handled a few moments, feeling a short rush of power. He liked the feeling. Charlie couldn't believe his luck: being in the right place at the right time, he made a nice little score for himself. Charlie thought about his situation a moment and thought about Big Red and he knew that this money was connected to him in some way. Charlie was unsure what to do with the cash. If he turned it in to the police, he knew they would ask him where he got it and keep it. Then Charlie went back to his initial thought to keep it.

A little later, Charlie checked the Top Hat bar and a few other places looking for Big Red. Not finding him there, he entered another bar called the Night Owl. He finally found Big Red sitting with a couple of sexy black women wearing low-cut dresses displaying their big breasts. Charlie walked over and approached Big Red who greeted him: "Hello there my little white brother! What brings you around here this late? Working overtime?"

"I have some important business to discuss with you in private," Charlie boldly answered and some of the patrons laughed at Charlie's boldness and serious tone and look on his face.

"CHILL!" Big Red said to the patrons who immediately went silent, "the little white brother is with me." Big Red stared at Charlie saying, "Come with me little brother."

Big Red walked to a private backroom of the Night Owl Bar with Charlie following, which made Charlie feel important. Once in the private room, Big Red sat Charlie down saying, "So, what's so important that you need to speak to me in private, little brother?" Charlie started by pulling the gun out of his pocket and Big Red was startled for a moment and reflexively froze until Charlie started speaking.

"One of your men dropped this." Charlie then went on and told Big Red the whole story. Big Red was surprised and impressed with Charlie's actions.

"How come you didn't keep the cash for yourself?" Big Red asked Charlie.

"Because you are a man of respect and an honorable man in the neighborhood and because I never forgot what you did for me that time with that pimp Leon," Charlie answered. Big Red just shook his head admiring Charlie's chutzpah.

"My little brother, you are a bigger man than a lot of men I know and anytime you want a job, when you're ready that is, you can have one with me. I need good men like you," Big Red told him.

Charlie took it all in and thought that this day he made a very valuable friend and connection for his future plans of being a big man one day himself, maybe even bigger than Big Red. Big Red handed Charlie fifty dollars for his honesty and then shook his hand. Charlie left the Night Owl Bar feeling ten feet tall and he liked the feeling even more than handling the gun in his hand.

Life went on for Charlie after returning the cash to Big Red. Charlie continued to live a mundane existence with his aunt and uncle who treated him no better than just a worker in their store. Charlie was not happy with his living arrangements, but he tolerated them, even though, sometimes, his Aunt Carmella would have some wine and tell him that he reminded her of his scumbag father. Charlie just let it go and thought that it could be much worse, but at least he had more freedom than he did at St. Patrick's and better food.

On his sixteenth birthday, Charlie told his Aunt and Uncle that he was going to go out on his own. Aunt Carmella got all bent out of shape with the news, even though she wasn't crazy about Charlie. To her, Charlie was only someone—to work the store as they got older and also to work the long hours the store required. Aunt Carmella let Charlie know it too, "You ungrateful little bastard. You used us and as soon as you're old enough you leave!"

Charlie's Uncle Anthony was silent and let Carmella vent her anger at Charlie as she always did, "You're a fuckin' bum, just like your father." Uncle Anthony finally said something like he could call the police if he left, but Charlie didn't care as he went upstairs and began to pack leaving his aunt and uncle to argue with each other. As Charlie packed, he wondered about his real father and what he was like and why they hated him so much. His aunt and uncle never gave any real explanation except that he was no good. Also, Charlie wondered why they never spoke much about his mother either. All they said about her was that she was a saint and deserved better than his father. They also talked a few times about how she died so Charlie would live, not going into any details, but making Charlie feel guilty about him living and his mother dying at childbirth. Charlie would think to himself it wasn't his fault. After all, he didn't ask to be born. Charlie didn't know what it was like to have a mother and father. All he knew was the orphanage and the nuns and the grief that went along with it. The only love he ever felt was from Sister Teresa. Charlie was cheated out of a normal family life, but he wasn't one to feel sorry for himself and thought to himself that someday he would show everyone who Charles Luzzi was. As he packed, Charlie said to himself, Someday! Someday! Someday starts today.

CHAPTER 4

A few hours after leaving his aunt and uncle, Charlie walked into the Top Hat looking for Big Red. Charlie figured he would ask Big Red for a job and collect on the promise he made to him years ago. Charlie didn't come with much. He had one suitcase and in it were two pairs of shoes, three shirts, three pairs of underwear and pants with four T-shirts, six-hundred and forty dollars to his name, and his dream of becoming somebody. At sixteen, he was ready to set the world on fire. Big Red, true to his word and knowing all about Charlie's past, gave Charlie some work. Big Red admired Charlie's guts at sixteen and thought the kid had balls, so he started Charlie out slow with cleaning out and working the candy store Big Red owned and having Charlie drop off some betting slips. In a short time, Big Red considered Charlie as family since Big Red was a bachelor and didn't have much of a family to speak of, just a sister and a nephew. Charlie was like a brother and Big Red would kid Charlie sometimes that he was the white sheep of the family. Big Red also paid Charlie well, two hundred a week and he also let Charlie use the backroom of the candy store to sleep and to take his showers. He didn't have a stove to cook on, but Charlie could eat at the bar whenever he wanted.

Charlie busted his ass for Big Red. He wanted to show his gratitude through his hard work and Big Red was pleased with Charlie's work ethic. Although he still went to school, little by little he started to phase it out. He found school too boring. The only time he felt challenged in school was when they gave him an IQ test and it was determined that he had an IQ of one-hundred and fifty six, near genius, but Charlie thought nothing of it. Charlie just assumed that his high IQ would help him with his future as a bookmaker and loan shark. Charlie had ability with numbers where he could almost remember everything without writing things down; all anyone had to do is tell him once. With each passing day, Charlie was working extra jobs for Big Red and he just about did every job Big Red gave him to perfection. He was now working weekends at the Top Hat bussing tables, stocking the bar, and cleaning up after closing.

On Saturday nights after closing, Charlie would mop up the private back room of the Top Hat where there were three booths and where some of Big Red's VIP customers would hang out after work and have a few drinks and snort some coke with the bartender Bobby. They would drink and laugh until the early hours of the morning, playing cards. Some of the local women would be there servicing some of the VIPs in the bathroom or in the poolroom on the pool table. Bobby liked Charlie and after getting to know him, Bobby let Charlie drink some beer while cleaning up. One Saturday after Charlie finished cleaning up, he was sitting at the bar drinking a beer when a pretty black woman named Sheri called out to him, "Hey Charlie, get your fine white butt over here!"

Charlie walked over to her. Sheri was a fine piece of black ass Charlie thought to himself, but she wasn't like the regular black working women in the Top Hat; she was the cream of the crop. Charlie often would check her out when she walked into the bar. She always wore tight, low cut, thigh-high dresses showing off her legs, her nice round ass, and big breasts. Charlie would get a hard on every time he checked her out and often thought about what a hot fuck she would be.

"Yes Sheri, what can I do for you?" Charlie asked her.

Sheri eyed him up and down as Bobby and some of the regulars looked on, "Come, sit next to Sheri baby," she said, patting her hand on the seat next to her. Charlie looked at Bobby, and Bobby nodded to Charlie to sit down. Charlie sat down and Sheri continued speaking. "I've been meaning to talk to you about something. You know you're not bad looking for a white boy," she said as Charlie stared at her breasts. "You like Sheri's tits?" she asked Charlie. He nodded yes as Sheri began to play with Charlie's hair and then pull him closer in to rub her breasts in his face. Charlie liked the way her breasts felt against his face; her skin was silky smooth and warm. Sheri moved her hand down and felt Charlie between his legs and spoke aloud, "Hmm, this boy is packing here; I think he's part black with what he got between his legs."

Some of the regulars laughed as Sheri asks Charlie, "So Sugar, you packing a pistol in there or you just glad to be sitting next to Sheri?"

After blushing, Charlie told her he was happy to be sitting next to her.

Bobby, looking, said, "Sheri, leave Charlie alone. He doesn't need to be your first or he will sure as shit give up women altogether after one session with you."

Sheri gave Bobby a little snarl as everyone laughed and then she looked at Charlie and said how utterly delicious he looked. Charlie kept getting friendly with Sheri as she gave him his first snort of coke. Charlie never did coke before and he wanted to fit in with the crew this night so he snorted as he saw them do many times, plus Charlie was a man now. At eighteen, he thought this is what grownups do and he also wanted to be cool like them. Charlie took a hit of coke when Sheri offered and Sheri noticed how Charlie's eyes bugged out after each hit.

"First time there Sugar with the nose candy?" she asked Charlie.

"Nooo! I've done this many times before," he said, trying to be cool, "I just don't think I've had this good of shit before," Charlie added. Charlie started feeling this rush to his head with the combination of beer and coke. He started to feel real good, smiling at everyone, cracking jokes with the regulars and snuggling up to Sheri's tits and kissing them. "MAN I'M HAVING A GOOD TIME!" Charlie shouted out and the regulars laughed at Charlie's being high and Bobby said to him, "Just don't tell the boss man we got you high there" Bobby laughed referring to Big Red, who wasn't around. "You hear me there GOOD TIME CHARLIE!" Bobby yelled out and everyone laughed and raised a glass to toast Charlie's first high and they all yelled out, "TO GOOD TIME CHARLIE!" They all drank and laughed and Bobby added, "YEAH! TO GOOD TIME CHARLIE, THE WHITEST NIGGER IN HARLEM!" They all laughed again and drank. From this day on, Charlie was referred to by the nickname GOOD TIME CHARLIE.

The partying continued and with each hit of coke Charlie got freer with Sheri, kissing her breasts, letting his hand wander between her legs and up her dress, and feeling her up. Finally Sheri took Charlie in the pool room where she stripped Charlie naked, sucked him off, had him do the same to her, and then she fucked Charlie four times breaking his cherry, one of the times on the pool table leaving cum stains all over it. Charlie wanted to fuck her more, but it was now daylight and Sheri's pussy was sore as hell from Charlie pounding it two hours straight. Everyone laughed as Sheri left the bar walking funny.

The next day, Big Red found out what went on at the Top Hat the night before and was really pissed off about Charlie doing coke and drinking so much. Big Red yelled at Bobby as he saw the shape Charlie was in the next day. He let Bobby know that if it happened again, he would fire him. Big Red was from the old school and he was protective of Charlie. Even though Charlie had a great time, Big Red felt his good times could wait. After Big Red finished yelling at Bobby and Charlie, he got all fired up again when he saw the cum stains on the pool table. "And how many fuckin' times do I have to tell you? I don't want nobody screwing on the fuckin' pool table. Now, I have to have the fuckin' cloth changed again!" Big Red said to Bobby and added, "It's coming out of your fuckin' pay." Big Red left the Top Hat in a huff.

Bobby was glad that at least no one ratted him out that it was Sheri breaking Charlie's cherry on the pool table the night before. If he found out about that, he might have yelled at them more. Bobby and Charlie had enough yelling and head bashing for the day as they were still hung over and feeling like shit. Charlie thought of telling Big Red about how the cum stains got on the pool table as he was proud of the fact that he lost his cherry and fucked the shit out of Sheri sending her home sore and smiling, but he wasn't sure how Big Red would react as he was in too much of a bad mood. So Charlie wisely kept quiet and after Big Red left, he and Bobby went back to work. Even with Big Red's yelling and unhappy with what went on with Charlie the night before, Charlie and Bobby laughed it off and Charlie had a grin on his face the rest of the day as he remembered how everyone toasted him and anointed him with the nickname GOOD TIME CHARLIE. Charlie felt important; he felt like somebody.

Charlie started to become a Big Shot with each passing day after that night in the Top Hat. Everywhere he went, his nickname got passed around the neighborhood and when they saw Charlie it was never just Charlie but it was "hi there Good Time," or, "There's Good Time Charlie." Also, Charlie's responsibilities with Big Red grew, as he became a full-time bookmaker with Big Red because of Charlie's ability to remember numbers so well without using slips. Charlie would think to himself who has it better than him. He had his bookmaking now, plus all the booze, drugs, and women he wanted every day—most everything he always wanted.

The next year blew by quickly with Charlie and with Big Red giving him more and more bookmaking opportunities; Charlie was able to save almost seven thousand dollars. Charlie was clearing five hundred a week and could have saved more, but he was into having a good time. GOOD TIME CHARLIE really liked the booze, drugs, and women. He became a big part of Big Red's crew and he got respect from everyone in the neighborhood. Even though he was white, everyone liked him. Charlie loved being in the neighborhood, but the times had begun changing as rival whites and blacks were fighting over the territory. Charlie never understood the difference; he never thought of Big Red as black or himself as white. The only color that meant anything to him was the color green, the color of money, because with the green came the power and the respect. Charlie noticed the changes that were happening in the neighborhood. There were lots of new faces, new attitudes and Charlie started thinking that maybe it was time for his next move to start a crew of his own and form his own business, but he had to get Red's okay before he would do anything.

Charlie sat down with Big Red one day and told him what he wanted to do. He wanted his advice. Big Red understood where Charlie was coming from. He was wise to the changes in Harlem and thought it was a big risk for Charlie to continue on in Harlem with the whites and blacks going at it. Some whites just might off Charlie, shoot him, because he was a white nigger, a white man working for the black man.

"Good Time, you are like a son to me, like the white little brother I never had and, as much as I hate to lose you, I do think it's time you moved uptown with your own Brothers where it will be a little safer for you," Big Red said. Charlie listened and tried to lighten things up: "You mean I'm going to stay this color forever," Charlie joked and they both laughed, but they both realized that Charlie had to make a move. After a few drinks Charlie gave Big Red a hug. Both promised to always be there for the other and that they would always be family. Charlie then left behind his Harlem roots.

CHAPTER 5

Charlie started looking a little more uptown to settle in. He moved up to Washington Heights on 161st Street off Broadway into a studio apartment and started looking for a business to get into. Charlie soon found a place to open up a bar on 171st Street and Saint Nicholas Avenue. This spot can't miss, he thought because it was five blocks from a hospital, near a Con Ed and other businesses, and centrally located in a predominantly Irish neighborhood. Charlie appropriately named the bar GOOD TIME CHARLIE'S.

Soon after opening up, Charlie started up a bookmaking operation and sold some drugs on the side. Charlie paid off some of the local police so he wouldn't be bothered. At nineteen years of age, Charlie had his life going the way he wanted, a business, his own apartment and lots of money coming in on a daily basis. The days of the orphanage, his aunt and uncle were a distant memory now, but he would often think about Sister Teresa and, even with his now busy schedule and his propensity for having a good time, Charlie found time to visit her.

Charlie had his bar up and running in no time as he marketed it well for the area. He hired local bartenders and waitresses to serve the drinks and the limited but popular food menu and even hired a local prize fighter named Tony "Pretty Boy" Thomas to hang out in the bar on slow days to draw more customers in. He catered to the area with lunch specials for the working-class patrons in the area making small profits on the food but maxing out with the liquor and beer, which was a bigger markup for him. He would have a happy hour with a free buffet, but maintained the drink prices with only one free drink for the hour. The bookmaking and on-the-side drugs were all icing on the cake for Charlie who was making money hand-over-fist. To make things easy for his hard working customers, he set up accounts with them at the bar so they could cash their payroll checks with him instead of leaving the bar to cash them at the bank where they might pass other bars and be tempted to go in. Charlie had every angle covered. Plus, everyone liked him, and his clientele just grew and grew. With the bookmaking, Charlie used Big Red's office to back him up even though there was a local guy named Gino who had been in the area a long time. Charlie didn't really care about this Gino guy, this was his place and his customers, and so he used Big Red.

Charlie worked hard to keep things going at his bar, but at night he partied even harder and he didn't worry too much about this neighborhood changing with the blacks and Spanish who were moving in. To him they all had green money and that's what counted with him. Charlie just made friends with everyone that came into his bar and he even partied with some.

One guy Charlie made friends with was a Cuban named José Matista who was a major player in the Cuban section of the neighborhood. They started out as drinking friends. Then later, José became a supplier to Charlie as he brought in some high-end drugs at a good price. Charlie didn't know just how big José was, but Charlie was able to find out in time that José was a made man among his Cuban connections and the Cuban Mafia which controlled the cocaine traffic in Washington Heights. José liked coming into Charlie's place because he was friendly to him. The other bars didn't treat him as well because he couldn't speak English well, but Charlie had no problem understanding him. Charlie and José also began to pal around together, going to after-hours clubs and picking up women. José loved large blondes with big breasts and Charlie would fix him up with some women he knew that José liked. José in return would fix Charlie up with some hot-looking Cuban and Spanish women, whom Charlie liked. On many occasions, they would party together, getting the women high on cocaine and then fucking their brains out.

One night after closing time at Good Time Charlie's bar, Charlie and José were talking over how much coke they would move and in what weight when two Colombian men entered suspiciously looking over the surroundings. As one of the Colombians stayed by the door, the other approached Charlie and José who had noticed them and were on their guard, ready to pull their guns if either Colombian made any sudden move. The Colombian who came in asked, "Are you Good Time Charlie and José?"

"So what if we are, who's asking and what's it to you?" Charlie asked, looking the Colombian directly in the eyes showing absolutely no fear and ready for any gunplay. The Colombian looked at Charlie and said, "Well, if you are, you have to pay protection to us to operate here in our territory."

Charlie looked at José and gave him the impression that he's ready to shoot these pricks for coming into his place and making demands, but José shook his head knowing what Charlie is thinking. José then told both to have a seat so they could talk. He spoke to the two Colombians in Spanish for a few minutes keeping a very cool head as Charlie wondered what the fuck was going on. After a few minutes of going back and forth, the two Colombians got up and left and Charlie immediately asked José, "What the fuck was said?"

José looked at Charlie and told him. "They said they will be back tomorrow for their money at 10 p.m."

"No fuckin' way those spics are getting a payoff!" Charlie said angrily. "I'll blow their fuckin' balls off first and shove them down their throats!" Charlie added with José smiling, "You trust me, Good Time?" José asked Charlie.

"Yeah, I trust you," Charlie declared.

"Then don't worry. I'll take care of those pricks," José assured Charlie with his broken English.

The next night the same two Colombians entered Charlie's place and walked over to the bar where José was sitting. Charlie was sitting in one of the booths looking on, as the bar was empty of patrons. One of the Colombians then asked José for the payoff protection money. José told the two men to sit down and have a drink and that he would be right back. As José got up, he motioned to the bartender, who happened to be one of his men and not one of Charlie's regular bartenders, to set them up with drinks and he then went into the bathroom. Once in the bathroom he made a quick phone call and then went back to the bar. When he came back, one of the Colombians told him that they want their money now and didn't have time to wait. As the Colombian finished speaking, four of the biggest Cubans Charlie had ever seen walked in. The two Colombians see the four large Cubans and got up to fight them, but they were no match for them as they quickly whacked them across their faces sending them sprawling to the ground. They kicked them repeatedly on the ground as José yelled, "NO BLOOD SHED IN THE BAR! OUTSIDE!"

Following José's orders, the bartender jumped over the bar with some duct tape and put it across the Colombians' mouths and tied their hands behind their backs and their ankles together. Then they dragged them outside the bar. Charlie was surprised how efficiently José's men took care of the two Colombian scumbags and asked José, "What are you going to do with them?"

José replied, "No more problems with those two punks my friend." José smiled and then said, "I have some good shit. Let's go find some pussy and party, Good Time." Charlie looked at José and laughed saying, "They don't call me Good Time Charlie for nothing, José." Charlie put his arm around José, locked up the bar and they left.

Charlie didn't ask José any more about the fate of the Colombians, but the next day at his bar he read in the papers about two Colombians found dead by a sanitation worker in one of the dumpsters near a Colombian club. Charlie laughed as he read how the two Colombians were not only shot but had their necks slit and their tongues pulled out through the hole in their throats. It was commonly known among the Cubans and Colombians as a Colombian necktie and a message to be sent out to the rest of their crews to not fuck with them again. After that, Charlie didn't get any more visitors from those gangs again.

As the weeks went on, Charlie and José were prospering and living large. They were selling their drugs at Charlie's place and even to the after-hours clubs they would frequent. José's suppliers were shipping a lot more to him and he and Charlie were moving it as quickly as it came in, their shit was that good. Charlie and José would just about celebrate every night with drugs, drinks, and pussy and Charlie was doing more drugs almost every day. Between work and partying, Charlie was barely getting three hours of sleep a night. He was burning the candle at both ends, but he was having too much fun and also picking up many bad habits. It wasn't enough to drink, do the drugs and get as much pussy as possible, but now he started gambling in the after-hours clubs. He played craps, roulette, and black-jack, as well as betting on all sporting events that took place, along with those that he carried at his bar. At his bar, Charlie had three TVs set up for his customers so they could always catch the top sporting events. The nights when the big sporting events took place, his bar would be jam packed. Good Time Charlie's was the place to be on sports nights and everyone would be placing bets and Charlie fell into the same trap. It wasn't that he really cared about the game or rooting for a team, Charlie just liked the added action and having money on a game was extra juice for him. Charlie would bet five hundred on the early game where the Knicks would be playing and then parlay it on the late game on the west coast like the Lakers.

In five short years, Good Time Charlie's bar had expanded into two other locations on the block where others went out of business. Charlie now added more bartenders. He now had five bartenders and eight waitresses in all. People from all over came to see Charlie who became well known throughout the New York area and even in Fort Lee, New Jersey where there were some hot after-hours clubs. Everyone liked Charlie; he was personable and knew how to show people a good time.

Charlie's drug business through José was getting bigger and bigger to a point where he had to take on someone extra to handle the workload. His name was Stevie, and Charlie took an immediate liking to him, as did José. Stevie was a little down and out, but he knew some people who could move a lot more coke for Charlie and José, so in time Stevie became a partner in the drug operation, since he was earning so much for Charlie and José.

Charlie and Stevie would also get high together and some nights when they would be high on coke they would get a little crazy and go into some of the bars in the Spanish and black neighborhoods to track down the people who owed them money. Charlie and Stevie were pretty brazen about it too. They would ask for the son of a bitch they were looking for with their coats open displaying their guns. They were lucky they were never shot going into places where they didn't belong, but nobody fucked with them either because they knew they were a little crazy and didn't take shit from anyone.

Charlie was also making friends everywhere he went. He made a connection with a half a wise guy uptown named Johnny Riff, who was half-Irish and half-Spanish. In a short time, the two men got together and opened an after-hours club uptown since most of the clubs were downtown. Charlie and Riff thought they would catch a crowd that didn't want to take the trip to the downtown clubs. Even more attractive to the uptown crowd, Charlie and Riff opened this club on a houseboat moored on the Hudson River at the end of Dyckman Street. They got a charter and named the boat the Atlantic Boat Club and Charlie was now into another money-making business. Once again, they paid off some cops to turn a head so they could operate freely and not worry about any busts.

CHAPTER 6

Charlie was now twenty-three years old and had come a long way since he was sixteen and working for Big Red. Even Big Red, who Charlie visited on occasion, was impressed with Charlie's success. He was a little fish in a big pond and was enjoying the life. Yet, the increased business opportunities and increased income brought an increase in doing drugs, gambling, and all around partying. Charlie didn't think about hard times, because he had never experienced nor seen a downside to the lifestyle he was living. Around Big Red, he saw a man who prospered and partied also. As far as Charlie knew, the money would always be coming in, so he might as well just keep on spending it and enjoying it. What Charlie didn't know was that, even though he was a little fish in a big pond, he was drawing the attention of some big wise guys around town as some of his businesses were cutting into some competitors.

Charlie was having problems keeping up with everything he had going on. He had Stevie and José helping him with the drugs coming in and going out and, sure, he had Riff helping him run the after-hours club, but he was still running his bar and the bookmaking operations himself. Big Red warned Charlie that the business was getting too big for him to handle and the workload was bigger every week. Charlie figured he would hire someone to handle his bookmaking, so he called on Gino the other bookmaker in the neighborhood to see what kind of deal he could work out with him.

Gino was one of those Old Italian goombahs who had been in the business forever. Gino was impressed with Charlie and his operation and his bar business and how he did it pretty much on his own. Gino, an old timer like him who had been around, made Charlie feel important. Gino was no dummy. He had to find out what type of people supported him and he found out that his people had more clout. Gino also observed Charlie and saw that he had turned into an out-of-control gambler, and he knew Charlie did a lot of drugs too and was into having a good time. The deal Charlie struck with Gino was that Gino would get one-third of the numbers profit and one-half the sports betting profits. Charlie liked this deal, because as he saw it, when he made his own bets he would be getting them for half the price and a chance to win the full amount. The only thing was that Charlie never wound up winning; he picked more losers than winners.

Charlie's bad habits prevented him from being a wealthy man. With the spending he did to show the ladies he took out for a good time, the gambling in the after-hours clubs and sports betting and giving out some of the coke to people he knew to impress them instead of selling it to them, Charlie was getting a little too loose with his business ventures and cutting into his own profits. He threw money around like it was nothing. Charlie also over-tipped everyone he came in contact with—the doorman, waitresses, and limo drivers. Most of this was due to the fact that Charlie was high all the time. Whether it was alcohol or coke, Charlie's thinking was clouded and he was getting more and more out of control with each day. Charlie now had unlimited credit in most of the after-hours clubs he went to and he was betting wildly, but he couldn't keep track of the money he owed because his mind was never clear. When he got hit with the markers that he owed he would pay up and it helped that money was still coming in from all his ventures. Every time he paid up, he vowed not to get fucked up and lose that much again, but he was Good Time

Charlie and the good times had to happen every night because that's what he was about.

Charlie was also still getting high with Stevie and they were getting a bad reputation of fucking people up with their hands when people were late with payments or some other bullshit reasons. Charlie liked the feeling he got when people would get scared of him. It was another feeling of power and respect he liked and again it came with his excessive use of drugs and drinking and he actually enjoyed fucking people up, especially lowlifes.

One Sunday afternoon when Charlie arrived at the houseboat, he had to park way down the block from his boat because of all the motorcycles parked outside blocking the entrance. Charlie was wondering what the fuck was going on. When Charlie got inside the club, he saw the club empty of his usual Sunday afternoon crowd and about ten bikers hanging out around the bar. They all had on black leather jackets with the lettering on them that said "Dyckman MC." Charlie walked over to Johnny who he had hired to help run the club and asked, "What the fuck is going on here Johnny? These guys aren't charter members?"

"Charlie, they're okay and they're good for business. They spend a lot of money and pick up the Sunday afternoon business," Johnny told him.

Charlie gave him a stare. "As long as they don't make trouble," Charlie said and proceeded to walk into his office in the back. Charlie began to make a list of the liquor they needed as it was a busy week and they were almost out of everything.

Meanwhile, Stevie walked in and was also annoyed with the bikers hogging up the space in front of the club. Stevie, not in the mood for any bullshit, walked up to the biggest biker in the bar, who looked like the leader of the bunch and asked him, "Can you please move some of your bikes from the front? You're blocking the entrance."

One of the bikers came up to Stevie and said, "Stick it up your ass. The Dyckman MC don't move their bikes for anyone."

Stevie stared at the biker.

Inside Charlie's office, Charlie was going over the inventory when he suddenly heard a loud bang and then a lot of yelling. Charlie rushed out of the office to see Stevie leveling one of the big gorilla bikers with one punch. The other bikers got ready to fight as Charlie came alongside Stevie with Johnny to his other side. Charlie stared at the bikers. "Ten to three, I don't think you boys have enough men here to make it a fair fight," Charlie said to them, smiling and then laughing at them.

The bikers charged into them and Stevie leveled two out cold with consecutive punches in about a span of two seconds, sending some of their teeth flying out of their mouths. Charlie knocked one out and sent another sprawling backwards into the jukebox so hard that it came on with an Elton John tune *Saturday Night's Alright for Fighting*. Two other bikers tried to grab Stevie, but he flung them both into the wall and turned quickly to kick another biker in the balls so hard that he squealed like a pig and just dropped to his knees. Meanwhile, Charlie took another biker by the head and smashed his head into another biker, knocking them both out cold while Johnny could only manage to take out one biker after a struggle. Stevie walked over to the two men getting up that he flung into the wall and, just for the fuck of it, pounded their faces until they were fully bloodied, "You fuckin' pieces of shit. So, you don't move your bikes for anyone, eh?" Stevie shouted as he alternated his punches with each of them.

Charlie went over and grabbed Stevie, "Okay enough, we don't want to have a murder charge here!" Charlie said, as some club members entered.

"What now?" Johnny asked.

"Let's throw them in the fuckin' East River," Stevie said, checking the cut on his face. They began to take them out one by one and toss them in the river with the help of the club members that walked in. As they hit the water, the bikers woke up and they started screaming at Stevie and Charlie, so Stevie started throwing their bikes in the river too one by one.

"You're lucky you're alive you scumbags and now you can walk home!" Stevie yelled as he threw the last bike in. "If I ever see your faces again, you'll be on the bottom of that river next time!"

Later, they were all drinking and laughing about how they kicked their asses and that those bikers were nothing but a bunch of pussies. That night the bikers did return after the club closed and they torched the club to the ground. Charlie looked over the cinders of what was once his club and said to Johnny, "Well, at least I didn't restock the place or it would have been more of a loss."

The big loss though was the location. It was a prime spot. They moved and found another club spot on 230th Street and Dyckman Avenue in an old hotel under the el.

CHAPTER 7

There was a change going on in Charlie. Sure, he was the Good Time man who liked the women, booze, drugs, and the gambling, but Charlie developed this dark side through his hanging around with Stevie. He enjoyed going around and busting people up when they couldn't pay up and he enjoyed putting the fear of God into people who tried to fuck with him because he was one tough guy and his reputation for cracking heads was becoming well known.

Charlie was also becoming too loose and free with his gambling, especially with Gino who just kept running a tab for Charlie and not letting him know what he owed. Gino gave Charlie all the credit he wanted and Charlie got careless and didn't pay at the end of each week as he should and the tab got larger and larger. Charlie figured Gino had it on paper and nothing was coming out of his own pocket, so he kept betting. This went on for six months and then finally Gino told Charlie one day that they had to speak seriously about his markers and all the money he owed. Charlie didn't think he owed that much; he thought at the most thirty thousand, but Charlie was paying more attention to his having the good times and wasn't paying much attention to what he was betting and that his losses were much more than the winnings he had.

Gino met with Charlie one day and they talked over the situation, "Good Time you owe seventy thousand large," Gino informed Charlie.

Charlie just stared at him with his cold stare that could make people piss in their pants. "Are you nuts? No fuckin' way I owe that much!" Charlie proclaimed, but Gino was just as serious as Charlie.

"No! I'm not nuts! If you want, come to my office and we'll go over all the bets for the past six months. I have all the slips and tapes of the phone-in bets. You can check 'em out for yourself and add 'em up," Gino told him.

Charlie didn't disbelieve him. Gino was no liar. That's why he was in business so long. Gino was the top bookmaker in the area and his rep was solid. Hell that's why Charlie was a partner with him. But Gino had a boss to answer to also and Charlie knew the deal: when the bosses called in markers, people had to pay up or suffer the consequences.

Charlie had let a lot of things go the past six months. He wasn't paying attention to all his businesses and transactions and was neglecting everything so he could have his good times. Charlie's association with José diminished and his dealing drugs for José went down. It seemed Charlie only used José now for his own purposes and he couldn't even cover the cost of what he was using as he was into José for a nice sum also, about thirty large. Charlie found this out about the same time Gino told him about his gambling debt and all Charlie could say to himself was "Fuck me, I blew a lot of blow." Charlie didn't do all that coke himself. He gave some away to the women he fucked, to Stevie, and to other snorting buddies he hung out with in the after-hours clubs. If he was at a party, Charlie would bring out the nose candy and make his contribution to the festivities. Sometimes, the party would be ten to twenty people, but Charlie always had enough to go around.

To top everything off, Charlie's businesses, his bar, and social club were also down about thirty percent. Charlie was basically strapped with everything he had going for himself at one time. He owed over one hundred grand and he had to come up with the cash. He was in a bind. He had to think of a way out quick; he didn't need this shit hanging over his head. After all, how could he have a good time knowing he owed out so much? Through it all though, Charlie still felt important—still a big man and people in his circles knew it.

Gino called Charlie up about two weeks after their last meeting over the money he owed and he asked Charlie to meet him at a bar called The Tropical Garden that night, right down the block from his place.

Charlie got there a little earlier than he was supposed to. He sat at the bar and bullshitted with the bartender about business in the neighborhood as they had a drink together. Gino finally came in a little late and saw Charlie at the bar and sat next to him. "Sorry I'm late, Good Time," Gino said. "The office had me on the phone, busting my balls about all these debts I have to collect," Gino added, and then ordered a drink. "How you doin', Good Time?" Gino asked him.

"Fine, I'm doin' good. I can use a few winners," Charlie replied. As the bartender put down Gino's drink, Charlie told him that Gino's drink was with him. "So, what do you need to see me about?" Charlie asked him, but Charlie knew what it was about.

"I need the money, Good Time. The office is on my ass and I need you to pay up," Gino apprised him. "And I can't give you any more time Charlie," Gino stated firmly.

"Well, I can give you five-thousand now and I'll come up with the rest soon," Charlie said, taking a swig of his drink.

"No can do, Good Time," Gino said in a serious tone of voice and a look that backed up what he said. "The office wants it all," Gino said, pausing a moment. "Look Charlie, I left you alone a couple of weeks to come up with the cash. When you made these bets, you said it was no problem that you always had the money, well now there's a fuckin' problem. The office wants the money and you, of all people, should know that when an office calls in a marker you have to fuckin' pay and not just a measly five fuckin' grand."

Charlie looked at Gino knowing he was right. "All right, give me a couple of days and I'll put a package together. What do you say?" Charlie asked as Gino's eyes looked around the bar a little perturbed.

"Okay Good Time, I'll stall the office for a few days, but I'm telling you right now you have exactly three days, three days," Gino emphasized to Charlie. "And if you don't have the money, it's out of my hands Good Time and you know what that means." Gino finished his drink and got up from his stool.

"Okay, three days," Charlie reiterated Gino's request and then asked him, "So, what's the line on the Knicks tonight?"

Gino looked at Charlie and replied, "You better take a rest for a while Good Time, until we get this mess cleared up. I'm outta here. I'll be calling you in three days Charlie."

Gino walked out the door to go make some pick-ups uptown as Charlie watched him leave. Charlie sat at the bar and had another drink as he wondered how the fuck he let things get so out of hand. He owed out over a hundred grand to Gino and José, and he didn't want to turn it into a situation where he had to pay a two percent vig (for vigorish; interest paid to a moneylender on a loan) on that kind of money each week when it was owed or he'd never get out of debt, especially with all his businesses doing so badly. Charlie thought hard about what he could do, but he put off his ideas and would worry about it tomorrow so he could go out and get drunk that night, do some coke, and get laid.

To Charlie's immediate left, he saw a stunning, big-busted redhead and a luscious brunette sitting together having a drink. They were evidently friends. Charlie thought, well, this would be a pleasant diversion for the evening. Before the clock hit midnight, Charlie had partied with the two bi-sexual bimbos in a nearby motel, drinking and doing some coke. Charlie had them both at once after he watched them do each other. Charlie was lying on his back with the redhead straddling him, riding him so hard he could almost feel his balls bouncing back up into his stomach and the brunette was grinding into his face as his long wide tongue was buried inside her. Charlie had a great vision too as there was an overhead mirror and he could see these two horny bitches going to town on him.

The next day, Charlie's problems were still there and didn't go away with another night of partying. Charlie was running out of tomorrows and he knew there was no way he could come up with the money he owed Gino's office. So Charlie decided he would meet with Gino's people and try to work a payment deal that he could afford with paying a vig each week and, if they didn't go for it, Charlie would just tell them to go shove it. After all, he was a somebody too and not just some small punk. Charlie felt that there was no way he was going to let them push him around because he had a reputation as a guy who could crack a guy's skull with one shot and, besides, he was Good Time Charlie.

Charlie called Gino in to his place the night before the money was due and he informed Gino that he wanted to meet his people at his office and try to work out a deal. Gino wasn't happy with what Charlie was going to do, but since Charlie didn't have the cash to pay the note, Gino knew this was the next step and he warned Charlie he shouldn't show up empty-handed.

Charlie just stared at Gino. "You let me worry about that, Gino," Charlie said with authority and added, "It's my problem and I'll handle it."

Gino and Charlie set the date for Friday when Charlie would meet the people at Gino's office or as Gino put it, "I'll introduce you to your new friends." Gino said it with a little sarcasm.

That night, Charlie left his bar and caught a cab uptown to check out a few of the after-hours clubs he liked to frequent. Charlie was upset the past few days as he thought about the Knicks game he wanted to bet heavy on and no one would give him action on it with the word out on what he owed and, wouldn't you know, the fuckin' Knicks won big.

Charlie made a pit stop first to see José to try to score some coke for the night. He caught up with José at a Spanish bar and restaurant he liked to hang out in called Zapata's. José, upon seeing Charlie walk in, smiled and invited him over to where he was sitting. José got up and hugged him and they sat and ordered drinks.

"Good Time, I need that cash you owe me soon," José informed Charlie in his broken English accent. "I'm getting ready to make a big buy and I need all the cash I can get my hands on," José told him and went on, "these people are in Florida and will only be there a short time and they only deal with cash up front."

"Sure, no problem," not wanting to let José know there was one as he knocked down his drink. "I need to go over and check things out at my club José." Charlie got up, realizing that he had to get serious about his problems.

"Stay here, Amigo. We can get some putta and party all night long man," José offered.

Charlie looked at him. "I better not, José. I need to keep my head clear the next few days. Business, you know," Charlie told José, knowing that he would be meeting Gino's people soon.

"Okay Good Time, just make sure you see me in a couple of days before I go to Florida," José said to him again.

"Listen José, I said no problem," Charlie repeated firmly.

Somehow, José wasn't too convinced as he sensed a problem as he watched Charlie walk out to catch another cab.

Charlie stopped by his club that he owned with Johnny, but Johnny wasn't anywhere to be found and the place was packed with people. Charlie was thinking, This place is packed. Why is business down thirty-three percent? Charlie asked one of his workers where Johnny was and he was informed that Johnny left to go whore around with some blonde and that he would be back later. Charlie was pissed off that Johnny wasn't around, especially on a busy night like tonight to keep track of the cash flow. Charlie stayed and had a couple of drinks and nursed them for about two hours until Johnny finally returned with the blonde bimbo he left with. He called Johnny over to where he was sitting and let him know that he was not too happy with him taking off on a busy night.

"How can you leave on a busy night Johnny?" Charlie asked in a mildly threatening tone with Johnny a little taken back, even though he's had a little too much to drink.

"What do you care, Charlie?" Johnny answered, getting gutsy with the liquor in him. "You're never here and, when you are, you're usually drunk or high on blow with a few of your freeloading friends." He went on, "I'm always carrying the load here so, if you don't like the way I run our business, then pay me off and you can have the place."

Charlie went into one of his cold stares. Johnny knew that stare because he had seen it before and he knew Charlie was livid.

"Listen, I'm the one that got this place started and made it a success. I brought the people in this club and it was always the deal that I would work the streets and get people in and you would work the club."

"Well, that's not how I understood this arrangement and as far as I'm concerned you can just buy me out, if you have the cash to do so and take the club and shove it up your ass because I've had it," Johnny firmly stated and continued on, "I've been hearing a lot of shit from people about you lately, Good Time, and I don't like what I've been hearing. Maybe it's better I buy you out Charlie, since you don't have the cash and you can leave here and never come back. Anyhow, you're never here anyway," Johnny said as Charlie stared at him. "So, what do you want to do Charlie?" Johnny asked as Charlie leaned into his so-called partner with his reply.

"You listen to me, you fuck. You're a little bit too fucked up to talk about this now, but tomorrow we will have this discussion again," Charlie told him with a cold as ice stare and pointing his finger in Johnny's face. Before Johnny could utter another word, Charlie spoke again, "Don't say another fuckin' word and make me put your head through the wall. We will talk and straighten this out tomorrow." With that, Charlie downed the rest of his drink and walked out of the club to catch another cab.

CHAPTER 8

Charlie was seething in the cab ride downtown to Houston Street on the west side, near the village. He had about a thousand dollars and about an ounce of coke on him which he turned into cash in one of the after-hours clubs on Houston. Charlie then went over to an after-hours club called The Zoo, which had a line around the block, but Charlie went to the front of the line because everyone knew him there. So Charlie slipped the doorman a ten spot and went in.

The Zoo was a place Charlie found very entertaining because of the diverse clientele that came there: straight people, gays, bi's, drag queens, transvestites, blacks, Spanish, Asians, just about anyone came to The Zoo and, on some nights, a celebrity or two might be hanging out, maybe Michael Jackson or Mick and Bianca Jagger. The common denominator was that everyone was there to get fucked up. Whether alcohol or drugs, people came in to get high.

Charlie went to the bar and got himself a drink from the bartender, a guy named Miss Mona, who Charlie knew for about two years since he started coming into the place. Miss Mona was a player with drugs and turned Charlie on to some of the other major players there, as well as giving him free drinks. Miss Mona also pointed out to

Charlie insight to who were the real men and who were the real women. It was hard to tell sometimes with the way they dressed and the last thing Charlie wanted was to be getting high and then making out with some fine piece of ass only to find a cock in his hand when he slid his hand under some lady's dress. Mona turned Charlie on to a piece of ass named Dizzy, a real hot number who was hanging out in the place that night and Charlie handed Mona a twenty spot with some coke wrapped inside.

Charlie watched as Dizzy came over to the bar. Dizzy was twenty one years old with a gorgeous face, standing about five-feet five in her red fuck me pumps, wearing a see through black fishnet top and no bra. Charlie took a long gander at her big firm breasts that stuck straight out with protruding nipples. She had a thigh-high tight red skirt displaying her shapely legs wrapped in fishnet stockings. She looked at Charlie and smiled. Charlie was hooked, in love and lust. He could throw her on the floor right there and fuck her silly. Charlie spoke with her after introducing himself and after a few minutes he knew why they called her Dizzy because it was obvious that she was a few French fries short of a Happy Meal. Charlie thought her name fit her perfectly.

After a few drinks and some hits of coke, Dizzy invited Charlie over to her place, a few blocks away from the club on 14th Street. She lived alone in a studio apartment, which Charlie liked. Once inside her apartment, Charlie took out a bottle of Finlandia that he scored from Mona before leaving The Zoo. Dizzy took out a gram of coke that she had left and puts it on the table and they started to party. It didn't take much. Dizzy was all over Charlie as they sat on the couch. She unzipped his fly and reached inside to stroke him, and massage him, and Charlie pulled her top off and was sucking on her nipples. Finally, Charlie took Dizzy over to her bed and they both stripped each other down while kissing and groping each other. When Charlie slipped a few fingers inside her, she was on fire and soaking wet.

Charlie just threw her on the bed and slid his manhood inside her and fucked her hard for a half hour straight. He was spent after fucking her so intensely and pounding her pussy like there was no tomorrow, but Dizzy was still horny even after coming three times. She wanted more.

"You want to try something with me baby? I'll get you nice and hard again so you can fuck Dizzy real good again," she told Charlie.

Even though he was worn out, Charlie was up for anything for him to get into that nice tight hole of hers again. So Charlie lay on his stomach as she asked him to do and she went into a small room as Charlie waited patiently for her to come back for round two. Charlie lay there, his eyes closed and all of a sudden Charlie heard this whip cracking then felt this stinging, burning sensation across his ass so fast he jumped up yelling, "OW!" Charlie turned and looked up to see Dizzy wearing thigh high, black long heeled boots with garter belts on each thigh and holding a bull whip. "YOU FUCKING LOONEY TUNE! WHAT THE FUCK DO YOU THINK YOU'RE DOING?" Charlie asked, rubbing his ass.

"Now, you just lie face down and enjoy," Dizzy told him as she got ready to crack the whip to Charlie again.

But Charlie, in one motion got out of bed and belted Dizzy right in her face, sending her sprawling backwards into the wall and cutting her lip open. Charlie was jumping around and rubbing the cheeks of his ass, trying to get the sting out of them. Charlie checked Dizzy who was out cold and he was hoping she would get up so he could belt her again. Charlie's ass was on fire. He never felt such a stinging pain like that and he thought for a split second that if the nuns did that to him back in the orphanage he would have been a real good boy. Charlie ran into the bathroom and tried to get the running water on his ass, but the fuckin' sink was too small, so he ran the bathtub water but forgot about it as he lifted the toilet seat and stuck his ass in the cold water. Charlie stayed there soaking his ass for a few minutes as the pain subsided a little, but not much. When he felt his ass, he saw a big cut across both his cheeks. "That fuckin' crazy bitch!" Charlie said to himself. As he got up still feeling the pain, he grabbed some lotion and baby powder out of the medicine cabinet and put some on his ass. Charlie then went back and got his clothes by the bed and started getting dressed. The pain just wouldn't go away, so he went back in the bathroom and grabbed the toilet paper and unraveled about half of it to stuff in his underwear to cushion his cheeks. As Charlie was ready to leave, Dizzy started to come out of the punch Charlie dealt her and Charlie noticed how badly he cut her lip open and that half her face was swollen.

She spoke to Charlie. "Where do you think you're going big boy?" she asked him in a half-conscious state as Charlie slipped his shoes on.

"Away from you, you dizzy fuckin' nut," Charlie replied, trying to tie his laces, but his ass pained him too much. Charlie just headed for the door to get the fuck out of there and before he left he could hear the water in the tub overflowing in the bathroom.

Charlie walked gingerly down the steps because the building had no elevators and then outside to hail a cab. As Charlie was hailing a cab, he heard Dizzy from her window. "THANKS, I HAD A GREAT TIME LOVER!" she yelled and shouted, "WILL I SEE YOU AGAIN BABY?"

All Charlie could do was look up and stare at the fuckin' nutty bitch as a cab pulled up in front of him. It took Charlie about two minutes to get into the cab as the driver wondered what the hell was wrong with him and Dizzy was still yelling out her window, "WAIT BABY, I'LL COME WITH YOU!"

Charlie looked at the driver and said, "Get me the fuck out of here quick! She's crazy!" He told the driver as they drove away, "Take me uptown, one sixty-eight and Broadway." Charlie still felt the stinging sensation from the bullwhip, which was as painful as when he was first hit. He had to lie on his side in the cab. He couldn't remember being in this type of pain. After a few minutes, he laughed to himself and thought about all the fights he had been in and how this puny broad had hurt him the most, and he knew now why they called her Dizzy. What person in their right mind would pull out a fuckin' bull whip on a perfect stranger she had just met? One thing Charlie thought was that she was a good piece of ass. With everything that was going on in his life at this point, Charlie thought that this night fit right in with his recent problems.

CHAPTER 9

Friday came too quickly for Charlie. It was time to meet with Gino's boss. There was still a little discomfort from the bullwhip incident, but the constant stinging pain was long gone. Charlie hooked up with Gino at his place and they went downtown to Eighty-first Street and Second Avenue into a classy after-hours club that catered to gamblers, a nice setup with crap tables, roulette wheels and tables, several blackjack and poker tables, and slot machines. It was classier than any other setup Charlie had seen. There were also two nice sized bars around the club, one in a lounge area and two dance floors also. The place wasn't open yet as it was before ten at night. The workers were just setting up.

Gino led Charlie to a back room of the club where Charlie noticed three gorilla-like men playing cards and drinking coffee. When they saw Gino, they acknowledged his presence. The biggest guy there got up and shook Gino's hand. He then pushed Charlie up against the wall and patted him down. It felt like lead paws going up and down his legs. Charlie was going to say something, but he checked himself since he didn't know these goons and there were three of them. When the big ape finished patting him down and announced that he was clean, Charlie was buzzed into a hallway that led to another back room with Gino.

"Why all this security, Gino? You would think we were going to see the pope," Charlie said.

"Maybe you're going to meet your pope, their wise guy," Gino replied with a smile as they came up on another two goons outside an office door. One of the goons opened the door to the back office, nodding and letting Gino and Charlie settle in their seats.

Inside a posh office, Charlie noticed a stocky man sitting behind a huge oak desk and behind him a redheaded woman. The stocky man was Tony "The Hammer" Squateri, the man who threw Charlie's father, Sal, off the roof some twenty-eight years before and the woman was Gloria, the woman Sal had been caught in bed with that night. Charlie was not aware of this connection to his father.

Tony was still in decent shape at his age, yet his age showed in his face with some sleep lines and wrinkles around his eyes. Gloria was still a piece of ass and kept herself well-preserved even though she was now pushing fifty, but still hot. Charlie thought to himself while checking out her large tits that he would fuck the old broad and that in her twenties she must have been some knockout. Gloria smiled at Charlie.

Tony motioned to Charlie and Gino. "Have a seat," Tony told them. After Charlie and Gino settled into their seats, Tony asked Charlie, "What's your name, boy?"

Charlie was a little taken aback by Tony calling him boy and thought to himself, *Who the fuck do you think you are calling me boy?* But Charlie didn't say anything because he knew Tony was a made man, a man of respect, meaning he had murdered someone on the command of a mafia boss.

Charlie just looked him in his eyes, not intimidated at all by Tony. "My name is Charlie Luzzi," Charlie answered in a strong, but calm voice.

"Do you know who I am, boy? Do you know whose money you owe here?" Tony asked.

Charlie just stared him in the eyes. "No, I don't know who you are," Charlie answered again in a strong, but calm voice.

"Well, my name is Tony "The Hammer" Squateri," Tony said loudly as if his name was supposed to strike fear at the mere mention of it.

Charlie remained cool. His facial expression didn't change even though he did know that name from working with Big Red's office. Charlie was neither afraid nor impressed with The Hammer. "Sorry, never heard of you," Charlie stated calmly.

Tony stared back into Charlie's cold eyes and started laughing. "You know, you got a lot of fuckin' balls kid. I like that," Tony said, while laughing a little more. Then Tony stopped laughing as he stared hard into Charlie's cold eyes. "I WANT MY FUCKIN' MONEY!" Tony demanded.

Charlie didn't know how to react, so he just sat there and stared at Tony and didn't waver at all at his order.

"DO YOU HEAR ME, BOY?" Tony asked.

After a few moments of silence, Charlie answered, "I do my business with Gino. He's the one I've been doing business with the past three years."

"FUCK YOU, YOU LITTLE ASSHOLE!" Tony said. "You were doing business with me, and anyone who does any business through Gino does it with me. Don't you think I know about what goes on? I know about your bookmaking operation out of your bar and you selling drugs and you've never had the respect to come see me, ask my permission to operate in my area and pay me my dues. WHO THE FUCK DO YOU THINK YOU ARE?" Tony asked, raising his voice again. He then lowered it quickly, "You think you're a good fella or a somebody? Tell me now! I'm waiting," Tony demanded.

Charlie kept his cool and just shook his head no, staring at Tony.

Gloria was looking on and noticed a slight resemblance to someone she knew before. "You look familiar. Who was your father?" Gloria asked.

"I never knew my father. He died before I was born, but his name was Sal," Charlie answered her.

Tony got a little pissed at Gloria for interrupting. "SHUT THE FUCK UP!" Tony told Gloria. "Can't you see I'm doing business here? Who cares if he looks familiar and who cares who his Dad is, just shut up!" Tony commanded her again. Tony then looked at Charlie. "How much do you have for me?" Tony asked him.

"Two thousand," Charlie replied.

Tony wasn't happy. "I can wipe my ass with two-thousand." Tony started asking Charlie about his businesses, but Charlie kept cool and calm about relaying what he had available to him. Tony was thinking fast as Charlie spoke and he didn't see the point in whacking Charlie for the money he owed. He saw a potential of someone who could make money for him and be a good earner as well as getting the hundred grand he was owed. Tony had to think about it. "What am I going to do with you, boy?" Tony asked and went on. "I mean, you act like you don't give a fuck. Do you intend at all to make good on this debt?" Tony asked Charlie bluntly.

"I always pay my debts," Charlie declared to him.

Tony thought a second and then told Charlie to think it over a few days and to come back on Sunday.

Charlie got up with Gino to leave as Tony warned him, "Don't make me come looking for you, boy."

"I don't run from anyone," Charlie replied, staring at Tony. Then he and Gino left as Tony watched him leave.

Tony admired the way Charlie handled himself; he had balls.

Gloria then spoke to Tony. "Don't you remember who his father was?" she asked.

"Yeah, I remember," Tony said, smiling, "He was the guy who was the Big Shot we helped be a big hit on Broadway," Tony said with a sinister laugh. "Let's hope he doesn't turn out to be like his father and follow in the old man's shoes." "He's handsome, like his father," Gloria said. Tony got out of his chair and slapped her across her face. She let out a squeal of pain and immediately held her face. "You never learn do you, you stupid fuck!" Tony said. "Get the fuck out of here before I throw you out." Gloria quickly left as Tony sat back in his chair and he began to think to himself that Charlie was going to earn him a lot of money.

On the ride back uptown, Charlie didn't say much to Gino. Charlie was thinking about the meeting and how he now felt intimidated, knowing that Tony was a made man and no one fucks with the mob. Charlie thought he could control the meeting and tell them what he would pay a week, but the meeting hadn't turned out that way. Gino let Charlie know that he had to deal directly with Tony The Hammer without his involvement anymore and said he was sorry it came to this, but Charlie knew he was full of shit; Gino was just looking for his cut.

CHAPTER 10

After Charlie got back to his place, he decided to find out more about Tony The Hammer, so the next night he went to see Big Red at the Night Owl. Charlie noticed a big change in the neighborhood since he had last been there. There were a lot of new faces. When Charlie entered the Night Owl Bar, he saw a lot of strange black faces he had not seen before, so he went to the bar and ordered a drink with everyone staring at him. The bartender then asked, "Are you the cops, man?" Charlie just looked at him. "Man, just make me a Finlandia on the rocks and tell Big Red his little white brother is here," Charlie said, not in the mood to be fucking around.

The bartender just smiled as everyone relaxed, as Charlie seemed cool to them now. After giving Charlie his drink, the bartender made a call and a few minutes later Big Red walked in with the bartender pointing him out, though he didn't have to. Charlie was the only white face in the bar. "Big Red, your brother is over there," the bartender said. "Did your Daddy fuck a white woman Red, is that what happened?" the bartender jokingly asked. The whole bar started laughing and Charlie smiled as Big Red grabbed the bartender to get him face to face. "You ever disrespect my brother again, I'll kill your black ass," Big Red told him. "When he comes in this bar, you show him the respect he deserves, you understand?" Big Red told him, as everyone in the bar stopped laughing and Big Red let him go.

"Excuse me sir, if I was out of line. I meant no disrespect. Please accept my apology," the bartender said to Charlie.

"No sweat," Charlie said. "Why don't you buy a round of drinks for the bar on me, Good Time Charlie," putting down a fifty and telling the bartender to keep whatever is left over.

"I heard of you, man," said the bartender. "You should have told me when you came in."

"Hey man, I said I was Big Red's brother," Charlie told the bartender, smiling as he got up from the stool with his drink to go with Big Red in the back office.

In the back office, Charlie and Big Red hugged and reminisced about the first time they were in the office together, the time Charlie pulled a gun out of his pocket and they both laughed about it. Charlie and Big Red spent most of the night talking over old times; it had been a while since Charlie had seen him. Charlie then asked Big Red about Tony The Hammer.

"He's a real bad dude there, Little Brother," Big Red informed him. "He's poison, no fucking good at all," Big Red added and asked, "Why do you ask, Good Time?"

Charlie was a little evasive with Big Red and didn't explain the jam he was in with Tony. He just let Big Red know that he might be doing some business with him.

"I wouldn't do any business with that crew if I had to. They are too greedy, mean and not to be trusted," Big Red stated. "Those Italians will bleed you dry and throw you away once you are all used up, Good Time. Tony is Sicilian and they would rather eat their own children than part with their money, and they love their children," Big Red said.

Charlie told Big Red he would forget about Tony and not get involved with him. Charlie then asked Big Red how his business was doing. Big Red let him know that it was tough times. People weren't gambling as much and the old timers were broke and dying off. He also let Charlie know that the new breed of hoods were killing each other off over the drugs they were pushing on the streets and people were afraid to go out at night and businesses were closing down because the area was so unsafe.

"Well at least you're still in business," Charlie said.

"I'm too old to change Charlie. I'll be here till they put me in a box," Big Red said laughing.

"That won't be for a long time Big Red," Charlie told him, holding his drink up to him.

"Amen, to that little brother," Big Red agreed, clinging his glass to Charlie's and they downed their drinks.

A little later, Charlie hopped a cab uptown to go see Johnny at the club. The cab driver asked Charlie what he was doing in that neighborhood which was kind of dangerous for a white boy and Charlie just told him that this was where he was from, where he was known as Good Time Charlie and he was just visiting his brother. On the ride to see Johnny at the club, Charlie thought about Tony The Hammer, as was Big Red who was in his office thinking about what Charlie might be doing to get involved with Tony.

Big Red wondered if he should tell Charlie about the story he heard about Tony and his father years ago, but Charlie had never mentioned his parents and Big Red figured why tell Charlie and have him try to get revenge on someone who could do him a lot more harm. Tony was ruthless and it would have been like committing suicide if Charlie went up against him. Tony had too much backing behind him being a made man and all. And now, Charlie was coming to him asking him questions about Tony and he just hoped that Charlie wouldn't get involved with him.

Charlie didn't find Johnny at the club, but caught up with him at his favorite Spanish bar up on Broadway. Johnny was busy trying to pick up one of the Cuban barmaids, but she showed no interest in him. She was being nice enough just to get a tip out of Johnny, like the twenty spot he would usually leave and some coke for her to do.

Charlie sat next to Johnny and ordered his usual Finlandia on the rocks from the barmaid and waited till she left before speaking to Johnny. "So Johnny, what's wrong with us?" Charlie asked.

"Nothing wrong, Good Time. I can run things fine on my own," Johnny replied.

"Why do you have this attitude with me all of a sudden?" Charlie asked in a serious, calm tone with Johnny looking at him.

"C'mon Charlie, I know what you're planning—to move me out and have some ginzo come in and take my place," Johnny said. "I'm not stupid, Charlie. I see the people coming into the club lately, asking our workers and our customers all sorts of questions." Johnny said. "And when I ask them who they are, they say they are your new business partners, Charlie. So what's the deal? Why didn't you come to me like a man, instead of going behind my back? That's something only a rat fuck would do. I mean, I thought we were like brothers, but you're not my brother. Fuck man, I was always straight with you with the club. I never stole anything from you. I split everything right down the middle and this is the thanks I get. This is how you repay me, well, thanks a lot, pal," Johnny stated.

"Just hold the fuck up, pal. First, I would never fuck you like that. I would never cross a partner of mine. You should fuckin' know that.

Second, I'm into hock with some wise guys and I don't know who those assholes are coming in our club, but I'm not taking them in as partners. You are my partner, so get that through your Irish-Spic head of yours, you fuck, and the next time you better come to me if you think that something is wrong instead of moping around like some cunt on the rag," Charlie told him.

Johnny smiled at him and they both laughed. After another drink, they both went into the men's room and did a few hits of coke. Johnny left the bathroom first as Charlie stayed to take a dump. As he did, Charlie thought about those pricks coming into his place thinking that they could just come in and take over like that. *Who the fuck do they think they are!* Charlie said to himself, fearful nonetheless that they really could come in and take over just like that.

Later that night, Charlie had to go face José and let him know that he wasn't going to be able to give him the cash he owed him, but that he would pay him in time. Charlie found José at Zapata's, and José waved him over. Instead, Charlie gestured to José that he needed to see him outside. José was too settled in with the women around him as usual and looking very happy, so Charlie went over to him when José waved for him a second time.

Once he sat down, Charlie ordered a drink and attempted to speak with José about the cash he owed. José immediately cut him off saying, "It's okay Amigo. You don't owe me anything." Charlie had a puzzled look as José explained, "Your people came over this morning and squared your tab with me, so we're back in business Amigo. I just have to let your people downtown know from now on what product you take, how much you take and what you owe," José stated and went on. "They say you have a little problem with holding on to money, so they are going to help you keep yourself straight."

Charlie knew what was going down now after speaking with José, and he had a few more drinks with José and left telling José he would be seeing him uptown. Outside Zapata's, Charlie was devastated and just stood there thinking that these fucks were taking over his life for a few stinking dollars that he owed them. Charlie was going to see that fuckin' Tony The Hammer and put a stop to this bullshit once and for all. He didn't like being squeezed this way and he was pissed and wasn't about to let Tony get away with it.

Charlie took a cab to his club so he could wind down a bit with a few drinks and check out the action there, but when he got there the club was closed down as he stared at the locked doors that he couldn't get into. "What the fuck is this shit," Charlie said aloud.

Charlie went to the nearest bar and went in to find some of his regulars there and they let Charlie know that the cops came over and closed it down because they got a call about some fights going on there. It was bullshit, Charlie thought. He paid those prick cops off every month, plus a nice chunk of change around the holidays. There was little Charlie could do this late at night, so he decided to go home and rest. He would find out what was going on tomorrow.

CHAPTER 11

The next morning, Charlie got a call to meet with Tony and that they would call him when they were ready. Charlie then met with Gino to rehash all the bullshit that was going on with him and Tony. Gino told him that he should have never bet unless he had the money to cover the bets he made. He told Charlie he only had himself to blame and that it was a good thing he wasn't in the hospital or dead right now. He told Charlie that business was business and their friendship was separate and that he had to square things with Tony. Before Gino left, he warned Charlie not to fuck with Tony and to go meet with him when he calls him and accept what he had to offer.

Three weeks went by and Charlie couldn't believe all the problems he was having with the precinct that closed his club down. He would open every night, but every other night they were closing him down, and he wasn't getting reasons why. His regular customers had no choice but to stay away because of all the police activity that was happening with the club. Finally, Charlie got in touch with the sergeant at the precinct and found out that the police captain was ordered to put the squeeze on Charlie and his club. Charlie wanted to see the captain so he could find out who was behind it, even though he had his suspicions. The sergeant let Charlie know that there was no way he was going to see the captain as he leaned over and spoke to Charlie in a low voice, "You listen to me you Italian fuck. The captain is only getting his orders from someone higher. Somehow you must have pissed off the wrong people and that's why you're being shut down, so get the fuck out of here, because if you keep bugging my ass I'll see to it that we close down your other bar too, you capisce you Guinea fuck?" the sergeant said.

Charlie had no other recourse but to leave, so he stormed out of the precinct. Outside, Charlie was furious about why these people were fucking with him and his livelihood. After all how could he pay them off if he was broke?

Charlie contemplated taking action against Tony The Hammer as he went over to see José and then on to Big Red to see if he could get some manpower behind him to go up against Tony. José told Charlie that there was no way he would go to war against Tony. He had too much power and was a made man and had the mob in his corner. He advised Charlie not to go up against him and to make a deal to pay off his note. José and his Cuban friends liked Charlie, but this was asking too much.

Charlie then went over to see Big Red and to confide in him what was going on. He caught up with him at his candy store. Big Red sensed something wasn't right with Charlie as this was another visit so soon after the last one. So, he knew something was up. He saw it in Charlie's face when he left last time. Big Red and Charlie retreated back to Big Red's office in the bar to talk over Charlie's problems with Tony.

"I need your help, brother, with a big problem I have with Tony The Hammer," Charlie said to Big Red and he went on to tell him the whole story.

"I can't believe you could be that careless and that foolish to let yourself get into trouble like this, especially with that Sicilian cocksucker," Red declared and went on, "I thought you were smarter and had more sense than that. It's my fault. I should have taught you more and not let you go so soon on your own. I think it was the drinking and the drugs that screwed up your thinking, man. It's easy to let the good times in and neglect your businesses," Red stated.

"I know, so what are we going to do about it?" Charlie asked Big Red and he looked at him.

"Can't do anything, Good Time. Who do you think I payoff? I've been in business with that scum for thirty years, holding off my big bets with him and paying him half my profits so I can operate here," Red informed him.

"I thought you said you wouldn't do business with him if you had to," Charlie reminded Red.

"That's right, I wouldn't, but I have to and I didn't know your situation at that time," Red said as Charlie pondered.

"So, I can't do anything?" Charlie asked.

"Chalk it up to experience, Good Time. The man has a lot of muscle behind him. Make a deal," Red told him.

Before Charlie left, Big Red told him that he and his crew were no pussies and that he could talk with Tony on his behalf and ask for a sit down to see what deal he could work out for Charlie. Charlie hugged and thanked Big Red for his help and said he would await his call after he talked with Tony and then he left.

Big Red sat there after Charlie left and tried to figure out how he could help out his little brother. There was still no way Big Red was going to tell Charlie about his father Sal and how Tony whacked him before he was born. That would only add to the problem. Big Red wished he had the cash to bail Charlie out, but times were tough for him also. He was barely keeping his head above water financially. Big Red made the call to Tony and he wasn't too receptive to Big Red's requests on Charlie's behalf.

"YOU FUCKIN' NIGGER, YOU HAVE NO BUSINESS GETTING INVOLVED WITH MY BUSINESSES!" Tony yelled into the phone banging his fist on the desk. "IF YOU CARE SO FUCKIN' MUCH, THEN COME UP WITH ONE HUNDRED AND FIFTY GRAND AND PAY HIS FUCKIN' NOTE OR SHUT UP AND GO FUCK YOURSELF, AND, IF YOU BUG ME ABOUT THIS SHIT AGAIN, I'LL HAVE YOUR BLACK ASS FOR LUNCH!" Tony shouted into the phone.

Big Red could be heard yelling back at him through the phone. "YOU GUINEA FUCK, I'VE BEEN AROUND TOO LONG FOR YOU TO SPEAK TO ME LIKE THAT! I MADE MY FUCKIN' BONES WHEN YOU WERE SELLING FRUIT ON THE FUCKIN' CORNER!" Big Red's voice came through the phone and resounded in Tony's office, referring to an expression wise guy Italians used indicating that they had killed someone for the family, but Tony was unrelenting and showed Big Red no respect. "YOU BLACK FUCK, YOU'LL SEE WHO THE FUCK YOU ARE REAL SOON!" Tony yelled and slammed the phone down. Tony then yelled to a couple of his men to come in the office.

Meanwhile, Big Red was reeling when he got off the phone with Tony and cursed the Guinea prick and vowed he wasn't taking any more crap from that greasy motherfucker. Big Red decided it was time to make a stand and he would talk to his men and decide how to proceed against Tony.

A little after ten o'clock at night, Big Red closed the candy store for the evening and started walking to his club to meet with his men. As he was walking, three shots rang out hitting Big Red in the chest and he fell to the ground with blood trickling away from his body all over the pavement.

The next morning, Charlie was up early and listening to the news on the TV when he heard about a gang-related shooting in Harlem. Charlie froze and realized that was close to Big Red's area and he went over and turned up the volume on the TV. Then he heard Big Red's name identified as the man shot three times in the chest and that he was at Saint Luke's Hospital in critical condition. The reporter on TV then went on to ask the public listeners to help with any info they might have on the shooting. Charlie got dressed in record time and rushed out of his apartment to go see how Red was doing.

Before Charlie could hail a cab, two men grabbed him outside his building and informed him that he had a meeting with Tony The Hammer and tried escorting him into a black Caddy, but Charlie started to tussle with the men. Then a third man came out with a gun and said to Charlie, "Settle down boy, this won't take long." Charlie got in the car and, once inside, he tried to protest: "What the fuck..." Charlie started to say, but one of Tony's men put the gun to Charlie's mouth. "Open your mouth again and I'll blow your fuckin' head off, understand?" he said. Charlie just stared at him and said nothing as he sat back and was quiet the rest of the ride.

Charlie was driven downtown to Mulberry Street and the Caddy stopped in front of a social club called The Sons of Sicily in Little Italy. Charlie, although Italian himself, never saw so many grease ball Italians in one place at one time. Most of them were dressed up in designer jogging suits wearing rings and thick gold chains with various Italian symbols of what looked like saints on them and they all seemed to be wearing black socks. Charlie smiled thinking how all these assholes dressed alike. Charlie was then taken to the back of the club where Tony The Hammer was eating pastries and having espresso with some old Italian men.

Tony looked at Charlie and pointed to an open chair and told him to sit, talking like he was a dog or pet. After Charlie sat down, Tony rehashed his predicament again with him and Charlie sat there as Tony rambled on about Charlie's shortcomings. Tony was speaking in a very businesslike tone. "Then you have that monkey in Harlem call me up and butt into our business having him tell me not to push you for the cash that you owe, and that chimp has the nerve to insult me too. He got me so angry I was ready to go up to Harlem myself and deal with him personally, but it seemed someone beat me to it as I heard on the news this morning," Tony relayed to Charlie, but Charlie didn't fully believe Tony's bullshit. Tony continued to speak, "So this is the way it's going to be, so listen real good to me. You owe me one hundred and fifty thousand large. I paid your spic partner and paid your gambling note and the interest in the time you owed Gino the money and jerked him around, not paying up. Your after-hours club is done, because you will be too busy now for that dump. You can keep your bar, but my people will run it for you and your profits will be taken out each week and go towards your debt. You will also pay one point on your note each week and that will last until your note is paid off in full and, in case you're no Einstein, that's fifteen hundred a week." Tony informed Charlie and then looked at his cold eyes. "Capisce?" Tony asked him and Charlie just stared back as Tony kept talking, pausing to take a sip of his espresso. "I've made some calls about you, boy. I hear you can handle yourself, plus you have a half a brain when you're not fucked up on booze and the nose candy and bet like a mama Luke, but that's your business and not mine, so you can still do as you please. There's something about you kid that I like—you remind me a little of myself at your age, but I was smarter and didn't indulge myself in the good times the way I hear you like to." Tony went on with Charlie just hearing him out.

Tony, it seemed to Charlie, just wouldn't shut the fuck up and kept talking telling Charlie that he was an orphan too when he came to America from Sicily at eight years old and how hard he worked to make something out of himself. Tony told Charlie how he fought for everything he wanted and kept it and made something out of himself. Charlie thought about clapping and whistling over his accomplishments and mock Tony, but Charlie just nodded his head a few times. Tony let Charlie know that he was now working for him and that he would draw a weekly salary and that money would be taken out each week towards his note but that there would be jobs where he could earn extra, and those special jobs would depend on how much balls Charlie showed and how well he did his weekly jobs. Tony was at the end of his lecture with Charlie and asked him if this arrangement was okay with Charlie and also let Charlie know that, if it wasn't, his man Bruno would just blow his brains out. Bruno was Tony's right hand man, a large man who stood six-foot two and built like a bull weighing two hundred and twenty pounds of solid muscle with jet-black hair.

Charlie really had no choice and played along for now and let Tony know his feelings, staring into his eyes. "The arrangement will be fine. I will work hard for you Tony, until my debt is paid in full, as I said I always pay my debts. But after my debt is paid, I will go on my own again," Charlie told Tony.

Tony agreed and the two men got up and shook hands on their deal. "Welcome to my family, Good Time," Tony said, still shaking his hand and Charlie felt one of the strongest grips he ever felt, so he gripped Tony's hand just as hard. "You're all right kid," Tony said laughing.

A few moments later, Charlie left escorted by Bruno, a little relieved knowing what he faced now. As Tony sat down, he looked at the old Italian men near him and said, "Yeah, he'll leave like his father—in a box." Tony laughed.

Outside the club, Charlie told Bruno that he would find his own way back uptown and Bruno told him he didn't give a fuck if he walked 'cause he wasn't taking Charlie back anyway, and, if it was up to him, he would have preferred blowing his fuckin' head off which he still

68

might do if Charlie didn't get out of his face. Charlie gave Bruno a cold stare. Charlie wasn't at all intimidated by Bruno's size because he had fucked up guys twice his size before and he knew he could do the same to Bruno if he wanted since he was as strong as Bruno and about fifteen years younger too. Charlie thought about getting into it with Bruno, but he didn't. He just smiled. "You have a nice day," Charlie said and he walked away thinking, "Someday, someday you Cro-Magnon mother fucker. We will dance. You and your fuckin' boss Tony will dance with me...someday." Charlie repeated.

Charlie immediately grabbed a cab to Saint Luke's Hospital and went up to the floor where Big Red was and quickly found out from the nurse that Big Red was still in critical but stable condition. The nurse also informed Charlie that he lost a lot of blood but because he is so strong that he might make it and only those who were family members could see him.

"That's okay, nurse. He's my brother," Charlie stated to her and the nurse's eyes opened wide in disbelief. "It's true, nurse. We just have different fathers, honest," Charlie said with a serious look on his face. The nurse just smiled and said it will be okay, but just for a few minutes.

Charlie went into Big Red's room and saw Red all hooked up to these tubes and the machine that monitored his heart. Charlie's eyes filled up as he hated to see Big Red like this and he knew it was his fault. Charlie went over and touched Red's hand and Big Red's eyes opened up.

"I'm sorry man." Charlie said, tears in his eyes.

"No, I'm sorry, little brother. I'm getting old and I got a little sloppy. I guess I shot my mouth off too soon. I fucked up," Big Red said and Charlie smiled at him.

"You don't worry about a thing, man. Everything is going to be okay. I made a deal with him I can live with and you did just fine, brother," Charlie informed him and added, "But, if I find out for sure he did this to you Red, I'll kill him myself."

"I thought you were a lover not a fighter," Red said and went on. "You just be careful dealing with them now. These guys are animals, ruthless," Big Red declared.

"I'm no walk in the park, either. Remember you taught me how to take care of myself," Charlie told him.

"Yeah, I did, little brother, but no stupid stuff for now. I want you around a while and I'll be up and around soon to keep an eye on you also, okay little brother?" Red said.

"No problem, I won't do anything stupid. Just don't worry about anything. I'll show them what I'm made of and take care of everything in time," Charlie informed him and then kissed him goodbye.

Charlie left the hospital and thought to himself that in the long run things just might work out fine. He would work hard with Tony's crew and become a man of more power as he worked himself up their ladder and just push everyone in his way out of his way as he knew he was smarter than most of them, but he had to pay his dues.

CHAPTER 12

For the next few days, Charlie mostly stayed close to his apartment, getting high on booze and drugs. He was just waiting to see when he would start work for Tony. He went out only to stop by his bar just to see how business was doing. Finally, a call came in and Charlie had to check in with his new boss Tony at Mulberry Street and get a list of places he was to collect from each day. He would have to check in every night after his run to hand over his collections back at the club to Tony or one of his men. Charlie thought this type of work was beneath him and simple shit he used to do as a teenager. Anyone could do this job.

Charlie's last stop of the day was in Chinatown and he was approached by two Chinamen who asked Charlie what he was doing in their neighborhood as they got in front of him.

"It's none of your fuckin' business, so step aside and there won't be any trouble," Charlie told them.

The taller of the two Chinamen got closer to Charlie. "Well, you better not be here to take my people's money, 'cause we will have trouble, round eyes," the Chinaman said in his heavy accent.

Charlie got ready to fight them both by stepping backwards and turning, making sure his back was to a wall and also going into a smaller enclosed area so, if they knew any martial arts, it would be tougher for them to use in a smaller space, especially if they were going to use their kicks. The Chinamen thought that Charlie was afraid and backing off so one of them tried to push Charlie backwards into the wall and Charlie grabbed him and drew his rising knee into his balls, sending him to the ground in excruciating pain. The other Chinaman was quick and cracked Charlie in the side of his face sending him backwards. Charlie immediately came back and grabbed the Chinaman's throat with his left hand while smashing him with his right, making his eyes rattle. Then Charlie took his left hand off his throat and punched him with his right. That last punch sent him sprawling to the ground gasping for air. Charlie then kicked the Chinaman hard in his stomach and head, knocking him completely out. The first Chinaman he kicked in the groin was getting up and Charlie just pummeled his face six or seven times, making his face look like chopped meat and sending him back to the ground. Charlie stood over the semi-conscious Chinamen. "Don't you ever fuck with me again you chink fucks, or the next time you will be dead," Charlie told them and spit on them as he walked away.

Charlie felt good about busting up the two chinks. He liked that feeling of power being able to deck people out, and he always felt good after fucking people up. When Charlie arrived back at the club on Mulberry, Tony noticed Charlie's swollen face from the Chinaman hitting him. "What the fuck happened to you?" Tony asked, as he went through the envelopes Charlie gave him. "Someone rough you up for your first day?" Tony inquired further.

"No big deal," Charlie calmly said. "Two chinks tried to jump me. They won't be doing that again for a while. You should see what they look like," Charlie stated.

"I did," Tony, said. "I was in a car following you around today. I wanted to see how you did for your first day," Tony added smiling.

"So, why didn't you help out?" Charlie asked, while Tony stared at him.

"I needed to see how you handled the situation. Besides they never got my money," Tony answered as Charlie looked pissed. "Look, I'm not going to be there every time you go out there and, besides, this is good that this happened on your first day and you handled it so efficiently. Now you have a reputation in Chinatown and it will now get around that you're a guy not to fuck with, so you should thank me for not interfering."

Charlie thought a second and he knew Tony was right. He didn't really need him to watch his back. He was tough enough to handle anything and do anything on his own. Charlie liked what he saw in himself that day.

Charlie fell right into place with Tony and his crew. Sure, he missed the freedom of owning his own businesses and partying like there was no tomorrow, but being with Tony and his crew wasn't as bad as he thought it would be. He adjusted easily to the new environment. He enjoyed collecting money, even though it wasn't his and when people didn't pay he liked fucking them up. Charlie was getting paid seven hundred a week for about twenty hours work. Tony also issued Charlie a beeper in case he ever needed him for some immediate extra work, which was hardly ever.

Charlie hardly went to his bar anymore as Tony now had all his people working there and Charlie just didn't want to face the questions from his regular customers on why all the changes. Plus it just didn't feel like Good Time Charlie's place anymore. Charlie also moved downtown to Little Italy to be close to the Mulberry Club since he was going to be working around there most of his time now.

Charlie would check in periodically with his old crew and on Big Red, who finally left the hospital, completely recovered from the bullet wounds to his chest. With Stevie, he felt bad about Stevie losing his job at his bar, so he hooked him up with José and gave Stevie his old drug connections. Tony didn't know about giving him one third of the profits and Charlie still kept the rest. So Charlie still had some things going for him, but on a much smaller scale. Charlie also let Stevie know that if Tony ever threw him some extra big jobs, he would surely include him in.

Charlie and José's relationship got a little strained since Charlie didn't like the fact that José had to report everything to Tony that he had to buy and sell. Charlie didn't trust him anymore, but this was the new arrangement and Charlie had to live with it. He figured he could live with it for the next two to three years until he paid Tony off. Charlie could also become more important and better known working with Tony's crew. For now, he was a little fish in a big pond, but he was getting bigger each day and people liked him.

Charlie signed over the charter of the club to Johnny so that he might be able to reopen in a few months. Johnny was pissed at Charlie and wasn't even speaking to him since Charlie fucked up a great business they had, but Charlie assured him things would get better again. Charlie also let Johnny keep the cash from the last few weeks they were open and also let Johnny turn whatever stock they had leftover into cash for himself. It was the least Charlie could do for Johnny. What Charlie didn't know was that Bruno, Tony's main man, gave Johnny ten thousand for the closing of the club and told Johnny that they would open up a bigger and better club for him to run in the near future and that Charlie would not be partners with him.

Charlie was doing pretty well in his job with Tony and the drugs Stevie was selling for him; Charlie was making a decent amount of money each week. Plus, Charlie kept himself straight and stayed away from the coke and the booze, which he did sparingly and not on a daily basis. Stevie was giving Charlie about five hundred a week, which Charlie thought was a little light, but he wasn't complaining because that was extra cash from Charlie's old clients Tony didn't know about. Tony did know about the fact that Charlie soon had Stevie selling drugs for Charlie to the clients Tony knew about and he liked that arrangement because it would keep the drugs out of Charlie's hands and keep Charlie more focused on his work without the temptation of getting fucked up on the drugs he was selling.

Charlie was asking Tony for more lucrative work after moving into his new apartment in the village. The place was a lot more money than his last apartment, so Charlie needed to make more. Charlie knew there were jobs that would bring him more cash and he felt he was ready for them, even though it might be more dangerous. Tony thought about it and told Charlie maybe he'd have something for him soon, but Tony knew all along that he was grooming Charlie for bigger and better things. Charlie's asking for more jobs was just playing into Tony's hands and Tony thought of himself as so smart to play Charlie this way, to do exactly what he wanted. Tony liked to think to himself, "That's why I'm the boss."

One Friday night, Charlie showed up at Tony's club for a job he had in mind and Tony had him waiting there a good four hours for him. Tony liked doing this sometimes to his workers to keep them waiting and getting them on edge on purpose. He liked to fuck with people that way. Charlie didn't mind so much though. He got a chance to look over the club, which was really a classy joint and starting to fill up with patrons. There were brass railings all around the club. The couches were made of the finest leather and the dance floors were parquet wood and were buffed to shine every day. The roulette, crap, poker and blackjack tables were the most expensive ones made and also cleaned to shine daily. This was an exclusive club and catered to people with MONEY. Everyone who frequented this club were people of means—politicians, lawyers, doctors, and businessmen. They came into this club dressed to kill and arrived in limos, Caddys, Lincolns, and Jaguars. Charlie thought how one day he would love to own a place like this in an exclusive area uptown. Charlie figured he could do it after he finished paying off that prick Tony. Charlie thought about the future and being on his own again. He thought it could have been right now with all the money he pissed away when everything was going good for him. He wanted to kick himself for letting it get away from him. Charlie attributed his downfall to being young and inexperienced and said to himself that it wasn't going to happen like that again.

Finally, as Charlie sat there, Bruno came over to Charlie and let him know that Tony was in the back and wanted to see him. Charlie never saw him come in and Charlie figured that there must be a back entrance to Tony's office. Once in the office, Charlie saw Tony with this big grin on his face and suddenly from under the desk this stunning blonde, one of Tony's waitresses, popped up licking her lips, just finishing giving Tony a blow job.

"Now, get back to work," Tony said, handing her something. "Come back later," Tony told her as she smiled and left. Tony looks at Charlie. "These cunts will do anything for a little coke, not a bad deal—a blow for a little blow," Tony stated, laughing and went on, "Makes her feel important too. She tells everyone what an honor it is to suck my cock."

Charlie tried to act impressed, even though he really didn't give a shit.

Tony started going into his reasons for Charlie being there. It was about an extra job he had for him and it had to do with a group out in Jersey he was thinking of doing business with. These were always chancy meetings. Tony knew it, but didn't tell Charlie so. He just told Charlie to meet a guy named Joe The Fish out in Jersey City early that Sunday morning. The meet was to take place on First Street near the docks in front of the Tide warehouse, which on a Sunday morning no one would be around and it would be a good place for an exchange.

"You'll be handing over a briefcase and getting sixty thousand in return, but you don't hand over anything until you count the cash and make sure it's all there," Tony informed him and went on, "and make sure you do the deal one on one in your car, no one else." Tony paused and continued, "Now, you are to do this alone and not pack a gun. Supposedly he is an honorable man and might get insulted if you bring a gun."

Charlie wasn't too crazy about the idea of going in alone and not packing. Charlie was no fool. He knew deals like this could easily go bad and he didn't give a fuck how reputable this Joe The Fish was. Tony let Charlie know that right after the exchange, he was to hook up with him at the Mulberry Street Club. Tony also told Charlie his cut would be two thousand for doing the job saying that was a generous cut.

Charlie thought, I'll see how the job goes and how generous it turns out. But he answered, "Piece a cake."

"It will be," Tony confirmed, adding that the briefcase would be at his apartment about five in the morning that Sunday.

After finishing their business, Charlie got ready to leave. But before leaving, Tony told him he could have a line of credit in the club for two thousand if he wanted to do a little gambling that night and Charlie took Tony up on it. After Charlie left, Tony laughed to himself thinking he'd get the job done now for free knowing Charlie was a born loser. Charlie made a prophet out of Tony as he wound up losing the two thousand Tony gave him as a line of credit. Charlie stumbled out of the club that night about three in the morning drunk. Charlie just thought to himself that he'd get them next time and win.

CHAPTER 13

The next morning Charlie woke up hung over and thinking about this Joe The Fish he was to meet on Sunday morning. The more he thought about it the more he didn't like the idea of going in alone and with no gun. He knew he was dealing drugs for that amount of cash being given to him, but there was no way he was going into this blind without any backup.

Charlie called up Stevie and met with him at his place to discuss the job Charlie was given by Tony. They both agreed that Stevie would back him up that Sunday morning. He would get there about an hour early just in case and park across the street. This would give Stevie an hour to look over the surroundings and to see if someone was setting Charlie up, then Stevie would just sit and watch as the deal went down and come in if it went bad. Charlie took a shotgun from his closet, wrapped it in some paper and gave it to Stevie. "Anything goes down, just come in shooting, pronto," Charlie told him and let him know he was going to be packing too, despite what Tony said. After going over their plans once again, Charlie and Stevie did a few hits of coke and decided to have a few drinks at a titty bar around the corner from Charlie's place.

"I go to this place sometimes. I know this one bitch you will like," Charlie told him, smiling as they walked down the block.

"Will she fuck me, Good Time?" Stevie asked. "I'm fuckin' horny as hell."

Charlie laughed. "She'll suck you and fuck you dry Stevie boy, but she's a little dizzy, in fact, her name is Dizzy," Charlie said.

"Well, I like a dizzy bitch," Stevie said as they entered the titty bar.

"Well, you're going to get what you asked for. Just run when she pulls out the bullwhip," Charlie said, laughing, with Stevie giving him a "what the fuck does that mean look."

Early Sunday morning, Charlie awoke at five from someone who was knocking on his door. He opened the door and let Bruno in. After the door closed, Bruno gave Charlie the briefcase with a set of instructions and with a few words of advice. "Don't fuck up this job, sonny boy, or your ass is mine. I don't like you and you don't belong with our crew, but that's Tony's choice, but I'll enjoy fucking you up if you fuck this up," Bruno informed Charlie.

Charlie stared at him. "What's your fuckin' problem with me?" Charlie asked.

"You're a fuckin' loser and I just don't like you," Bruno spate out.

Charlie sized him up and just smiled. "No problem on my end. I'll be back later and maybe we can talk some more Bruno, just me and you, without your trained monkeys around," Charlie said to him, making sure to stare in his eyes and show Bruno he didn't sweat his bullshit and could fight with him anytime.

After Bruno left, Charlie left for Jersey City to meet with Joe The Fish in a car that Bruno brought over for him to use. Charlie got there a little earlier than eight o'clock, when he was supposed to be there and looked over the desolate area. He saw Stevie's car parked across the street, but couldn't see Stevie and he figured he must be slumped down so as not to be seen, but he couldn't go over and confirm it, in case he was being watched.

About ten minutes later, a black Cadillac pulled up alongside his car with the window coming down showing two men in the front. The man in the passenger's seat, about fifty years old, asked Charlie after he lowered his window, "You Good Time Charlie?"

"That's me," Charlie responded.

"Tony said you were young. I'm Joe, Joe The Fish," Joe informed him and invited Charlie to get into his car.

"That's not the way I understand this will happen. You have to come into my car, alone," Charlie told him.

"What's the matter kid, you don't trust me?" Joe asked him.

"Just following orders," Charlie told him.

"Okay, orders are orders," Joe said as his window went up.

Charlie noticed him talking to his driver before he got out of the Cadillac. As Joe made his way around to the passenger side of Charlie's car with a briefcase in his hand, the driver of the caddy also got out and tried to enter the rear door of Charlie's car, which was locked. Charlie looked at Joe, peering into his passenger window. "Just you Joe, don't you trust me?" Charlie asked him.

Joe ordered his driver back into the Cadillac and to park a little ways up at Charlie's request, until he called him. After the driver did so, Charlie let Joe in the car.

"Aren't you a little young to be doing a deal like this?" Joe asked Charlie.

"I may be young, but I've been around the block a few times and I'm not stupid," Charlie replied and added, "so don't underestimate me."

"Yeah, sure kid," Joe assured Charlie. "So where's my merchandise?" Joe asked and Charlie pointed out the briefcase behind his seat on the floor.

"First, we count the cash in the briefcase," Charlie informed him.

"This is bullshit kid, I don't work that way. The cash is here in the briefcase. Let's just make the exchange." Joe stated.

"Look, this is my first job and my orders are to count the cash before handing you the briefcase, so do you want to do this or not?" Charlie asked him and Joe smiled.

"Sure kid," Joe agreed and opened up the case for Charlie to look at the money, which looked like it was all there as Charlie flipped through a couple of stacks and didn't want to push the issue by counting it all.

"Okay, just place your briefcase on the backseat and take the briefcase on the floor and look it over if you want," Charlie calmly stated.

Joe did exactly what Charlie said. Joe opened up the briefcase, which contained heroin and Joe sampled some by cutting into one of the brown bags with a small knife and putting some of the powder into a small tube filled with some fluid, and then shaking it up to mix the contents. "This shit is on the money," Joe said and then waived his hand to his driver.

"Hey, the deal is over, just walk back to your car with the shit," Charlie said. Then he noticed, not only the driver getting out of the car, but someone else and both wearing trench coats. Charlie immediately knew something bad was going down seeing guns underneath their coats and he quickly reached and grabbed his gun under the seat as Joe tried to stab him with a small knife to his neck. Charlie whacked Joe in the head with his forty-five making him drop the knife and sending him into the passenger door. Joe reached for a gun in his pocket and Charlie whacked him again with his gun and took away his gun. The two men from the caddy were getting close to Charlie's car and ready to shoot him as their guns were now drawn to fire. Stevie wheeled up behind them with a shotgun out his window and pointed at the two shooters' backs. Stevie emptied both barrels and cut them both in half just as they were going to shoot Charlie. Joe was then reaching for a second gun strapped to his leg and Charlie began to tussle with him and as he did the gun went off right under Joe's throat with Joe's blood and brains flying all over Charlie's face and clothes. Charlie looked and saw the top of Joe's head blown off. Joe must have had those special hollow point bullets loaded in the chambers to cause that much damage.

"HEY! YOU OKAY?" Stevie yelled to Charlie from his car.

Charlie nodded to him yes and stared at the headless man for a few moments. He instinctively removed Joe of all his money, belongings, rings, bracelets, and doing this at the same time being scared and peeing in his pants, thinking about having not only the heroin in his car, but the cash too. Charlie then opened the door and kicked the dead man out of his car.

"WE GOT TO GET THE FUCK OUT OF HERE!" Stevie yelled and Charlie told him to follow him and they drove away.

As luck would have it, Charlie found a self-service car wash not too far away from the shooting. His fully tinted windows concealed the mess inside his car, but he couldn't take a chance of going through the toll booths going back into New York and someone seeing the inside. Charlie pulled his car into an empty stall in the car wash and began to hose himself down and clean up as much blood as he could from the interior of his car. He got so sick that he puked his guts up while Stevie was laughing at him.

"And this was supposed to be a piece of cake. No problem my fucking ass," Stevie said, still laughing.

After Charlie finished cleaning up his car enough to make the trip back into New York, he told Stevie to meet up with him later at his place as he had to meet with Tony first.

Charlie got to the Mulberry Street club and walked right into the back where Tony would be with the two briefcases as everyone stared at him and saw the dried blood on his clothes as he walked past Tony's two bodyguards.

Tony saw Charlie coming and saw the dried blood all over him. "What the fuck happened to you, you get shot?" Tony asked him with little concern.

"NO, I DIDN'T YOU FUCK. THEY TRIED TO KILL ME. DID YOU SET ME UP?" Charlie bellowed with Tony telling him to sit and calm down assuring him he did no such thing and asking him if he wanted a drink

Charlie told one of Tony's men to bring him a bottle of brandy and top shelf, not that cheap shit.

"So, what went down?" Tony asked Charlie.

After downing a brandy, Charlie told Tony the whole story of what happened with Joe The Fish in between downing a few more brandies.

Tony couldn't believe that these guys tried to pull this shit with one of his men. "Those fuckin' scumbags, some people will pay," Tony told Charlie. Then Tony told Charlie that he did real well and that he was glad he acted on his own and went with back up, he showed good sense. He also congratulated Charlie on his first kill and that he made his bones on his first job. Tony was so happy that he not only came back with the drugs, but the money too. He ended up giving Charlie five thousand for him and Stevie since they were almost shot on the job, but Tony warned Charlie about using someone like Stevie next time and that he should use someone more inside the crew.

Bruno was watching what was transpiring between Tony and Charlie. He became jealous of Charlie scoring some major points with Tony and his crew. On top of everything, he got five grand to boot on a job which should have been offered to him.

A little later after Charlie showered and changed clothes at the club, he left the club and the bloodied car Bruno brought over for him to use. He caught a cab back to his apartment and he hooked up with Stevie. He gave Stevie twenty five hundred dollars; half the amount Tony gave him for the job.

"Is that all the money that fuck Tony gave you?" Stevie griped. "Is that all he thinks your life is worth?" Stevie asked Charlie. "Well, we should have kept all the cash and said that they came with nothing," Stevie said, making Charlie think a moment that they should have. Stevie hung out with Charlie for a while and cut out after a few hits of blow and went to go see Dizzy and get laid.

Charlie had a few drinks and took another shower and thought about what happened that morning. He was calm now and liked the fact that he killed that lowlife bastard Joe The Fish. Charlie felt powerful and superior. He never killed anyone before and he felt good about it. Plus he got paid seven thousand for doing the job and he took another fifteen hundred off of the dead man which made for a nice day's pay. He could get used to that kind of cash. But he thought about what Stevie said and keeping the sixty grand for themselves, and how would Tony find out if they came to the meet with cash if they intended to kill them. But after thinking it over, he knew Joe the Fish would bring cash just for show as to bait them more, so he had to turn over the cash and that scored him a lot of points with Tony and his crew. Couple that with his first kill for Tony and Charlie became that much more respected and feared within the family. Now maybe that fuck face Bruno will give me the respect I deserve, Charlie thought.

CHAPTER 14

Over the next few weeks Charlie was really fitting in with Tony's crew like a pair of old shoes. He even started wearing those designer-jogging suits and the black socks he was making fun of not long ago. Charlie was also totally neglecting his old lifestyle uptown and the life he loved so much. Charlie was getting respect from everyone inside Tony's crew as well as from people outside who knew about him. Charlie was someone to fear now as word got around that he was an enforcer for Tony and Charlie was becoming more and more important to Tony each day. Every job that came up, Charlie wanted it, no matter what it was or how dangerous it might be, and Tony didn't mind giving Charlie as many jobs as he could handle because Charlie was so professional and efficient in getting the job done without a hitch and without any trails leading back to Tony or his crew. Charlie became one of Tony's top soldiers, so there were no more gofer jobs for Charlie as Charlie was making a fortune for him and too valuable to waste on menial jobs. Charlie moved so far up the ladder so quickly that he was now getting all his orders directly from Tony and stealing some of Bruno's thunder and position with Tony. These changes infuriated Bruno and put more of a wedge between him and Charlie because usually Bruno would be a go between for Tony and his soldiers. Tony just liked

Charlie. He saw a lot of himself in Charlie and started to see Charlie like the son he never had. Tony saw in Charlie a kid with intelligence, a quick thinker, a loyal soldier and most importantly a kid with a lot of balls and not afraid of anything. This was a good situation for Tony too, because as long as Charlie was in debt to him he could own him and there was the fact that Tony killed his father and for some reason Tony felt it necessary to own Charlie. Tony thought that he could always keep Charlie in debt to him since he was a born loser and lost most of the money he made from the jobs he did for Tony by gambling at Tony's club. Tony thought that he was one smart cookie by letting Charlie live to pay off his debt because he already wound up way ahead of the game.

After about six months, Tony let Charlie start up his own little crew to drum up any other business he could without interfering with Tony's businesses and having to kick back a percentage to him since Tony let him have that freedom to earn more. Also, any jobs that they pulled outside Tony's territory were to be done on his own time and which again would not interfere with Tony's jobs and, again, kick back a percentage. Charlie didn't mind this because it allowed him to earn more and get out of debt faster.

Charlie took on three men to start his own little crew. Stevie was one of them, of course since Stevie was his friend and had as much balls as Charlie. Charlie also took on a young kid he had his eye on named Jackie D, a gutsy pretty boy who was an expert wheelman and fast on his feet. The third was an ex-cop named Frank who was thrown off the force for excessive force and being on the take and instead of openly charging him and having him embarrass the NYPD, they just let him go. They were all Irish too, which Charlie liked because he could keep them at a distance from the Mulberry Street club. Only Italians were allowed there, and plus he didn't have to worry about people like Bruno probing them for any information about Charlie's side businesses. This was all okay with Tony as Charlie was making him money hand over fist and the less he had to use his own crew. He gave the jobs to Charlie without paying any extra. It was good business and less of a risk on his part.

About this time, Charlie started dating this hot babe named Connie Greco who turned out to be the daughter of a made man named Bennie Greco and who was with another crew. Charlie didn't think anything was wrong with dating Connie who looked like a movie star with a firm tight body. Before Charlie would fuck her each night, he just liked to watch her naked in bed, feeling herself up and playing with herself. She liked men watching her too while she caressed her huge thirty-six double D breasts and fingered herself. It really aroused her and it aroused Charlie too.

"You want to fuck Connie?" she would say, teasing Charlie as he stared drooling at her voluptuous body.

"I'm going to fuck you real good" and he would as he made himself hard.

But Connie was trouble as her father was pissed knowing that his little innocent Mafia princess daughter might be sucking off and fucking a soldier from another crew. Bennie had heard things about this Good Time Charlie and didn't want his daughter Connie to go out with him. She cost Charlie a lot of money too, as she was spoiled rotten from her goomba father and enjoyed the better things in life. Charlie would spend the cash on her too because her ass was that good and he loved fucking her.

Between Tony and Bennie, two made men, there was no bad blood, but Tony worried that Charlie's running around with Connie would create some. Bennie would tell Connie to stop seeing Charlie, but she didn't listen because she was hooked on Charlie as much as Charlie was hooked on her. Sexually together, Charlie and Connie were like two depraved animals and they did just about everything to each other. The more Bennie objected to Connie seeing Charlie, the more she wanted Charlie, telling her father, "He's good to me Daddy, he buys me nice things and takes me places." Bennie would just get furious and tell her she has everything she could possibly want and to stay away from the two-bit hoodlum. Sometimes, she would get so upset she would run to Charlie crying and Charlie would get pissed because her father didn't accept him.

"What's his fuckin' problem with me? I'm not a nobody?" Charlie would say and go on saying, "I'm a respected man. I made my bones."

The situation got worse between Connie and her father Bennie in the next few weeks as Bennie forbid Connie and Charlie to see each other or he would disown her and deal with Charlie personally.

Charlie decided to talk with Tony about it to see if he could have a talk with Bennie and calm him down about his daughter seeing him.

"We have a problem, Tony. Bennie's hassling me. It's all because I'm going out with his daughter. What can you do about it for me?" Charlie asked in a cocky tone of voice as he sat across from Tony who was eating a plate of spaghetti at the club.

Tony let Charlie know his feelings. "Bennie is a made man, Charlie and you should respect him and his wishes and you're a stupid little shit if you think we're going to go to war with Bennie over your prick," Tony informed him and went on, "I suggest you stop seeing his daughter, too. His wishes are to be respected." Tony twirled a forkful of spaghetti in a spoon. "Charlie, who the fuck do you think you are anyway? You think 'cause you whack a few people and smack people around that you can disrespect a made man?" Tony stated and started to get a little angry too at Charlie's cocky attitude.

"What's this shit, Tony? I thought you were supposed to look out for me, being part of your crew and all," Charlie said, as Tony took a sip of red wine after swallowing a mouthful of spaghetti.

Tony sat back in his seat and stared at Charlie. "Look, I brought you into my crew 'cause you owed me. You don't mean a fuckin' thing to me and I owe you shit. I don't have to speak to no one on your behalf, especially a good fella. You work for me. I'm the fuckin' boss here, so get your ass out of my sight. I don't want to hear anything more about this bullshit and you are to stop fucking around with that cunt or I'll let Bruno talk to you about it," Tony stated, pushing his plate away, visibly pissed off. Charlie decided not to push it anymore with Tony and he just left the club.

Charlie just learned a valuable lesson with Tony and knew just what he was to Tony. He was nothing more than a source for Tony to get richer and to maintain his power. Charlie then decided to keep his nose clean for now and not disrupt his situation with Tony.

Two years passed while Charlie was still working hard for Tony, busting his balls to make a buck and doing every job he could. Charlie was almost all paid up on his debt to Tony. With all the interest and the original note, Charlie paid over two hundred thousand and owed less than seventy grand now. Another turn was happening—Charlie actually started winning lately at the club, so much to the point that Tony thought about cutting him off 'cause he was afraid Charlie might win the money he owed. Charlie figured within six months he would no longer be in debt and he could go out on his own again.

Tony was getting worried now, because the arrangement was that he would let Charlie go once he was paid up. So, he had to think of something where he could get Charlie deep in debt again so he wouldn't lose his best earner for him and his crew.

On Saturday, there was a big party for the big boss for the whole New York area and just about everyone was there, including Charlie. When you are invited to a bash that the big boss throws, you don't say no. At the party, Charlie ran into Connie and the fire they had was still there. They slipped away from the mainstream of the party and found a phone booth downstairs by the restrooms, where Connie pulled Charlie inside and started kissing him.

"You still want me after all this time?" Charlie asked her.

"I do want you," she demanded. "And I know you want to stick it in little Connie, don't you?" she asked.

Before Charlie could answer, two men started yelling at Charlie. It was Connie's father Bennie and her brother Bennie Jr. who noticed them slipping away from the festivities at the party. Bennie, Jr. was known by two nicknames as Quiet Bennie, but you wouldn't know it the way he was yelling and also Bennie 'The Shiv' because of his expertise with a knife.

"GET YOUR FUCKIN' HANDS OFF MY DAUGHTER!" Bennie yelled.

"GET YOUR FUCKIN' HANDS OFF MY SISTER!" Bennie Jr. yelled almost simultaneously to Charlie.

"YOU FUCKIN' LOWLIFE!" Bennie added, as Charlie stepped out of the phone booth. Once out, Bennie smacked him across his face.

Charlie just reacted and in a split second he punched Bennie out with one punch breaking his nose with blood squirting out. Charlie saw Junior reaching and pulling out a knife from his pocket in his suit jacket. Again, Charlie reacted with another knockout punch and Bennie Junior fell on top of his father as Connie got a little hysterical.

Some of Tony's men who had seen what was developing at the party came downstairs at Tony's request and they grabbed Charlie and dragged him outside before any more trouble could materialize from Bennie's men. Tony was told what happened and got all pissed off and confronted Charlie outside the catering hall where the party was taking place.

"You stupid fuckin' baboon, you just signed your own death warrant!" Tony told him. Charlie, still seething himself, told Tony to let him go back inside and let him finish them off if that was the case.

"I was only defending myself, Tony. I just reacted to them. I'm sorry if it was wrong, but I wasn't about to let them kill me," Charlie relayed to him.

Tony just told Charlie to get the fuck out of there and he would call him later at home. "Go straight home, you hear me!" Tony said emphatically.

Charlie took a cab home, first stopping off to get a bottle of Finlandia to go along with the blow he had at home. At home, he sat drinking and snorting, waiting for Tony to call. Charlie wasn't taking any chances on there being some sort of retaliation, so he kept a shotgun close by just in case. Charlie passed out waiting for someone to call or someone to unexpectedly come after him, but nothing happened that night.

The next day, he got word from Tony to meet with him at a vacant warehouse off the Hudson River at eight in the morning and Charlie wondered why such a desolate location to meet and not the club. Charlie thought that this might be it, that Tony would kill him off for Bennie at his request. Also, Tony rarely got up before ten o'clock for anything. Charlie wasn't taking any chances so he called Stevie and he came over to discuss with Charlie his new dilemma. They took a ride over to the spot where Charlie was to meet Tony and gave it the once over. They decided that Stevie would secure a spot in the main warehouse about an hour before the meet and where he could oversee everything in case something bad went down. Stevie told Charlie he would watch his back and even would bring his high-powered rifle for this meet in case it was a setup and he had to pick them off at a distance.

The next morning at seven-forty, Charlie got out of a cab near the warehouse and walked over to a spot where Stevie had a good look at him. Stevie was in position after he had parked his car out of sight and walked into the warehouse forty minutes earlier. Charlie looked around and saw that Tony hadn't arrived yet, so he waited. Ten minutes later, a black Cadillac pulled up into the warehouse parking lot. Charlie could see that Bruno was in the front with the driver and Tony in the back with a bodyguard. Tony got out of the car as did Bruno and the bodyguard, but only Tony walked over to where Charlie was standing.

Tony came up to Charlie. "Let's walk, kid." He pointed towards the river. "We need to talk," Tony said and some awkward silence was prevalent as they started to walk.

"You haven't called me kid in quite a while," Charlie said, breaking the silence.

"Well, no smart adult would make a stupid mistake like you did the other night and punch out a made man and his son," Tony firmly stated as they walked.

Charlie took notice of Bruno following them, still staying a ways back but with his hands in his pockets and within shooting range. Tony's bodyguard was checking out the surroundings as if he was looking for someone. Tony stopped and so did Charlie, near the edge of the lot right close to the water. Charlie was quickly sizing up the situation in his head in case there was any shooting and he spotted

Stevie's shadow in the window of the warehouse. He knew Stevie had a tough shot to get Tony, so he knew he would have to shoot Tony if anything went down, but he knew Stevie's first shot would be Bruno and after that they would worry about the bodyguard and the driver.

"So, what can we do about this problem, Tony?" Charlie calmly asked. "I know they want me dead, even though they provoked the situation. She was the one that came after me, Tony. I stayed away from her all this time and she came after me at the party, honest to God Tony," Charlie said, pleading his case. Charlie was scared but wasn't showing it as he glanced over at Bruno. Tony wasn't speaking now and Charlie didn't like the look on his face. Charlie got a little queasy in his stomach as he thought about taking out his forty-five and blowing them both away before giving them a chance. Hell, they couldn't kill him twice for committing two wrongs, he thought, but then Tony spoke, sensing a little desperation on Charlie's part.

"Well, I might have a way out for you," Tony informed him.

Charlie, not knowing what he meant, nonchalantly moved in a better position to shoot at Tony and Bruno while speaking. "What do you mean?" Charlie asked as Bruno stared at him. "How can I make good on this problem?"

"Do you know you broke Bennie's nose and Jr.'s jaw?" Tony asked.

Charlie nodded no.

"The only good thing about this was that it was in public and some people saw it and some people were impressed about the way you defended yourself, but the fact remains that Bennie is a made man and you shouldn't have touched him or his son," Tony informed him and Charlie just let him talk. "Another thing in your favor is that Bennie is not one of the big boss's favorites and he has sent word down that you can compensate Bennie monetarily, buy your way out, instead of Bennie taking it out with your blood," Tony stated to Charlie.

"How much?" Charlie asked him.

"Two hundred thousand, Good Time," Tony told Charlie. Charlie barked at the enormous amount. "Look Charlie, you did a lot of damage not only to their faces but their pride. Two-hundred thousand is not a bad amount for you keeping your life in this case," Tony said and suggested, "I'd pay if I was you."

"Where am I going to get that kind of cash?" Charlie asked Tony. The door was now open for Tony to bury Charlie into another debt and keep him working for him for at least another four or five years as Tony told Charlie he would help him out.

"You know I have a soft spot for you, Good Time," Tony said to Charlie.

Charlie thought, Yeah, you have a soft spot for the money I can earn for you. Charlie thought it over and accepted Tony's offer, thinking that, at least, he will be alive to pay off this debt, but remarked to Tony that he was his goose that laid the golden eggs, meaning that Charlie was the best earner and Tony was getting a good deal too.

Tony didn't want to hear shit and let Charlie know that he had plenty of men like him and that he really didn't need to do this for him. Tony also said another remark like that will get him swimming in that Hudson with the fish. Before the meeting was over, Tony also let Charlie know that he didn't like the fact that he could see beneath Charlie's jacket that Charlie was packing for this meet and that he disrespected him by doing so as Tony walked away he gave Charlie some more advice. "I guess we'll have to go back to square one with you Kid and you're going to have to show more respect, you hear me you prick?" Tony asked, staring at him.

Charlie stared back, showing no fear.

Tony waved to Bruno to come along with him, but before he followed, Bruno looked at Charlie and shook his head.

Charlie knew he wanted to waste him right there. Charlie thought to himself about Tony being upset about the pistol. He would probably be angrier if he knew Stevie was there to back him up. Charlie watched as Tony got in the car with Bruno and the bodyguard and they drove away.

Tony was in the back of the car speaking, "I can't believe the balls on him packing like that."

"I told you he was no good. Say the word boss and we'll go back and waste the little prick," Bruno offered.

"No, I've got plans for that boy. He just has to learn to keep his place and know I'm the boss. Besides, on a meet like this, I would have done the same fuckin' thing. Good Time is no dope. I wouldn't even have been surprised if he had someone in the warehouse backing his ass up," Tony thought aloud. "All I know is I got what I wanted out of this."

Bruno knew it was having Charlie stay on and work for Tony another four or five years which didn't sit well with Bruno because he saw Charlie as a threat to his position with the crew in the long run. Add to that, Tony could count on Charlie as a soldier that everyone feared, a guy who wasn't afraid to punch out a made guy and also who impressed the big bosses.

Charlie was still standing at the same spot where Tony left him and was mentally beating himself up for his careless quick temper and punching out both Bennies. He thought that he should have just left it as a slap Bennie gave him, because now he was buried with another big debt and still owned by Tony for another four years instead of being done with him in two or three months. One thing that made him smile was the fact that the big boss himself took notice of him and valued him as a man of respect.

CHAPTER 15

Over the next few months, Charlie got meaner and tougher with just about everyone around him. He was looking for scores outside the families that would help him get over his debt with Tony. Charlie once again sought out José who could give Charlie inside information on independent drug dealers and deals that might be going down, that had no ties at all with any of the New York families or José's connections, and didn't need anyone's approval. Charlie would cut José in for half of whatever he made after he would muscle in on a drug deal and steal the buyer's money and the seller's drugs. Then kill them both off. This turned out pretty profitable for Charlie as he made nearly eighty thousand for himself in a span of seven months. He would use Stevie, Jackie or Frank or, sometimes, all three, depending on what each job called for and how many lowlifes they would be going up against. Charlie would pay them off out of his cut. Pretty soon, there were no more independent drug dealers and deals going down because Charlie and his crew wiped them out. It would probably be a while before some other independent dealers take the chance again.

Charlie still needed more scores, because he wanted to pay off Tony as soon as possible and be free and on his own again. Charlie felt he was too smart to be stuck working for Tony and that he should be his own boss. By now, he had learned his lesson about letting the drugs, booze, and good times control his life.

Charlie got wind of some realtors and real estate investments where he could double his money in a short period of time. They let him know about a brownstone in Greenwich Village that was going for a bargain price at three-hundred thousand and that they could probably turn around and sell for seven hundred and fifty thousand.

The realtor who got Charlie involved was a guy named Joel Treser from Jersey City. He put Charlie's eighty grand down for twenty-five percent of the investment. As Charlie would find out though, this Joel Treser pulled this little fraud maneuver on about seven or eight other people who were looking for their payday that would never come about. As it turned out, Joel never even purchased the building, but issued out phony paperwork that indicated he had made the purchase. Joel made about eight hundred thousand on the scam.

Charlie was fucked all around because he gave Joel cash and couldn't make any formal claims to get his money back. The government would be all over his ass. Charlie had been showing his bar's income at twenty grand a year. How could he explain the eighty grand he was looking to get back that he invested with this fraudulent realtor?

Charlie went looking for Joel one day. Joel had been keeping a very low profile after scamming everyone. He took Stevie and the ex-cop, Frank, with him to Joel's place of work. The secretary let them know that Joel had not been around for a while. One of the other realtors told Charlie and his friends to leave or he would call the cops.

"Fuck you asshole. Tell us where your boss is and we'll leave," Charlie told the realtor who instructed the secretary to call the police. As she reached for the phone, Stevie took it out of her hand and ripped the phone out of the wall. Charlie then grabbed the realtor and turned him upside down and put half his body outside a nearby window.

"One more time, I'm going to ask you. Where's that no good fuckin' prick Joel?" Charlie asked the realtor.

"You wouldn't dare," said the realtor and Charlie just let the dickhead go. He fell two stories to the pavement and it sounded real painful for him when he hit the ground. Charlie jumped out the window to the sidewalk and was next to the realtor, who was grabbing his broken leg in pain. Charlie stepped on his leg. The realtor screamed in more pain, while Stevie watched from the window laughing.

"One more time, where's Joel?" Charlie asked. The realtor gave Charlie his address, as Stevie jumped down to the pavement with Frank. Stevie grabbed the realtor's wallet and told him that he better be right with the info because now he knew where he lived as he removed the realtor's ID. Stevie also told him that this never happened.

Frank had to get back home, so he left Charlie and Stevie to head out to Joel's home address. The realtor, who wound up at the hospital, turned out to be Joel's brother-in-law and had called Joel to warn him.

At Joel's house, Charlie and Stevie rang and knocked on Joel's door for about ten minutes before leaving the front of his house because no one answered.

"What do we do now?" Stevie asked. Charlie told him to park up the block and they'd stakeout the place for a while.

A few hours later, Stevie snuck up on Joel's house and peeked in the window. Someone was inside moving around. He went back and let Charlie know that someone was home, so they went up and knocked on the door again. This time Joel's wife called out asking who was there and then threatened to call the cops if they didn't leave. They said they wanted to speak to Joel.

Joel's wife wouldn't open the door. Finally, Stevie just broke it down. He and Charlie went looking for Joel.

"He left. He ran out the back when you came knocking!" Joel's wife exclaimed. It was apparent she was right because Joel wasn't around anywhere. "Now, you get out of here or I'll call the cops!" she told them both.

"Do it bitch and your husband is a dead man, so shut your fuckin' trap!" Stevie told her.

"So kill him. I don't give a fuck about him anymore anyway. He's a selfish prick, so get the fuck out of my house!" she repeated.

Stevie took out a bullet from his pocket and showed Joel's wife, telling her that one of them could have her name on it.

Charlie then told Stevie, "Let's go!" and they left.

Joel's wife did report the incident to the local police after they left, but Charlie and Stevie were already back in New York by the time they showed up at her house. Charlie was pissed that he didn't get his hands on that fuck, Joel and, on top of everything, they had to involve his wife and Charlie hated to get any other family members involved in any personal business he had with someone. Also, something Charlie didn't know was that Joel's wife had a sister who worked at the district attorney's office in New York.

After a few days, Charlie had no success in finding Joel. To his surprise, Joel called him and said he didn't want any trouble and he wanted to work out a deal. Charlie then agreed to meet Joel at a restaurant after Joel told him how scared he was. Charlie entered the downtown restaurant and sat opposite Joel in the booth.

Joel started explaining, "I don't want no trouble, but I don't have your money yet. I had to pay some other nasty people."

Charlie grabbed Joel and looked right into his eyes. "I don't give a flying fuck about anyone else, you little scumbag. If I don't get my money in two fuckin' days, I'm going to hunt you down and kill you, you little bastard, and then I'm going to kill your fuckin' parents for having you and you can take that to the bank," Charlie told Joel in a commanding, but cool manner. Charlie than got up looking him dead in the eyes and reiterated to Joel who was visibly shaking. "Two days, you mother fucker, you be back here with my money at noon or you meet your maker. Understand me?" Charlie asked and Joel nodded yes. Charlie left and went back to his apartment.

Two days later, Stevie drove Charlie back to the restaurant where he was supposed to meet Joel at noon. Stevie waited outside in the car as Charlie went in to collect his money. Charlie entered the restaurant and walked over to a booth where Joel was sitting.

Charlie didn't even bother sitting down, "You have my fuckin' money?" Charlie asked in a strong voice.

Joel looked scared to answer, "No, but..." Joel started to answer, but Charlie cut him off.

"No, nothing, make your peace with God, scumbag, because you're a dead man." Charlie said. Before he knew it, four FBI agents swarmed around Charlie grabbing him and one shouting, "FBI! You're under arrest!"

Joel was wired both times he met Charlie and everything Charlie said was on tape. They had Charlie cold. Stevie was watching from his car, but there was nothing he could do but watch as Charlie was whisked away in an unmarked car.

Stevie decided to follow Joel as he left the restaurant. Stevie recognized Joel from the photos he saw when he was at his house. Stevie followed Joel everywhere. Finally, Joel entered a travel agency downtown, not too far from where Charlie was arrested.   Curious, Stevie went into the agency after Joel left. A fifty bill gave him the information—Joel was taking a trip back to Israel in about four months. Stevie knew this prick was going to make off, not only with Charlie's money, but with money from other people he screwed on the brownstone deal.

Meanwhile at the courthouse, Charlie was being interrogated for what seemed like hours. Although he was caught dead, Charlie didn't volunteer any more information, even though the Feds had everything on tape. Charlie just let them know that he had business dealings with Joel and was looking to get the money back that Joel owed him. That was as far as his cooperation went. Charlie's record was spotless as Charlie had no prior convictions, not even a traffic ticket. Charlie called a lawyer he knew through his connections with Tony and the club. He was arraigned and let out on only five thousand dollars bail. He was home that night. While in court, Charlie saw some people he dealt with in his businesses over the years.

Charlie was home and still reeling over that Jew fuck Joel using the Feds to nail him, besides stealing his money. Charlie asked his lawyer earlier about the money he invested with Joel for the brownstone and his lawyer told him he had to look over the papers he signed with him before he could give him any solid advice. The only thing the lawyer told him was that he could charge Joel for grand larceny and fraud to recover his losses, but he probably wouldn't get his money back. No matter what, Charlie's threat to Joel was not a wise thing to do and he was looking at some time in prison. Charlie came up with twenty grand for his lawyer, who gave half of it to the judge who was to hear his case. Since the Feds were involved, they would be looking for the maximum sentence on Charlie, but by greasing the judge's palm, he knew he would get much less time.

Charlie's case came up fourteen weeks after the arrest and closer to when Joel would be leaving the country. Charlie couldn't take any chances of killing him. Charlie did have several conversations with Stevie about it though. "That Jew cocksucker is not to leave the country alive." Charlie relayed to Stevie a few times.

"It will be my pleasure," Stevie assured Charlie.

At the courthouse, Charlie was given a one-year sentence by the judge as his lawyer worked hard on his behalf to get him the leanest time he could. Joel left the courtroom thinking he was home free. Charlie forgot about going after Joel legally knowing the Feds would give him more shit as to how he was able to come up with eighty grand on a twenty thousand a year income. Charlie knew he was going to do time, no matter what, so he would see that Joel was taken care of his own way.

Joel never had the cash on him in America. All the money he screwed people out of had been sent to an account in Israel in which he had over a million socked away. Joel was going to leave the country and not even tell his wife he was going. He was ready to leave her in America to face all his problems.

Before Charlie was shipped off to Riker's Island to serve his time, Tony laced into him, "You fuckin' asshole, you're going to owe me big time now. You're going to be working your ass off for me when you get out."

Charlie really wasn't interested in what he had to say. All he did say was "Okay, boss," but he thought to himself, if this prick Tony keeps pushing him he just might waste him when he gets out, steal all his fuckin' money, and retire to an island himself one day. After meeting with Tony, Charlie was sent off to Riker's.

Two weeks later, Joel told his wife that he had to leave on a business trip.

"It's just business, honest honey. I'll only be a few days," Joel said with a straight face, but lying through his teeth. Then, he kissed her goodbye and left with a small piece of luggage. Outside, Joel got in his car and drove over to his office, arriving there after six in the evening. No one was around as he parked in the lot. Joel had his papers, passport, and the Israeli bankbook locked in his safe at his office so as not to take a chance on having his wife find the papers at home. Joel planned on leaving without telling anyone.

As Joel got back to his car in the lot, he opened his trunk and threw in another piece of luggage he had ready at the office. As he turned to get into his car, someone cracked him over the head from behind. He fell to the ground, out cold.

Later, Joel woke up in the back of a moving car. He was tied up and a rag stuffed in his mouth. As he tried to get loose, he could only make some mumbling noises.

Stevie, who was driving the car, turned to Joel on the back floor. "So, you're up, you fuck. I guess you don't remember me in the courthouse. Nah, you were too busy smiling. Well, I don't see you smiling now, scumbag," Stevie said as Joel's futile attempts to get loose were wasted. "Relax there, Jew boy. Enjoy the ride. It might be your last one." Stevie informed him, smiling and laughing. Then, turning up the volume to the car radio, he sang along to a Frank Sinatra tune, *That's Life*. "That's life. That's what all the people say. You're riding high in April, shot down in May." Stevie sang and then broke in to say, "Hey Joel, you Jew Fuck, this could be your epitaph." Stevie started laughing his ass off.

About two hours later, Stevie drove to a secluded area in Bear Mountain, got out, and removed Joel from the floor of the back seat.

He pulled him out and threw him on the ground. Stevie then untied his legs, while keeping his gun pointed at his head. He told him to get up and walk. Joel was so scared he peed in his pants. As he got up, he mumbled through the gag, trying to plead for his life.

Stevie yelled, "WALK! YOU FUCK!" He started kicking to make Joel walk. This went on for about half a mile. They reached an area where Stevie told Joel to stop walking. He untied Joel's hands, while Joel had collapsed to his knees, sobbing. Stevie told him to take off his gag as he kept his gun pointed at him. Joel untied the rag slowly. Stevie then threw Joel a shovel that Stevie had been carrying and told Joel to start digging.

Joel began begging for his life. "Please, don't! I'm sorry I did this to Charlie!" "Please, let me go! I'll make it up to you! I'll give you money! All the money you want! I have over a million dollars. Just don't kill me!" Joel begged, tears in his eyes.

"And how are you going to pay me?" Stevie asked.

"I have the money at my house, the whole million. I'll give you all of it. Just let me live," Joel said again, thinking that he was convincing Stevie.

Stevie pulled out a bankbook and threw it at Joel's feet. "Home, my ass, you sure the money is not in a bank account in Israel, you fucking, lying, sack of shit?" Stevie asked.

Joel's face told Stevie that he was lying.

"DIG!" Stevie commanded.

"NO! NO! I WON'T DO IT!" Joel fired back.

Stevie shot Joel in the foot and he screamed with pain as Stevie told him again to dig. Joel reluctantly grabbed the shovel and began to dig, crying, begging for mercy, and trying to convince Stevie for the next few hours how he could send the money back to Stevie from Israel, but his pleas were falling on Stevie's deaf ears.

Stevie finally told Joel to stop digging as he saw the hole was big enough. Stevie had Joel throw the shovel in front of him and Stevie picked it up and held it. "If you have any prayers you would like to say before you go, now is the time." Stevie informed him.

Joel got a sudden burst of courage. "FUCK YOU, YOU MOTHERFUCKER!" Joel yelled. Before he could say more, Stevie whacked him in the head with the shovel.

Joel yelled out "NO, PLEASE!"

Stevie tucked his gun in his pocket and began wailing away at Joel's head with the shovel.

"I'M SORRY, PLEASE!" Joel begged, but Stevie just kept whacking Joel's head with the shovel. Even when Joel fell into the grave, Stevie was still smashing the shovel against his head and kept at it for about five minutes with Joel putting up his hands trying to stop the assault. Blood occasionally spurted upwards and on Stevie. Finally, Stevie stopped and watched Joel's dying body lie there. Stevie pulled his gun and shot him once in each hand and then once in each leg. Stevie then spoke, "Goodnight, Jew boy." Stevie fired one more time into his head, making sure he was dead. Stevie then poured some lime into the grave that he had brought to the spot a few days earlier while scouting for a spot to do the job on Joel. Stevie then covered up the hole and buried Joel and then pissed on the grave. "That's for Good Time, you prick!" Stevie said aloud.

Stevie got back to his car and drove back into the city admiring the jewelry and watch he took from Joel after he killed him. He also took about three grand in cash he had on him, this was a bonus he got for doing the job since he was doing this job as a favor. Stevie thought that he had earned this money with this kill he did for Charlie as well as so many others that he should be entitled to a fifty-fifty split with Charlie and not work for chump change.

CHAPTER 16

Charlie wasn't feeling comfortable with his incarceration. It reminded him of being back at the orphanage, but worse and there was nothing worse than the orphanage. On top of everything, Riker's was way overcrowded. Also, being white and Italian made Charlie a minority there with ninety percent of the inmates being black and Spanish. He found that the guards had it out for him too. Charlie got into words with a guard. "You don't want me to take your punk white ass to five main," the guard warned, referring to a part of the prison called the house of pain where fights and stabbings were a daily occurrence, but the sergeant told the guard to take him there anyway because he didn't like Charlie's attitude. So, Charlie went there.

Charlie got into it with a big Spanish man, who thought Charlie would be a pushover because he kept to himself, but after Charlie opened up his head with only two quick hard punches to the Spaniard's face in front of the other inmates, no one fucked with Charlie after witnessing the damage he could do. Charlie spent most of his day in his cubicle working out doing pushups and just waiting for his release date out of this shit hole.

Charlie got a break one day when he was summoned to be a bodyguard for a famous ex-baseball player for the New York Yankees who was doing six months time at Riker's for drug possession. They gave the ex-Yankee some special treatment and let him stay in his own room in the infirmary, the garden spot of Riker's and he requested that, if there were any big Italians at Riker's, he would like to have him for company and more important protection when he mingled with the masses. Charlie fit the bill. This worked out well for Charlie who got the use of better surroundings where he watched color TV, made phone calls, and ate decent meals from the fresh food brought in daily for the ex-Yankee.

Charlie had it good and the only drawback was to hear the ex-Yankee punk cry about being setup, hearing all his other bullshit, and having to work out with him, but it was a small price to pay. The ex-Yankee acted like he was a wise guy, too, while hanging with Charlie and he tried to impress Charlie with some mob figures he knew. When he mentioned one name to Charlie, Charlie let him know that he was a deadbeat and at one time beat the shit out of him for not paying a debt. With that, the ex-Yankee saw it was pointless to try to impress Charlie further. The ex-Yankee was also able to have women come in from the outside so he could get his rocks off and, since he liked Charlie so much, he had some come for him too. One time, they were both busy fucking two sluts that were brought in when Charlie heard the ex-Yankee crying from the other room. He went to investigate, thinking that something was wrong, and he just saw the ex-ballplayer sobbing in the corner with the girl just looking at him. Charlie just shook his head and walked back to his room thinking: boy, some role model he is…if his fans could only see him now. He smiled and laughed to himself.

The time with the ex-Yankee helped Charlie's time at Riker's go more quickly. He was ready to get out soon, but he had to work off ten pounds that he gained eating all that good food he was getting.

Charlie knew he would have to go see Tony once he got out. The last month at Riker's Charlie thought how he would have to work hard for the guinea fuck and he hoped that Tony wasn't charging him more interest on the money he owed while he was in prison. As Charlie thought more and more about it, he wasn't about to let Tony roll all over him like before. Charlie now wanted more respect than he got from Tony in the past.

The day Charlie got out, Stevie was outside waiting to drive him home to Greenwich Village. Stevie told Charlie about what happened with Joel and all, giving him every little detail about Joel's one-way trip, and laughing about it.

"Did you find any of my cash on him?" Charlie asked.

Stevie let Charlie know about the bankbook from Israel and that Joel only had a few hundred on him.

"Too bad he didn't have all that cash he scammed off that brownstone deal Stevie. We'd be sitting pretty right now," Charlie stated with Stevie agreeing. They had a laugh at the fact that the rat fuck was buried in a grave up at Bear Mountain and never had a chance to spend the money in the Israeli bank.

Later, Charlie was back at his apartment with Stevie and he didn't realize how much he missed being there and he was glad he had paid the rent ahead for the last year so he would have a place to come home to. Charlie was happy to be in the real world again as he took a deep breath of the free fresh air.

"Why don't you take a shower and we'll go out and get some pussy. You must be as horny as hell being cooped up in that fucking dive," Stevie said.

"I had plenty of sex while I was in the joint," Charlie told Stevie who got this dumb look on his face that Charlie might have gone queer.

"No fuckin' way you're like that," Stevie said aloud.

Charlie laughed while telling him about the ex-Yankee who was getting him pussy while they were in there together.

"You're about the only prick I know who can go into prison and wind up having a good time," Stevie said.

"Well, they don't call me Good Time Charlie for nothing," he said, smiling and laughing as Stevie pulled out some coke from his pocket.

"Get any of this inside?" Stevie asked.

"No man, it's been a while since I had the high," Charlie said and grabbed an old bottle of Finlandia from one of his cabinets in the kitchen. He and Stevie started snorting and drinking like old times. "I'm back, baby. I'm back with a vengeance!" Charlie said. "Ready to go, man, all revved up with no place to go!" Charlie joked. In actuality, he had somewhere to go, to see Tony The Hammer, but it could wait. As for the next two days, Charlie partied with Stevie with drinks and blow, and some sluts they picked up along the way.

Finally, Charlie knew it was time to go see Tony. One morning Charlie entered the Mulberry Street Club. He was greeted happily by everyone, except for Bruno who showed contempt.

"So, here's the loser fuck out of stir. Did some chubby tough guy bust your cherry inside, fruit lips?" Bruno said, insinuating that Charlie took it up the ass.

Charlie just stared at him. "One day Bruno, me and you are gonna dance and it will be just you and me, no one around," Charlie told him in a calm, threatening tone.

Bruno stuck up his middle finger telling Charlie here's more if you want it. Charlie shrugged it off and headed for the back of the club to see Tony who was sitting in his usual spot. Tony looked up at Charlie, "You've been out two days. What, I'm not good enough for one fuckin' phone call to let me know what's going on?" Tony inquired, looking a little peeved.

"But boss, you know everything anyway," Charlie told him with Tony agreeing and reminding Charlie not to forget it.

"You still owe me a lot of cash, Good Time. When will you pay me?" Tony asked.

"I've been gone a whole year and this is the first thing you say to me, no how you been, how did it go?" Charlie suggested.

"Hey, it wasn't me who got you behind bars. You did that all by yourself. You should just be happy I don't ask you about that eighty grand you lost in that bad investment deal you got into instead of you paying me with that kind of cash first. And then you top it off by not coming to me to handle it for you, so you wind up going to prison and it's your own stupidity that got you there. So, we're still left here with a two-hundred and fifty thousand debt and you lost about ninety thousand in pay you would have made over this past year," Tony informed him.

"Hey, what about the profits from the bar and my drug connections with José?" Charlie asked him

"You don't get paid off on the drug connections if you are not on the outside to work or supervise them and your bar profits barely covered the cost of the interest the past year," Tony said, relaying the hard facts to Charlie.

Charlie sat there going over it in his head. "Well, fuck it then. Give me some work and jobs to do so I can pay you off as soon as possible. I'm tired of having this over my head and I want you and this debt off my back for good," Charlie stated.

"Okay, take another day off first and get your head straight, so you can work with the right attitude," Tony suggested.

Charlie got up to leave. "Listen, sorry about my attitude. Just please, start me off with some good scores," Charlie said.

"We'll see what we can do for you, Good Time. I'll either call you later or you can just stop by here tomorrow afternoon," Tony told Charlie as he left.

Tony noticed a change in Charlie. Sure, he just did a year in jail and he's low on cash, needs work, and wants to get out of debt quickly, but there was a difference in Charlie. Tony had to keep a close eye on him. Charlie was still a good earner so he would line him up with some good jobs, get him back in the swing of things, and then see what happens with him. Tony felt that, even though Charlie followed orders and was a good soldier, down deep Charlie didn't have the respect for him that he deserved and that in time he might be a danger to him.

Charlie was quickly lined up with some jobs and it was business as usual for Charlie. It didn't take him long to get back into the groove and things went along well for him for a while as he worked his tail off to get out of debt with Tony.

Charlie was almost thirty years old now. In the past three years, he paid Tony almost three hundred thousand dollars. Even with the interest payments and the very large note, Charlie was almost all paid up again with Tony. Tony thought he could keep Charlie buried into the loan forever and kept giving Charlie gambling credit at the club so he could lose and keep adding back to the debt. But Charlie actually had won more than he lost in the last three years, due mostly to the fact that he was gambling most of the time without being high on booze and blow.

Charlie was also thinking about settling down and actually having a family. As odd as it may have seemed, Charlie wanted a happy family life, something that he never experienced in his whole life. Charlie liked his women though and liked fucking different girls every night, but there was something missing, a steady relationship would be nice for a change. Even though he had no idea what to do in relationships like that, Charlie started to keep his eyes open for someone who would make him a good wife and mother to their children.

Charlie was a few months away from being out of debt with Tony. He was now clearing two hundred grand a year and, soon, all that money he made would be his and he thought that wasn't bad for some poor kid from St. Patrick's orphanage.

Charlie started hanging out again in the bars uptown and his own Good Time Charlie's bar. He counted on it soon being his again and he started to let the customers know that also. The bar was still doing well with the hospital crowd and other businesses in the area that brought in customers. There were some good changes also: a new school dorm was there not too far from his bar and that could only mean young adults spending money on the weekends at his place. Since Tony was smart enough to put in a dance floor with a DJ and a few pool tables, these improvements attracted a nice crowd every night.

One Friday, Charlie was at the bar and talking things over with Gino and how he wouldn't mind settling down and raising a family.

"Why don't you marry a nurse? They usually make good wives and mothers and they wash your balls too," Gino joked.

Charlie told him that he liked the flashy types with big tits.

Gino told him to marry a nice Italian nurse with family values and have a whore of a girlfriend on the side. They both were laughing when three nurses happened to walk in and sat to have a drink. Gino and Charlie eyed them.

Gino offered Charlie a bet. "Bet you fifty you can't get that one in the middle for a date, Good Time."

Charlie checked her out. She looked a little preppie, but she had nice Italian facial features, a real pretty face, nice size breasts, shapely legs and a perfectly rounded ass. "You're on pal," Charlie said with confidence. He went over to talk with the three women while staying behind the bar.

"Can I help you ladies?" Charlie asked them. They ordered drinks with him. The one in the middle that Charlie bet on ordered a Beefeater martini on the rocks. Charlie focused his conversation on her as he made their drinks. "Beefeater Martini? Are you having a rough day Gia?" Charlie asked her, reading her hospital nametag.

"Yes, we're in the middle of working a double shift. The martini is my dinner, so quickly, please. I need it," Gia said. He smiled at her.

"No problem," Charlie said as he put their drinks in front of them. "These are on me since you ladies are having such a rough day," Charlie told them, smiling.

Gia gave him a big smile back while they all thanked him. "Hope you don't get in trouble with the owner for giving us free drinks. Maybe we should pay," Gia said, pointing to the regular bartender at the other end of the bar and Charlie laughed.

"Don't worry. I'm the owner. My name is Charles Luzzi. They call me Good Time Charlie around here and it's a pleasure to meet you ladies. Enjoy your drinks," Charlie said.

They thanked him again as he went back and sat down next to Gino who was smiling.

"Smooth, Good Time, real smooth," Gino said.

Charlie then called over the bartender and told him to buy a round for everyone and not to charge the three nurses on their next round either. Gia confirmed with the bartender to make sure Charlie was the owner because she never saw him around. The bartender let her know

that Charlie didn't come around much because he had other busine
downtown.

Charlie then went back over to Gia after they thanked him for
second round and asked her out for dinner that night, but she coul
make it. She did give Charlie her number, however. Charlie took
number, collected on his bet with Gino, and then Charlie left to
over to see José and Stevie to see how business was going with t
drug connections.

At the bar, the three nurses were talking about Charlie and on
the nurses relayed to Gia that he was some sort of big shot wise
and Gia raised her eyebrows saying, "Well, he sure is cute and I hav
uncle who's a wise guy and I love him to death. He was always goo
me and helped pay for my college."

CHAPTER 17

Two weeks went by and Charlie called Gia to go out for dinner. She accepted saying, "I'd love to."

While at dinner, Charlie found out that Gia was a few years older than him even though she looked younger. She wasn't like any other woman Charlie dated. Most were bimbos who would fuck him for some blow and drinks. Gia was educated and when she talked, you knew it because she made sense. She also had class, Charlie thought and made him look classy when they walked together. Charlie liked this type of relationship for a change and he treated Gia like royalty and she liked being treated that way. Charlie took her to the best restaurants and clubs he liked going to and she enjoyed it, she also did drugs with Charlie as well as drink with him.

Gia was from a lower middle-class Italian family and she got used to the nightlife that Charlie was used to. It was exciting to her to be with this big shot wise guy who liked showing her off. Charlie didn't confide in her what he was and she was okay with him just telling her that he was a salesman. It added spice to their relationship she thought because she knew what he really was. Gia also figured she wasn't getting any younger and that Charlie could provide her with a much

richer lifestyle than she was used to. Seeing how all her friends were married already with kids and living in nice houses, she felt that Charlie was the one for her. Sexually, she liked the way Charlie fucked her too and she pretty much liked everything Charlie did to her. One night when they were both wired on booze and coke, she told Charlie she wanted him to bang her up the ass and Charlie gave it to her good that night.

Charlie was happy with the way things were going too. It seemed that they were both at the same point in their lives where this relationship satisfied them both.

Charlie and Gia finally tied the knot and got married at City Hall in Queens after about six months of steady dating. Both were not even sure who really proposed either, as it was decided after a night of partying. They went and had a great time on their honeymoon on Paradise Isle and then a week in Florida as they talked about how anxious they were to get their life in New York started together when they got back.

Back in New York, Charlie was still doing his usual jobs for Tony, but was taking a lot of time off to spend with Gia. He couldn't get enough of her. Charlie was spending all his nights with Gia because she worked mostly in the mornings and afternoons. Besides, evenings were his only times with her and most of the cash Charlie made at night on certain jobs slacked off. Finally after a month, Charlie was losing out on too much money because of being home every night. He had to get back to the night jobs that came up, so he told Gia to start working part-time because he would make enough money for them. Gia would tell Charlie that when she had a nice house to live in she would start working less.

Charlie had finished paying off Tony, but was still doing jobs for him and breaking away from him and his crew slowly as all his businesses were his again and he knew that there would be a lot more money coming in now for him and he could buy that house for Gia in two or three years. He could tell she was getting antsy and it worried Charlie a bit.

Charlie got an idea and decided he would tell Gia all about his lifestyle and that he wasn't a salesman. She laughed and confided in Charlie that she knew all along. Since this was cool with her, that night Charlie took Gia out to a Broadway musical and then dinner at The Russian Tea Room. After dinner, Charlie then asked Gia if she wanted to go over to Tony's club, do a little drugs and drinking and then go home and fuck like rabbits. Gia told Charlie she didn't want to drink or do drugs anymore, but she'll go to the club with him. Charlie asked why the sudden change, because his little loving party girl wife was taking some of the fun out of the evening. "Everything's okay with you?" Charlie asked with some concern.

Gia just smiled. "Everything is fine, you big jerk. You're going to be a daddy, Mr. Good Time Charlie," she informed him.

Charlie's jaw just dropped as he was floored. Charlie got up and kissed Gia and told her, "We better get you home. You need your rest," Charlie said.

Gia remarked, "Don't worry. It's not like I'm going to break."

On the ride home, Charlie promised her that everything was going to be great and that he would take care of everything. Gia said that she knows he will. Then Gia started to say that things were going to get expensive: they could use a bigger place, a house; they are going to need baby clothes, baby furniture; see the doctor every month.

Charlie was smiling. "Not to worry Babe, Good Time Charlie will take care of it, nothing but the best for my family," he stated, but knowing he would have to go into hock with Tony again to make sure his family would be provided for. At least this time it was for a good reason, he thought to himself. What's another three years that I have to work for him anyway? I have a family now.

So, Charlie went to see Tony at the Mulberry Street Club to discuss some business. When Charlie got there, they got into an argument over the businesses that Charlie owned with Tony saying that Charlie still owed him sixty grand for all the improvements he made over the years in his bar and that, until he paid that off, they owned the bar together. Charlie had been counting on all the income from the bar for his needs and didn't think he would still be splitting with Tony now that he was paid off. Charlie was pissed, but he needed Tony now. His family needed things. He needed a large sum of cash now, and couldn't wait to earn it. After bickering back and forth for hours, Charlie finally agreed with Tony on a deal they both could live with. Tony got what he wanted—having Charlie buried in more debt. Charlie got what he wanted—money to get a nice house on Long Island and immediate financial security for his family. Tony gave Charlie a big break on the percentage interest on the money he was now lending Charlie and asked Charlie not to say anything to Bruno because he never gave Bruno or anyone a deal like that. Tony made some major concessions, but with Charlie he knew he would get his money back tenfold and it was important just to keep Charlie working for him. After their meeting, Tony invited Charlie and his wife out for dinner.

That was a big offer Charlie thought because Tony rarely did things like that. "Thanks Boss, we'll see you tonight then," Charlie told him.

"Good, in the meantime, why don't you and your wife go house shopping this afternoon," Tony suggested. "And let me know how much you'll need for it." Charlie agreed and left. After Charlie left, Tony smiled to himself, thinking, this jerk will always be mine and tonight at dinner he'll let his new wife know how much money she can spend. Charlie will probably be back asking for more than he originally thought. "God I love my work," Tony said aloud and gloated to himself, "and this is why I'm the boss." Tony then began singing.

That night Charlie and Gia drove over to have dinner with Tony in their new shiny black Chevy Corvette. Charlie bought it thinking it looked so cool, like the Bat-mobile. Soon, he would also buy Gia a new car right after they picked out and moved into their new house.

During dinner, Gia felt that she found Tony pretty charming and she wondered why Charlie was sour on him most of the time when he mentioned him to her. At dinner, Tony handed Charlie a large envelope with two hundred thousand inside and told him, if he needed more to let him know. There was enough money in the envelope for at least a down payment on a house on Long Island. During dinner and out of the blue, Gia referred to Tony as uncle and Charlie nearly choked on his shrimp when he heard that. Tony was acting like a saint during dinner telling Charlie that he was like a son to him and he would do anything for him

Charlie thought, "Sure, you prick, as long as I keep making you millions and you can gouge me for interest on money I owe you and, if I was sick or unable to make you the cash, I'd be shit out of luck because then you wouldn't give me the time of day."

After dinner while Charlie and Gia were driving home, Gia began praising Tony's good heart. Charlie was ready to upchuck his dinner if she kept at it, so he told her to stop talking about that dirt bag. Then she started talking about other things, "So, where will we go tomorrow to search for a house?"

Charlie suggested that tomorrow they should go to Freeport; he heard from some people that it was a good area. Freeport was about a forty-five minute ride from New York City on the south shore of Long Island and it was close to the ocean. Most of the houses there were brick houses with big driveways. Italians liked that shit.

The next day, they decided to save time by going into a real estate office to see what the going prices on houses in Freeport were. They hooked up with a realtor named Jan, a tall blond lady in her fifties, probably Jewish with all the rings, bracelets and necklaces she was wearing and with her nose up in the air attitude as she spoke. "It's a rough buyer's market right now and prices are sky high, honey," Jan said.

Charlie wasn't in the mood to be snowed so Charlie cut to the quick with her and told her what they were looking for. "And, please don't call me honey. That's bee shit," Charlie said, much to the chagrin of Gia, but all Charlie was doing was trying to make this as painless and quick as possible without all the bullshit. With that, Jan just told them to come with her and she would show them a few houses that would fit their needs.

"By the way, do you have financing?" Jan asked, as she showed them the first house.

Charlie thought, We haven't even picked out a fuckin' house yet and she's worried about how we will pay for it. "Listen lady, just find us a house we agree on and let me worry about how we'll pay for it," Charlie stated.

"Yes, but I wouldn't want to waste each other's time," Jan said in that uppity tone of hers.

Charlie was getting a little pissed with her. He was thinking that maybe she was thinking, Charlie being in a jogging suit and Gia in jeans and a shirt, and not dressed to her uptown taste, that maybe they didn't have the money to afford a house in Freeport. But Charlie thought, can't she see that $30,000 dollar ring on Gia's finger? Did she think it was glass? Charlie just told her to keep showing them houses and that it will only be a waste of time if we don't find a house we like.

Jan showed them about four houses in different areas. None were to their liking, but they noticed some houses in an area they did like when driving to the houses she was showing. These houses had nicely trimmed lawns, big driveways, and were in stylish brick. Gia kept telling Jan what she wanted and Jan said for what they were looking for that they should go another half-hour drive farther into Long Island and that she was just trying to stay within a price range she thought they could afford.

Charlie lost his composure. "Listen lady, do you think I'm some sort of fuckin' bum? You have no idea what I can afford, so just show us a house according to what we are looking for or we'll go to another realtor," Charlie bluntly told her. "So, either show us a house that my wife would like or we walk," Charlie added.

"Look, I'm sorry if I offended you in any way," Jan said and went on, "It wasn't my intention, I think I have something for you. Please, just sit back and relax and I'll take you there." She took them to a house that was situated away from the main road. It was a four-bedroom colonial brick house with a large neatly trimmed lawn and a large driveway with evenly trimmed bushes, a large backyard and swimming pool. Charlie and Gia's eyes lit up when they saw it. Jan immediately let them know the price to save time if it was out of their range, reduced to one hundred and eighty thousand from two hundred grand. It seemed the owners were anxious to unload it since they already moved to Florida and came down on their asking price.

"We'll have to see the inside before we make a decision," Charlie told her and with that they went inside. Jan escorted Gia around inside as Charlie sat on the steps outside to smoke a cigar. Ultimately it would be Gia's call anyway. If she wanted the house, he would get it.

Charlie saw one of the neighbors and he got up and went over and struck up a conversation with him asking questions about the house and the owners. Charlie found out that the owners had been there for forty years and just wanted to be in sunny Florida year round now. He also found out that they originally bought the house for twelve thousand and that the house had been on the market for some time.

After he finished conversing with the neighbor, Charlie sat back down on the steps and thought about it, while waiting for Gia's decision. Jan and Gia returned to Charlie on the front steps and Charlie saw in Gia's eyes that it was a go, that this house was it. After some negotiations with Jan privately, Charlie walked away with a hundred-fifty thousand dollar cash deal on the house.

After closing the deal, Charlie took Gia out furniture shopping, buying everything new for the new house. Between the house, closing costs and furnishing the house and also getting Gia an El Dorado Cadillac, Charlie wasn't left with much out of the two-hundred grand Tony spotted him the night before, but Charlie figured it was money well-spent and in another three or four years he would have Tony paid off again. Charlie was happy though: Good Time had a wife and a kid on the way, a nice big house, and new cars. He had the whole nine yards and most of all a family life he had never had before. Gia was also living on cloud nine. Life was good. She had a husband who was a good provider and she was pregnant with her first child. She had eventually caught up with her girlfriends who were all married and living the family life, but she did better for herself—she had a bigger home, a finer car, and a constant flow of cash at her disposal.

CHAPTER 18

As they settled into their family life, they started to entertain their friends, his and hers to show off the new house they had bought. Gia didn't care for Charlie's acquaintances and asked Charlie to stop inviting them over because they drank too much and did drugs. Charlie didn't care for her friends, which consisted of stuck-up drunken lawyers and doctors and a few other major assholes that Charlie had absolutely nothing in common with. Charlie didn't like when they probed him with questions about his line of work. Gia would always interrupt and say he owned a restaurant supply company in New York.

"Great, now I know where to go when I need some pots and pans. I'll let you know," one doctor said once to Charlie at a party.

Charlie just smiled at him asking, "Do you have a good shovel?" He was esoterically referring to his line of work and that he wouldn't mind burying the good doctor one day.

"No, I don't think I do," the doctor innocently answered.

Gia was getting close to her due date and she had stopped working, which meant Charlie was the only one bringing in the cash. Since she was home so much, she wanted Charlie to stay with her more, but his staying home meant he was losing out on making money for them to live. Gia had her way to get what she wanted, too.

"You can always make money, but you can't always get a great blow job from your loving wife while you're at work," she would seductively tell him. Usually after a session like that, Charlie would wind up staying home and taking her to lunch, shopping, then dinner, and wind up spending $300 on bullshit stuff instead of going out to make some money.

Gia finally gave birth to a baby girl and they were proud parents. Gia named her Alison. As they agreed, Gia would name the girls born in the family and Charlie would name the boys. Why Gia chose Alison, Charlie never knew. It had absolutely no Italian ring to it at all. Charlie, even though he was happy about the birth of his baby girl, didn't feel any different. He thought with the birth of his first born that it would cause a change in him, but he felt no different and he wondered if there was something wrong with him. As a person, Charlie still felt incomplete. The family lifestyle did not affect him the way he thought it would. What's the big fuckin' deal? He expected that maybe in time his feelings would be different.

With the new expenses of his new born and with Gia not working, Charlie had to step up his pace to make some cash again. Gia was still spending money like they were Rockefellers, not realizing what a burden she was putting on Charlie. She thought Charlie's resources were endless. Charlie had to go back and do some extra jobs to score extra cash, so he went back with José and Stevie and did more work with pushing the drugs, which meant not being home nights. He had no choice if he wanted to keep the new luxury family lifestyle he was in.

After about a year, Gia grew very unhappy with Charlie not being around at night. Their home life was not a happy one. Charlie would still be drinking and snorting the nose candy every night as he always did when around José and Stevie, and every morning Charlie would come home high on the booze and blow. Gia wasn't thrilled about that and complained endlessly to Charlie about it, "You're a father now. You have responsibilities. You have to cut this fuckin' drinking and coke out!" She would yell and continue to chastise him. "When are you going to fuckin' grow up and be a man?" she would say. Every time he was ready to go out for the night, she wanted to break his balls. "You're going out again!" she would scream. "Where the fuck are you going now?" she would ask and, before he went out, she would pry a thousand out of him and tell him that she had company coming over the next night and that he had better not go out the next night.

Charlie would wonder, What the fuck happened to that shy loving girl I married?

"Fuck you and your company, you fuckin' nut job!" Charlie would tell her and storm out the door.

She's turned into fuckin' Godzilla, Charlie thought to himself driving off and leaving her in a fit of rage. What the fuck did I get myself into with that screwball? Charlie wondered. Well, at least she gave me a beautiful daughter I love, Charlie would think, resolving his situation in his mind.

A few weeks later, Charlie had a real big blow up with Gia letting her know that, since he was stopping his drinking and coke, she had to cut down on her spending. They really were going at it and Gia got Charlie fuming with a comment about him having a real good job like her doctor friend Donald or as she called him "Donny!"

"Well then, why didn't you marry that dickless fuck instead of me?" Charlie fired back at her.

"You're right. It's my fault. I should have married him, but I married you and I'm stuck with you," she spitefully stated and adding that she got caught with the glamour of him being with the mob, but telling him that he wasn't even a real good one like his boss Tony.

Charlie stared at her raising his index finger to her. "If it wasn't for my daughter, you could go fuck yourself," Charlie said in a calm voice and walked out of the house.

Gia followed him with Charlie thinking she was going to apologize, but she asked him instead for money to buy stuff for a pool party she was throwing the next day.

"Fuck you! Get your doctor Donny friend to pay for your parties and buy the booze for your alcoholic friends for a change," Charlie told her and left thinking that she had some balls to ask for money after all the shit she said.

The next few weeks they hardly spoke to each other. Gia would get things good between them by giving Charlie a night or afternoon of hot sex the way they had when they met, but the peace never lasted that long as the arguments would start up again and they would go another few weeks with silence. This was a cycle that lasted for a few years with Charlie seriously starting to think about making a move to get away from the psycho bitch. Charlie knew he wasn't the perfect husband either but Gia knew what he was when they married and that his job meant that he had to work nights. But Charlie just couldn't take her bitching anymore. Gia now felt that Charlie wasn't good enough for her anymore. She had outgrown him and it drove Charlie away.

CHAPTER 19

Now at 34, Charlie felt he was going nowhere fast. He was determined to make things right in his life again. His drug connections with José and Stevie were earning more now. Problems arose with Stevie who was acting a little ungrateful and getting greedy, forgetting that Charlie had gotten him started with this business which made them a lot of dough in the past few years. On the other hand, Stevie felt that Charlie used the connections when they suited him, such as when he needed the cash. Stevie didn't think it was fair. Charlie was giving him half the profits, but Stevie wanted more now.

"I put you in business, made you a full partner, even overlooked the fact that I know you're skimming some off the top too, and this is how you thank me?" Charlie told Stevie one night.

Stevie said he was the one working his ass off every night and that Charlie only came around when he needed the extra cash. Charlie and Stevie almost came to blows that night throwing old favors in each other's face.

"Don't you ever mistake my kindness for weakness, you stupid Irish prick!" Charlie warned him.

"And I'm not some fuckin' lackey, you can just use, you fuckin' grease ball!" Stevie fired back at him and Charlie got that cold look in his eyes.

"You better check yourself, pal. Is it going to be you and me or one of us alone? Decide now," Charlie dared him in a low commanding voice with Stevie backing down for now.

"Not today, tough guy, but maybe another time," Stevie stated.

Charlie didn't know what to make of that answer, but it ended their argument that night and Charlie went to see José at Zapata's.

Charlie sat with José, who as usual had a couple of lovelies sitting with him, and José was happy to see Charlie. Charlie partied a little with José and they went to the bathroom to do some coke together and José seeing his old buddy wasn't in the best of spirits invited him to a private party at his pad with a few hot bitches.

Charlie and José partied for a few hours with the two women. They drank, snorted some coke, and Charlie took the shapely brunette wearing the tight blue dress into one of José's bedrooms. He had her suck him hard and then he fucked her doggy style while she leaned against the dresser draw and Charlie could hear José pounding the young blonde bitch in the next room,

"Yeah, fuck me! Fuck me!" Charlie heard the blonde say from the other room and then moaning real loud as she came. He and the brunette laughed at the young blonde's vocal pleasures. Inside the bedroom where José and the blonde were, José finished pumping the young blonde.

"Ay caramba, baby! You have one tight little fuckin' chocha!" José exclaimed. "How old are you?" José asked.

"I'm fifteen," the blonde said with José saying, "Shit, you jailbait baby." The blonde told him that's okay and asked him if he wanted to fuck her up the ass now.

Later, after Charlie and José were done with the bimbos, they gave them some coke and sent them on their way. They got into a conversation about Stevie and Charlie asked what was going on with him. José let Charlie know that Stevie was getting a little out of hand and looking to take over all of his contacts and cut Charlie out altogether. José also let Charlie know that Stevie was pushing a lot more stuff lately, not cluing Charlie in, and keeping the extra profits he had been making,

"Also, he asked me not to tell you about it cuz. It was none of your business," José relayed to Charlie and continued on. "He's been bad mouthing you all over, amigo, saying that you are getting fat being a downtown man and that us uptown people weren't good enough for you and that you only use us when it's convenient for you."

"Do you think that, José?" Charlie asked him.

"Good Time, we go back a long time and you always been square with me. For me, the only reason I deal with Stevie is because you brought him in, otherwise, I wouldn't." José added, "Also, he's a junkie, amigo, with a hunger for both coke and money and I heard from someone that he might be trying to make a big deal with those Dominican pigs and you know, my friend, if he does that, he'll be cutting us both out."

Charlie's mind was racing.

"You know what could happen if he goes with those Dominicans and what it means Good Time. Those fucks are animals and would slice their own mother's neck for a dollar and you know it would be trouble for us too," José added.

Charlie knew this was a situation he had to handle personally. He had seen this happen to a lot of people before, punks who let the lifestyle go to their heads thinking that they were better than their bosses, and craving more money and power and totally neglecting the chain of command. He saw this in himself with Tony and he wanted to take Tony out so many times, but you had to have that respect and loyalty for the people above you who treated you right or total control was lost and total anarchy would exist. Charlie knew this, but it was obvious it was escaping Stevie who was out of control.

"Don't worry, amigo, like that one time you asked me to trust you and that you would take care of a certain situation," Charlie stated with José nodding to him. "Back then, you put your trust in me and trust me to handle this," Charlie told José.

Charlie was very upset about Stevie, thinking how stupid can he be to try and take on him and José. Charlie thought about the situation and needed to investigate further to make sure his solution would be the right one. By the way Stevie was acting lately, he knew that José wasn't bullshitting him.

Charlie let a few days go by and met with Stevie on some business and Charlie accompanied him on some collections that day. Charlie was subtle in his approach with Stevie in trying to feel him out to make sure everything José had told him was true. Charlie wanted to give Stevie every opportunity to prove him wrong, but it was becoming apparent that Stevie was getting ready to branch out on his own, as there was an air about him when speaking to their customers. The way he talked with some of the connections saying "me" and "I" a lot instead of "us" and even speaking over Charlie when questions were asked directly to Charlie. Charlie likened that kind of talk to Gia who would now say "my house" and not "ours" anymore.

Charlie let a lot of things slide with Stevie over the years. Maybe, it was the fact that Stevie did him that big favor years ago taking out that Jew Joel, but Stevie was getting too greedy now. Taking advantage of Charlie's old connections after Charlie set him up in business and being friends is one thing, but business is another. You just don't do what you want and take a friend for granted and take so much off the top. Charlie faulted himself a bit: maybe he should have been stricter with

Stevie, but, then again, how could he know Stevie would wind up like this.

As they hooked up with José at his apartment, Charlie had it out with Stevie, letting him know that he was not doing right by him. Stevie felt that Charlie shouldn't get involved in how he runs this side of the business anymore, "Listen you fuck, I'm still the boss here. I made you what you are today, so who the fuck do you think you are, you Irish cocksucker?" Charlie asked him. "I made you and I can break you!" Charlie told him.

"No! You listen to me, Mr. Good Time. You don't have the weight uptown anymore and neither does that Cuban fuck!" José Stevie fired back, getting real cocky. "You fuckin' guys are dinosaurs, old shit and washed up, and I'm hooking up with some heavy hitters now. I only stayed with you guys for old time sake and felt sorry for you two, but it's over now and there can't be two head guys so I'm the one." Stevie looked at Charlie and José.

Charlie was trying hard to remain cool as he tried to talk some sense into Stevie. "I think you better cool it, kiddo, and wisely rethink what you're saying real hard because it could affect your health," Charlie stated, solemnly staring at Stevie.

Stevie glared back at them both, telling them he was done with them and left saying he'll see them around.

Charlie looked at José. "I will handle it," Charlie assured José.

"Handle it soon, amigo, cause if you don't I will," José said, still fuming a bit.

This was a tough situation for Charlie. He liked Stevie and looked at him like a brother over the years. They partied together, killed people together, watched each other's back over the years. Charlie knew it was the coke and his greed for money that was taking over Stevie. Those things were erasing the bond they developed over the years. Charlie owed Stevie one last chance to straighten his ass out.

Charlie thought long and hard about the Stevie situation and it lead to a lot of personal revelations about himself also. He hadn't felt like Good Time Charlie in a long time. That fellow left him a long time ago and it seemed everything in his life wasn't right anymore. Somewhere he took a big detour in life that had taken him to this point and pitted him against someone that used to be a friend, but it was the nature of the business he was in. It was a business where friends and enemies were tough to distinguish after a while. Money was always the deciding factor and that was the life that Charlie chose for himself and he knew he had to live with the good and bad of it.

Stevie wasn't around for the next three weeks and wasn't answering any of Charlie's calls. Charlie didn't care too much for this type of snubbing Stevie was giving him and was wondering what Stevie was up to. Charlie started going around to his drug customers and learned that Stevie was trying to sell them coke at a lower price. Charlie knew he must have made a deal and now was being sponsored by the Dominicans and was trying to take away his customers. What Stevie didn't count on was Charlie, who was a trusted and liked supplier for years and his customers weren't going with Stevie. This also put Charlie and José on their guard as they expected some type of repercussion from Stevie since his plans weren't going the way he thought.

Stevie finally called Charlie and asked to meet with him to discuss their problems and try to come to an agreement. Stevie had told Charlie, "Hey, we're like brothers. We should be able to work this out."

Charlie knew he couldn't work it out and thought, Yeah, we're brothers, like Cain and Abel. Without totally trusting him, he agreed to meet him. Charlie could hear on the phone that Stevie was fucked up on drugs as he slurred his words. This made Charlie more concerned as they agreed on a place and time. Charlie said he would bring along José since he was involved too. Stevie wasn't receptive to that idea and told Charlie he just wanted it to be the two of them, so Charlie agreed.

After his phone conversation with Stevie, Charlie talked with José about the meet and where it was. Charlie thought it might be a setup and he had to take the necessary precautions after José let Charlie know that the place he was meeting Stevie was a Dominican hangout.

The next night Charlie was up at 235th Street at a place called El Bandito. He walked into the bar at about eleven o'clock and ordered a drink. The place stank of stale beer and the poor ventilation system didn't help much for the stagnant air. The bar had only three customers, which didn't look like trouble to Charlie. About fifteen minutes later, Stevie walked in and sat down at a table in the corner, waving Charlie to come over.

Charlie walked over to the table and sat down. "And hello to you too," Charlie said with some sarcasm. As soon as he had sat down, five Spanish guys entered the bar, looking it over. The bartender didn't seem to recognize them as they sat at the bar and ordered some beers.

"You want a drink?" Charlie asked Stevie.

"No, I'm here on business, not to socialize," Stevie stated.

"So start talking," Charlie said.

"Look, you're finished, Good Time. I'm the man in the neighborhood now and I'm taking over," he boldly told Charlie. Then he let him know that he had made a deal with a well known Dominican drug dealer named Diablo from Charlie's old territory and connections. Diablo was pushing everyone out. "You can't just come and go as you like uptown anymore. Times have changed and this area is mine now. You left a long time ago and it's time for someone new to take over altogether and that's me," he told Charlie.

"Is that why the customers are staying with me, you little shit?" Charlie asked. "You were only in business because of me. I gave you the customers and the means to supply them with José. Otherwise, you would have been shit, a nobody—and the territory and all are still mine."

"Well, not anymore," Stevie smugly suggested. "Your buddy, José, got a call saying to meet you and just like you've been brought here to meet your fate. José will meet his," Stevie told him. He waved to the guys at the bar and they came over with guns drawn on Charlie. They had Charlie stand up as they patted him down to see if he was packing. Then Stevie introduced his new supplier, Diablo, to him.

Diablo was smiling as Charlie spoke.

"I didn't bring a gun, Stevie. I thought this was to be a friendly meeting between two old friends and partners, pal," Charlie said, giving Stevie that cold stare.

"Well, you made a mistake, Good Time," Stevie said.

Charlie knew now that it was a setup and Stevie was no longer good to him.

"Let's go. Your time is up. It's time for you to meet the grim reaper, as they say," Stevie said to Charlie.

Charlie smiled. "So, this is how you repay me, after all I did for you?" he asked Stevie as Stevie got up and motioned to him to start walking,

"Sorry Charlie, it's business, nothing personal," Stevie said.

Charlie stopped at the bar and stared at him. "One more drink, a toast to old times," Charlie suggested to Stevie.

Stevie nodded his head. "Sure, why not, for old times," Stevie agreed liking the idea because it made him look important to his new crew around him to have this big wise guy make a last request.

Charlie and Stevie gulped down a double shot glass each of Jack Daniels.

"Have to do it right, pal, go out the right way, one more snort in the bathroom, if you don't mind," Charlie said, reaching in his pocket to take out a vile of coke.

Stevie looked at the five Dominicans.

"When I finish this, I'll be right when I meet my maker. It's really good shit," Charlie said.

Stevie laughed. "Sure, Good Time, can't deny you your last requests," Stevie said as he told the Dominicans to wait there and he walked Charlie over to the bathroom and they went in. "Wish there was another way out, but there isn't," Stevie told Charlie.

"Maybe so, but I need one more blow," Charlie said, taking a snort of coke from the spoon from the vile and then handed the vile to Stevie.

As Stevie took one big spoonful up his nose, José came up from behind him from one of the stalls, put a forty-five pistol to his head, firing once and blowing Stevie's brains out all over the bathroom wall.

"What a waste of good coke," José said as Stevie dropped the vile to the floor, not far from where his lifeless body fell. José had been waiting there a while for Charlie.

Charlie looked down at Stevie's dead body. "Stupid fuckin' Irishman, he's so fucked up on blow that he forgot that I always cover my ass in situations like this," Charlie said. He and José went back out to the bar area where all five Dominicans were lying face down on the floor and all tied up. José had come earlier with some of his soldiers and took the place over, tying up some of the regulars in the basement with the usual bartender. José had set up his own man behind the bar saying he was the bartender's brother filling in for him while he was sick.

José walked over to the Dominicans and pumped one bullet into each of the heads of four of them. Then he came to Diablo. "Maticone!" José said to Diablo, "You try to fuck with me puta? Now, I show you who is the life in this neighborhood," José said. He took out a knife, cut off Diablo's clothes and then started peeling off his skin as he sliced it off with a filet knife.

Diablo was screaming the most excruciating sounds so they stuffed a handkerchief in his mouth to muffle his sounds. José continued to slice up Diablo as the other men were drinking, laughing, and playing the jukebox to drown out the sounds Diablo was still making noise even though he was gagged. José then stopped to take a few hits of coke and put some on Diablo's open wounds. José then shot Diablo's balls off and Diablo finally passed out. José threw some water on his face to wake him up so he could slit a hole under his chin. Then he pulled his tongue through it, and then shot him in the head. José then told his men to take the bodies and leave them in the streets somewhere so that everyone will see them and know who did it. José then smiled at Charlie saying, "Let's have a drink, amigo, and go get some chocha."

"Sure, sounds good," Charlie said, shaking his head smiling. He just saw a side to José he had never seen before. And it actually scared Charlie a bit and Charlie didn't scare easily. Charlie was a little remorseful about what just happened with Stevie, but it had to be done. It was either him or Stevie. He just never thought Stevie would get so greedy as to kill him over money. Charlie and José had a drink with Charlie saying I hope you never get mad at me like that.

"Good Time, I know you will never give me reason. You are an honorable man. But this fuckin' Diablo, I knew he was behind this and I hate these fuckin' Dominicans and they deserve what they get," José stated.

Charlie knew the deal: it was the same with all the Tony's and José's in the world—pay up and never cross us or you pay with your blood. Charlie had respect for José though, more than Tony. Their business dealings in the past were always profitable and their relationship was a good one. Watching José retaliate with Diablo made him realize he should keep a little distant from José. Charlie wanted to handle this whole situation, but he now knew why José insisted on being in on this because of Diablo and the Dominicans. José took enjoyment in offing them and putting their bodies in the street as an example. Charlie's way would have been just to shoot everyone and that would have been it.

CHAPTER 20

Charlie had trouble functioning the next few months after the incident at El Bandito. He felt bad about losing Stevie. He had been a good backup man and had as much guts as anyone, but he had to kill him. Charlie found himself becoming more and more like Tony each day. He didn't give a fuck about anyone, but concentrated only on business and making money. Charlie needed to find a new backup man to replace Stevie, since he had a big workload to handle uptown and downtown. The only two guys he could turn to were Jackie Dee, the young kid who was a good wheelman, or Frank, the ex-rogue cop. One good thing with all this: he didn't have to pay them the kind of money he'd paid Stevie. That meant most of the profits were still going to be his and all he had to do was to show them the ropes and introduce them to his customers.

One day, Charlie was doing a job for Tony uptown where he used to live with his aunt and uncle. He decided to pay them a visit at the store since he had not seen them in a while. When he got to the store, he saw that it was closed with a sign: "Closed due to illness, will reopen at later date." Charlie was in a bit of a rush so he didn't want to go upstairs to see what was going on, but he planned to call later to make sure they were okay.

When he did call a few times later that day, he got no answer. Feeling guilty, Charlie made a special trip to go see them. When he went to the apartment, no one was answering. A next door neighbor heard the knocking and came out to see who it was. Charlie remembered it was Mr. Luigi.

Mr. Luigi was trying to make out who he was. "WHATA DO YOU WANT?" he yelled in his broken English accent.

"Mr. Luigi, it's Charlie. I used to live here remember? I'm looking for my aunt and uncle. Do you know where they are?"

"Oh Charlie, little Charlie, God, you gotta so big, but I thoughta your aunt and uncle said you were dead!" Mr. Luigi said.

"I'm not dead Mr. Luigi. I'm alive, so where are they?" Charlie asked him again.

"Your uncle, I'ma realla sorry Charlie, but your uncle, he passa away yesterday," he informed Charlie.

Charlie was slightly saddened at the news. "So, where's my Aunt Carmella?" Charlie asked him.

"She's I guessa at the funeral home righta now," Mr. Luigi told him, and let him know it was the one on one hundred and tenth street near St. Mary's Church.

Charlie thanked him and left to go to the funeral parlor and pay his respects.

At the funeral parlor, Charlie saw his aunt walking towards the parlor office with a man named Vinny, who was one of the funeral parlor directors and an acquaintance of his aunt and uncle. Charlie walked over to his aunt and followed her into the office. She was crying and shaking her head as Vinny tried to console her.

Charlie went over to her. She looked up at him.

"Who are you?" she asked in her heavy Italian accent, but she did recognize Charlie. It was just the way Italians acted when someone doesn't come around and they pretended that the person must be dead and that they don't know you when they see you.

"Aunt Carmella, it's me, your nephew Charlie Luzzi," Charlie told her.

Vinny looked at Charlie with a surprised look saying, "I thought you were dead."

"Why does everyone think I'm dead?" Charlie asked, a little pissed.

"Because you lefta fifteen years ago and never cumma back, you jadrool," Aunt Carmella said, trying to make Charlie feel guilty.

"Well, I'm here alive and well, so can we cut it out with that stuff," Charlie said and his aunt started crying.

"My Anthony, my Anthony he'sa dead, he'a gone and not comma back," she said and she lost her balance and started to keel over, but Charlie grabbed her and put her back in the chair. Then she started to ramble on about how he suffered so much after Charlie left, working the store by himself and that's what killed him. Charlie knew she was trying to make him feel guilty. He thought to himself: Well, he must have loved suffering, the old fuck. It took him only fifteen years to die. What Charlie didn't know was he really died when his aunt was helping him stock the shelves at the store. Uncle Anthony said something she didn't like and she hit him in the head with a can, causing him to fall and cracking his skull on the floor. But she told everyone he died when a can fell on his head. Then he slipped on a wet floor and hit his head again on the floor.

Charlie was sympathetic to his aunt as she shed her tears and told her that he would talk with her later that night. She told him, "Without my Anthony I will die tonight because I have no one to take care of me and I have no money and I'm better off dead." She just rambled on and kept faulting Charlie saying that, after he left, the business went bad. Charlie couldn't believe this old bitch was pinning everything on him and, if he knew the truth how his uncle died, he'd probably kick her teeth in and shoot her himself, but Charlie was actually feeling bad for the old bag. Aunt Carmella went on about how she had no money and she didn't know how she would pay for the funeral saying maybe she should get a cheaper casket. Charlie asked Vinny about the cost of the funeral and the casket and he told Charlie if she doesn't get a cheaper casket it would be about six thousand dollars.

Charlie then looked at his aunt. "Aunt Carmella, don't worry about the cost. I'll take care of it," Charlie said as he took out a wad of bills and gave Vinny three thousand dollars. "All right, here's half and I'll give you the rest tomorrow," Charlie told Vinny and with that his aunt suddenly stopped crying.

"Charlie, please taka me home. I don't feel very gooda."

Charlie got her home and decided to spend some time with her and talk a while.

"Whatta you been doin' alla these years?" she asked.

Before he answered, Charlie was thinking that this was the longest conversation he ever had with her without her cursing him and his whole existence. "I'm in sales, Aunt Carmella, a restaurant supply business," Charlie said.

She told Charlie that she thought she heard his uncle say that he had wound up in the same type of business as your father.

"Well, he was wrong," Charlie said and quickly changed the subject, asking about a life insurance policy that his uncle had on himself and that it was paid up when he was living there.

"No, no, he hadda nutthing!" Aunt Carmella emphatically denied, but Charlie wasn't sure if he could believe her or not. "You maka mistake," she added.

Charlie inquired more about her finances. He had thought they saved a lot of money from the profits from the store because they never spent much and she just said that they had made just enough to get by the last fifteen years and never saved much. Charlie had no reason to doubt her. After a while, Charlie left saying he had to get up early for work and left her his beeper number in case she needed anything. After Charlie left, his aunt went into her bedroom and was going through her drawer and removed a box and opened it. In it, she looked over her bankbook, which showed about ten thousand dollars in savings and the policy she said she didn't have that was worth fifty thousand dollars. She also had his will there in which he left ten grand to Charlie, but she would never tell Charlie. As she tore it up, she thought, "Fucka him, he's in da Mafia like his scumbaga fatha. He don'ta needa the money."

The next day Aunt Carmella called the insurance company about the policy to get the money she had coming to her now that her husband died. She gave them the death certificate and they did the rest.

After they buried Charlie's Uncle Anthony, Charlie gave his aunt one thousand dollars to help her out with the bills, thinking she needed the money. She not too convincingly thanked Charlie for the money as he left saying, "I'll check on you in a few weeks, Aunt Carmella." Charlie left happy and feeling good about helping out his feeble aunt. After all, his uncle was still his blood. She was his wife, and it was the right thing to do.

After a month, Charlie went to visit his Aunt Carmella. He wanted to ask her if he should get her some help in the store. Once there, he noticed that the Fusco Market, the name of the store, was replaced by a Spanish Grocery instead. Charlie asked the new owners where his Aunt Carmella was and what happened to the store, but they only spoke Spanish. So, Charlie went upstairs to his aunt's apartment and knocked on the door. A stranger answered the door asking him what he wanted. Charlie inquired about his Aunt Carmella Fusco and the guy who answered the door couldn't give him any answers saying he saw the apartment when it was empty and didn't know or meet the previous tenant. Finally, Charlie knocked on Mr. Luigi's door and Mr. Luigi told Charlie that she picked up and left. He also let Charlie know that he heard she got a lot of money from his uncle's insurance policy and that he heard her cursing when she left the apartment about why it couldn't be more.

Charlie left the building a few minutes later. "That fuckin' old bitch conned me!" Charlie exclaimed. "What fuckin' balls she's got, scammed the fuckin' pants right off of me." He started laughing to himself, "Well, better her than some stranger, I guess."

Things at home for Charlie had completely deteriorated by now. He and Gia were going in different directions now. Charlie still took care of the bills, but that was about it. Charlie had a place in Manhattan again, not too far from his bar, and came home when he wanted to, which was about three times a week. He still loved his daughter and liked spending time with her. He took out insurance policies so, if anything happened to him, Gia and his daughter Alison would be taken care of. Gia had her Mom move in full-time so Alison would have company when she went out shopping or with friends or with Doctor Donny who she was fucking now. Gia still would screw Charlie, too, when he came home, sometimes, but it was to get extra money out of him and Charlie figured she was still a good fuck and he liked the way she sucked him off, so he figured he might as well get something for his money. Depending on their moods Charlie and Gia would talk nicely and maybe fuck or start fighting. They knew their marriage was no longer a marriage and Charlie felt it was mostly her fault. He put up with all the bullshit now because his daughter, Alison, was worth the price he paid.

Charlie was back with his loose bimbo-like women. The last thing he wanted again was a relationship. He dated women who were strippers, did drugs, drank, and even some high-priced hookers whom he never had to pay.

Tony was getting on Charlie's case lately because he wasn't doing enough jobs for him and he wasn't receiving enough of the money he owed him. Charlie was paying back Tony though at a good pace, but it seemed when Charlie came to the club, Tony liked to break Charlie's balls in front of the old timers there because he enjoyed doing it and because he was the boss. Tony also liked to ask around and check up on Charlie and his outside business dealings knowing that Charlie was a little shrewd and might be holding back on him.

Charlie took a real tough job for Tony, one that just he and Tony knew about. It was a hit on a made man that Tony wanted Charlie to do personally. Charlie didn't like doing the hits anymore, but this was a twenty thousand dollar payday that Charlie couldn't pass up. It was a chancy situation for Charlie too because, if he was caught, he would have to take the heat alone. The mark was Bennie Greco Jr. and it was ironic that Charlie got the job. Bennie Jr. was taking some business away from Tony in Chinatown and muscling in on some of his spots. Chinatown was a gray area for the Italian families as it was pretty much an open territory, but Bennie was enticing some of Tony's old customers that he had for thirty years and on top of everything, he was bad mouthing Tony with the Chinks saying, "Fuck that Tony, he doesn't own Chinatown." But Bennie Jr. was making a big mistake of fucking with the Sicilians' money. Tony thought of calling for a sit down with Bennie Sr. and the big bosses, but this would have made him look weak with the families, plus Bennie Sr. was one of the bigger boss's Godson, and they might side with him anyway. Tony handpicked Charlie because even though he did work for his crew, it was common knowledge that Charlie was only working for Tony because he was working off a debt, plus, if Charlie did get caught, the past bad blood between Charlie and Bennie Sr. and Jr. would be enough to explain the hit and no one would blame Tony.

CHAPTER 21

In preparing for the hit, Charlie started by tailing Bennie Jr. in Chinatown to nail down his routine and he found out that Bennie Jr. was doing a lot of business with the most notorious gang in Chinatown called the Fun Chins. Charlie then sought out the gang his crew did business with called the Hip Sings. He went to the Mott Street restaurant called Hung Fats where they hung out. Charlie chatted with a couple of the leaders about the rival gang and he told them about a problem he was having with them. They really didn't give a shit about Charlie's problems; in fact, they really didn't care about greasy Italians and just wanted the round eye people for their business and money. When Charlie let the Hip Sings' leader Chang, know that Bennie Jr.'s dealings with the Fun Chins could result in a big drop in their business dealings then they started to listen. Charlie then told them that they should sit tight. He would think of a solution and he would contact them for their help. Charlie asked them, if they could get any inside information on some of Bennie Jr.'s deals with the Fun Chins, to let him know.

Charlie thought that the best opportunity for the hit would be when the feast would take place the following week. Meanwhile, the Hip Sings had someone infiltrate the rival gang and got word on a big buy that Bennie Jr. was going to make from the Fun Chins this coming Saturday afternoon. Charlie figured this would be the best opportunity to pull off the hit on Bennie Jr. Charlie was also going to use some of the Hip Sings to do the job and contacted the leader Chang to see how many people he could use and that he needed men that were reliable and that could keep their mouths shut afterwards. Charlie also knew that Chang would want to be there since he was their leader and so as not to lose face with his gang.

That Saturday, Charlie was hanging outside The Mulberry Street Club sitting in a car across the street. Every other Saturday Bennie Sr. and Jr. would stop by Tony's club to have some espresso with the old timers and also break Tony's balls a little because Tony was not one of their favorite made men. Charlie had a purpose for being there, when Bennie Sr. and Jr. left the club to go to Chinatown, Charlie was outside.

Bennie Sr. saw Charlie. "What the fuck are you doing here you fuckin' mutt!" he said with Jr. looking on, wanting to have it out with Charlie.

Charlie took a step back saying, "Listen, what happened between us before I'm sorry for and I paid you a lot of money to show my respect, Don Greco." Bennie Sr. liked hearing that name in respect as Charlie continued talking, "and let me also say, Don Greco, that I know what your son is doing in Chinatown."

Bennie Sr. cut him off. "Look, it's a free country, we can do whatever the fuck we want in Chinatown."

"Understood, Don Greco, I meant no disrespect. It's just that I think you might be paying too much," Charlie insinuated. Bennie Sr. asked him why should he care anyway and Charlie told him that he could get him a better deal with someone else in Chinatown who had quality stuff and save him money too.

"Hey, you work for the Hammer," Bennie Jr. insisted. "Why the fuck would you want to help us all of a sudden. We're not stupid! What's the angle?" Bennie Jr. asked.

Charlie then let them know that Tony owned him and only worked for him because he was in debt and that his loyalty was only to money and not any one man. Charlie let them know that Tony was the one who loaned him the money to pay them for the incident he had had with them years ago and that's why he was in debt with him.

"Look Don Greco, I know you're godson to one of the big bosses and I'm looking to move out from under Tony's thumb and debt soon, and I know I can help you here if you help me to maybe get a job with one of the big bosses and get Tony off my back," Charlie suggested.

Bennie Sr. and Jr. were suddenly open to Charlie's ideas knowing Charlie's rep for uncovering the best drugs possible for the least amount. Bennie Sr. was thinking that Charlie was one stupid fuck because, if he introduces him to a drug connection where he won't pay as much, then what would he need Charlie for? Bennie Sr. and Jr. were on their way to a big buy and they knew they would have some time before their meeting and they were thinking that maybe they could make a pit stop to see Charlie's connection and see just how good his stuff was. Bennie Sr. then asked Charlie if he had time to take a ride with them in their car now, since they were on their way to Chinatown.

Charlie thought perfect, but made it look as though it was an inconvenience right now. After a few moments of acting as though it wasn't a good time, Charlie agreed to go as he got in their car with Bennie Jr. driving, Charlie in the front with him directing him where to go and Bennie Sr. in the back.

Later, they pulled up into a lot. Then, they got out and Charlie led them to a basement apartment. Charlie was thinking that they must have the cash with them and that it was probably in the trunk of the car since he noticed a key on Junior's arm which was probably for a briefcase on a chain. They entered the building. Three Chinese men got out of their way when they saw Charlie. They entered the large basement where they encountered another four Chinese men, the leader Chang and three of his men playing cards.

Charlie made the introductions and Bennie Jr. immediately started talking business, asking about the stuff they had and at what price and whether it was much better than he was getting from the Fun Chins. Chang even let him sample some as Bennie Jr. gave it the fluid test, looking for it to change color for cocaine, and then gave his Dad the nod that the shit was better than he sampled with the Fun Chins. Bennie Jr. asked about how much they had available.

Chang told them, "I can move as much as you want, as soon as you want."

Bennie Jr. said he wanted to see and Chang brought him over to a desk with huge draws and opened them up and it was full of coke.

Bennie Jr. made a slight blunder, anxious to do the deal, saying, "We can do the deal today?"

His father looked at him as if to say, we're not sure of these people, and he called Bennie Jr. to talk in private.

Meanwhile, Charlie slipped out the back door as they talked over business.

As Bennie Sr. looked to say something to Charlie, he noticed he wasn't around and he sensed something wasn't right as he looked at his son. Chang's three men pulled out hatchets from underneath the table with the playing cards.

Bennie Sr. and Jr. started to draw their guns, but Chang's men flung their hatchets so quickly that it cut both Bennies right in the stomach and chest cutting them wide open and blood started gushing out from their wounds.

Charlie came back in the room and told Chang and his men that he was pleased with the results and told them to sit tight: he would have one of his men come down and pay them for taking out the two Bennies. Charlie made a call and twenty-five minutes later Jackie Dee showed up with a briefcase and he put it on the card table. He told Chang to open it up and count it. As Chang went over to open the case, Charlie readied himself and so did Jackie because they knew that once Chang counted the cash, he would kill both him and Jackie and pin Bennie's hit on them. Chang wasn't stupid. He knew this hit would bring a lot of heat down on him, so he used Charlie to get Bennie down there so they could do the hit.

As Chang clicked the levers to open the briefcase, the other six gang members looked on. The other three that were watching the door escorted Jackie down into the basement. As the briefcase opened, it exploded in Chang's face blowing his head off and killing him instantly. The other six gang members reacted as they went for Charlie and Jackie. Jackie had already pulled out two guns, throwing one to Charlie while shooting at the six gang members hitting two, with Jackie firing at them also. Frank, the ex-cop, came in with a machine gun and blew two of the gang members out of their shoes as Charlie finished the other two off, emptying his gun into both making sure they were dead. Frank sent a few more rounds into all of them, making it final.

After the shooting, Charlie looked over the dead gang members and said, "Really good work, guys." And Charlie went over to the big desk and took out the coke that was inside the draws and split it between his guys saying, "Here's your payment, guys. You got about fifty or sixty grand apiece there," Charlie told them. He kept the same amount for himself. He let them know that, even though the building was empty and a little isolated, they should get the fuck out of there and they left after setting the basement in flames.

Outside, Charlie forgot about the key Bennie Jr. had on his arm and the money that was in the trunk of the car. He was about to go into the flaming basement again to get the key, but he heard police sirens not too far away and he didn't have time to get the key. "Mother fucker!" Charlie said aloud as they got into Frank's car with Jackie Dee driving and they were out of there in a flash. As they were driving away, four police cars came by them from the opposite direction, making Jackie and Frank laugh.

Jackie and Frank dropped Charlie off at the Mulberry Club as they went over to Charlie's apartment to wait for him. When Charlie went into the club, he politely pried Tony away from two old timers and he told Tony that everything went down without a hitch and that he got two for one.

"What do you mean?" Tony asked.

"I mean you won't have to worry about Bennie Sr. or Jr. anymore and I have it set up where the Chink gangs in Chinatown will be blamed for the hit," Charlie informed him. He told him that he was tired and needed to go home and relax, and that he would fill him in on the details if he wanted to hear them another time, and Charlie left.

Tony watched as he left. He was worried about the way Charlie swaggered out of there like he owned the place. Charlie was someone that Tony actually feared now. He worked for Tony a lot of years and Charlie was approaching a point where he wasn't afraid to take on anyone and he had the smarts and muscle to do it too. Charlie was one dangerous man, but was he dangerous to me? Tony thought. He dismissed all his thoughts knowing that Charlie respected his position but he did think that Bruno should watch his ass now because Charlie could, if he wanted, take him out. Tony likened Charlie to himself when he was younger. He saw it in Charlie's eyes when he would stare at him.

Charlie was walking home and thinking that he pulled off a good solid hit and no one would know it was him, except Jackie, Frank, and Tony. He knocked off two made men and two scumbags who had cost him a lot of cash a while back and he was glad he had them whacked. As far as the families would know, Bennie Sr. and Jr. died in a drug deal gone bad. Charlie liked the look on Tony's face as he walked out of the club. He knew that Tony was impressed with him and the way he handled it. Charlie went another step up the ladder.

With the coke Charlie scored in the job and the payment he got from Tony for doing it, he was close to having Tony paid off again. That made Tony start wondering what he could do again to bury Charlie into another debt. With Charlie's payoff, Tony would lose that edge he always had over him, plus he would have to start paying Charlie for the side jobs and all the other businesses Charlie had going for Tony. Tony resigned himself to the fact that Charlie was a born loser like his father Sal and that Charlie would fuck up somehow, so he would have him back in the hole, one way or another.

CHAPTER 22

Now, once again, almost out of debt with Tony and having greater success with his businesses, Charlie had become lax in his ways, increasing again his overuse of alcohol and drugs on a daily basis.

However, Charlie didn't neglect things this time. He made sure his wife was taken care of as far as the household bills went and saw to it that his daughter always had new clothes and money for school. Still, he was seeing less and less of them as he was Good Time Charlie again, doing more drugs and drinking.

Gia was afraid of Charlie's temper. She was glad that he didn't find out yet she was fucking Doctor Donny whom she was seeing. She feared what Charlie might do to him and that he wouldn't give her money anymore either. Gia got shrewd with Charlie by using their daughter to get more cash out of him, instead of using sex, since Charlie had a huge soft spot for his little girl.

Charlie had Jamaican drug connections he used on and off for the past few years when supply was less than the demand. The quality wasn't up to snuff like his usual, but good enough for his customers in the crunch. They always told him that he should push some weed for them, but Charlie had always shrugged it off because the money was in powder, plus Charlie never really had time for it. There was a demand for it in his circles too so he decided to listen to the Jamaicans to see what they had to offer. Jamaican weed was the most popular in the area right now. Charlie figured it could be extra cash, seeing as how the Jamaicans were getting richer by the minute selling it.

Charlie approached Tony on the Jamaicans about what they had to offer. Tony wasn't crazy about Jamaicans as he wasn't crazy about the spics either. "What the fuck is it with you, Charlie, and these connections? First a question about the spics, which I don't mind so much, and now these Rasta monkeys. You're a fuckin' guinea, not a moolie," Tony said.

"Tony, all I see is green. These guys are more honorable than some of the guinea fucks we've done business with in the past and they always pay up front," Charlie informed him.

Tony thought things over in his mind and told Charlie he wanted to meet the head man in charge of the operation before he would talk a deal. This sounded just like what Bennie Sr. and Jr. were attempting to do with his Chink connections in Chinatown.

Charlie knew where Tony was coming from. He would meet the head man and start dealing with him directly and probably cut Charlie out of the deal or give him a very small slice, but Charlie had no choice. He didn't have Tony's money—resources he needed to make a large buy.

Tony gave Charlie the green light to go ahead and follow up with the Jamaicans and set up a meeting with the main man and this included Charlie taking a trip to Kingston, Jamaica where Charlie would meet with him first. Then Tony would come down if everything looked good. Charlie didn't mind; he could use a working vacation and a little sun. The Jamaicans took three weeks to set up Charlie with a meeting down in Kingston, so Charlie was off on his meet with the head man.

Charlie was accompanied by two Jamaicans on the flight: a guy named King who was his New York connection and his bodyguard, a big tall man who said nothing on the whole flight down. The plane landed in Montego Bay and another two Jamaicans met them at the airport and drove them to their destination. As they drove in a beat up old Mercedes limo, Charlie was told by one of the Jamaicans that it was once owned by the Pope which explained the bulletproof bubble glass around it. Charlie checked out the beautiful blue skies, took long deep breathes of the tropical clean air, and thought this would be a nice place to retire. It was a nice balmy day and Charlie liked the change. King told Charlie that they would meet with his boss after he got settled in his hotel in Ocho Rios at the new Hilton Hotel. Charlie got a suite, compliments of King's boss.

At the hotel, Charlie took a shower and got settled in and decided to go down to have a drink at the bar. King met him there and he ordered a special drink for Charlie that was part of the Rasta's religion: a rum called Bacardi 151, Campari, and Jamaican beer. It was the kind of cocktail that could make you breathe and shit fireballs after drinking it. King told Charlie about Jamaican religious tradition and that drugs and drinking were okay with them. Charlie liked their religion.

"You drink this drink man and smoke our ganja weed and you see God for sure, Mr. Good Time," King told Charlie

Later that night, King took Charlie to a club called The Number One. It was appropriately named too, as it was Jamaica's number one hot spot for drinks, music, and overall partying. They partied with the owner named Jack Rube, in his private lounge, drinking and smoking weed.

Charlie was feeling good. "Jack Rube, didn't you shoot Kennedy or was it Oswald?" Charlie jokingly asked.

"You crazy man!" King told Charlie and they laughed as Charlie looked at some of the people around him. He saw Keith and Mick and Bob Marley. It was obvious this Jack Rube had some elite clientele, especially with the music industry. Charlie took out about an ounce of coke and put it on the table,

"Enjoy my friends. Have a blow on me," Charlie said, smiling.

They all started taking hits saying that was quality shit and some even asked if he had extra so they could buy some, but he told them he only had enough to party with. Charlie did, however, give Keith and Mick a few grams each, letting them know he loved their music. They thanked him saying to look them up when they play the Garden in New York.

When Mick and Keith left, Rube said in his Jamaican accent, "Fuck those cheap bastards. They think because they are famous they can get everything free."

Charlie laughed as he dug a spoon into some of the coke and took a hit. He partied all night with his new Jamaican friends and even hooked up with a young, pretty Jamaican at the end of the night, who sat in his lap grinding him into a raging hard on. She was wearing a short dress and had no underwear on so Charlie just unzipped his pants and slid up inside her and he fucked her right there as some of the Jamaicans were doing the same.

The next day, King had called to set up the meeting with his boss Jaba, but still had to wait for them to call back. So, in the meantime while waiting outside by the pool having drinks, King introduced Charlie to a hot native girl named Beverly, Bev for short, who had a body that wouldn't quit. She was a redhead, too, and the contrast between her skin and her hair reminded him of Big Red, but he was darker skinned. Charlie flirted with the girl a bit and kidded with her about her red hair as she let him know that her grandfather was

German and her grandmother was an Island girl, but whatever the mix was Charlie would fuck her if he got the chance.

"Is that your true hair color?" Charlie asked her.

"Hmm!" Bev cooed for him a bit saying, "Well, if you're a good boy, you just might find out. That is, if you want to." She went on, "King, tell me he's Italian. I find Italian men so sexy."

"Man, I'm glad I came down here," Charlie said to her. "I'm having a good time, Bev, and did you know that's my nickname Good Time?" He asked her.

"No, but that's a good nickname and we should get along great Good Time 'cause I'm Good and Plenty, baby," she told him and Charlie laughed.

As it turned out that day, the meet with Jaba didn't take place, so that night Charlie hooked up with Bev. They partied all night, drinking and snorting and fucking like rabbits and Charlie found out that she did have a bright red bush to match her hair color.

Bev would suck him off saying, "Hmm! I like the white man's cock. Make me feel like I'm licking and sucking on a vanilla pop." She then sucked Charlie, swallowing all his cum.

"And Charlie says, I love my Good N' Plenty," Charlie said jokingly referring to the commercial that was popular in the 60's and 70's. Then Charlie rolled on top of her to fuck her again.

The next morning he awoke with Bev still there next to him and naked. He was hard and fucked her awake and she started moaning with pleasure. After they both came, she was saying, "Oh, that's the way to start the day, man."

Back in New York, Tony was plotting some strategy to get Charlie back into debt with him or at least make it so that Charlie's businesses wouldn't be as profitable so he could work more for him. Tony resented the idea now that Charlie was making all this money. Less of it was being kicked back to him.

Tony first contacted one of Charlie's men—Jackie Dee and had him come to the club to meet him. Jackie Dee was scared shitless because he wondered what Tony wanted with him to have a direct meeting. The word was out that Tony didn't like the other guy Charlie used, Frank the ex-cop, and Jackie. They were not welcomed in any of Tony's clubs anymore. So, when Jackie sat down to talk with Tony at one of his gambling clubs, he was shitting a brick, but Tony let him know right away that he would never tell them to stay out of his clubs.

Tony then started asking Jackie all sorts of questions about Charlie and his businesses. Jackie was answering all his questions too because he was frightened and didn't want to piss him off. Tony asked Jackie how much he made with Charlie and Jackie told him.

"Doesn't sound like it's enough to me with all the work you do for Charlie." And then Tony asked him if he would like to work for him if Charlie ever left the uptown area and Jackie said he would.

Then Jackie let Tony know that he thought Charlie was really happy with being uptown and thought he would never leave and that after his trip from Jamaica he was going to stay uptown full-time and forget about working downtown.

"Well, you never know what someone is going to do until they finally do it," Tony said to Jackie. Tony began chatting with Jackie about some bullshit stuff as he had already got most of the information he wanted on Charlie. Tony then brought in Bruno and told Bruno to give Jackie two-hundred in chips and let him do some gambling in the club. It was on him tonight and, also, he could drink as much as he wanted for free.

As Bruno escorted Jackie into the casino, Jackie thought that Tony wasn't such a bad guy and wondered why Charlie dumped on him all the time.

Tony sat back down in his office and thought that this was pretty easy, "Fuckin' Irishman is as dumb as a dead ape," Tony said aloud to himself and laughed thinking about his next move.

Back in Jamaica, it was afternoon and Charlie was getting antsy waiting on the word to meet with this Jaba guy already and King was telling him, "Relax man, we will see Jaba when he calls us." And King went on to tell Charlie that things were done differently down here. Things were more laid back, unlike New York where everything had to be done yesterday.

Later, King got the word and they took the Pope-mobile into Kingston to meet with Jaba. On the ride, Charlie and King had some drinks from the bar in the limo and did a little blow on the way. Charlie observed how old and rundown things looked in Kingston with the houses looking like little shacks, which made Charlie ask King, "Are we in the right area?"

"Yo man, this is where we do business, man, but Jaba lives all the way up there," King informed Charlie, pointing up to the top of the hill where Charlie could see a large white house. The driver took them up this long path leading there after turning off the main road.

"I'm going to get a fuckin' nose bleed up here," Charlie remarked as they got to the top.

King laughed saying, "You're a funny man there, Good Time Charlie."

They were driven into a huge barn at the top of the hill. Inside the barn, there were about five Jamaican bodyguards walking around with automatic weapons. Charlie also saw and smelled these large bails of weed all around the place and the intoxicating aroma made him dizzy. As they drove in, another six armed guards came over and started speaking real fast and Charlie couldn't make out what the fuck they were talking about, but made out one remark, "Hey man, you Al Capone?" one guard said as they smiled and laughed. Jaba, the head man, came over.

"Good Time man, let me introduce you to Jaba," King said, pointing to his boss.   Charlie and Jaba shook hands saying their hellos.

"So, you are Good Time Charlie. My people speak well of you, that you are a Mafia man, a man of respect they say," Jaba said to him.

Charlie said, "I'm just a businessman trying to do a deal."

"Yes, but you are a man of respect and trust and that is a good thing," Jaba said

"And I'm looking to do business and make a lot of money too," Charlie told him with Jaba giving him a big smile showing his teeth of all gold with his name Jaba written in diamonds on his front four teeth.

Charlie couldn't resist commenting on them. "NICE SET OF CHOPPERS!" Charlie mused aloud.

"The better to eat you with," Jaba said smiling and laughing, as the rest of the men around them started laughing.

CHAPTER 23

Back in New York, Jackie was leaving the club when Tony came over. "Leaving so soon?" Tony inquired.

"Yeah, I have a little business to take care of," Jackie said. Before Jackie left, Tony told him that he was having a party the following night and asked him to come by with Charlie's connection, José, and saying, "There's going to be a lot of hot women at the party so I won't take no for an answer and Charlie should be back in time for the party too."

Early the next day, Jackie hooked up with José and let him know about the party Tony was throwing. He told him that he could probably have his choice of any hot blonde there and that Charlie will probably be there since he was coming back from his Jamaican trip, so José agreed to go.

At the party that night, José and Jackie were treated like royalty as Tony made sure Bruno and some of his other men tended to them like they were VIPs. José and Jackie both had a blonde on their arm as they drank, getting liquored up real good, and gambled at the club with Tony spotting them a few hundred in chips each. About three in the morning, one of Tony's men offered José and Jackie a suite each at the hotel across the street from him. Since they were in no condition to drive, they figured why not and they could take the blondes with them and fuck them. They were also invited to have breakfast with Tony The Hammer the next morning.

José agreed, saying, "Sure, anything for the big boss."

José and Jackie went up to each of their rooms with their blonde bimbos for the night and a bottle of champagne, compliments of Tony. José was all over his blonde bitch once inside the room feeling her ass and breasts. Jackie was doing the same with his date for the evening, but these girls were professionals and handled drunks before. They each got their man to take a shower first as they slipped them each a drug in their champagne glasses. When they came out from their showers, they each were greeted by the women lying in bed nude and with a champagne toast to a night of sexual fun. Both Jackie and José passed out from drinking their spiked champagne before they could even have the two sluts get their mouths on their cocks. The two blonde women that Tony had hired and paid, then got dressed and relieved each of their dates of any drugs and money they had on them as a tip and left the suites with the doors unlocked.

Later that morning, Jackie awoke with a splitting headache and could hardly stand up. Jackie saw that his cash was gone and thought when he saw Tony for breakfast he would ask who this cunt was and where she lived 'because he wanted to break her fuckin' neck. Jackie got dressed and thought he would check on José in the room next to him and see how he made out. Jackie knocked on the door several times without getting an answer, so he turned the knob and let himself in. Jackie stopped dead in his tracks and froze as he caught sight of José lying in a pool of blood on the bed. José's chin was sliced open, and his tongue pulled through the opening, making Jackie think that it was a Colombian necktie and it was a hit.

What Jackie didn't know was that Tony was behind the whole deal making it look like it was someone else doing the hit on José. Tony thought by killing off José, who was Charlie's major drug supplier, he could cut into a large source of income that Charlie was making. When the police got there, they considered it a Colombian drug hit and the investigation went no further, with nothing to implicate that Tony had a hand in it, especially since this was his territory and he had the police chief from that precinct in his pocket.

Tony acted all innocent about the hit and asked Jackie questions about what happened after they had gone to the hotel for the night and acted concerned asking if he was all right. Tony made a few suggestions such as that José was probably followed that night and it was lucky for Jackie they didn't kill him too. He told Jackie to lay low for a few days just in case the same people who hit José might come after him. Jackie agreed.

Down in Jamaica, Charlie was putting a deal together with Jaba in which he got some real good prices for his top quality stuff. Charlie called up Tony to let him know that the deal was too good to pass up, but Tony let Charlie know that he was going to send his top man Bruno down and negotiate the final details.

Charlie contested, saying, "I don't need that fuckin' cafone down here. I have the deal I want."

Tony fired back. "I don't give a fuck what deal you can make. Bruno is the one who will secure the deal for the family or there will be no deal at all," Tony stated firmly.

Charlie felt infuriated with Tony because this was his baby that he put together and he didn't want that big dumb Neanderthal Bruno fucking up this deal. Tony remained adamant about the deal going his way or no way at all. Charlie had no choice but to agree. Tony then told him when he introduced Bruno to Jaba he was to head straight back to

New York because there were some problems he needed to discuss with Charlie personally and he would explain it to him when he got back. Charlie, again, tried to persuade Tony to not let Bruno come down and to let him seal the deal, but Tony just hung up on him. Charlie still didn't know yet about José. That was something Tony wanted to tell him when he got back.

That night Charlie partied again with King at The Number One Club with Jack Rube. On this night, Charlie was rubbing elbows with the likes of Peter Frampton and Joe Cocker. Charlie thought, Hell, I'm just like these rockers and all I have to do is learn to sing and I'll be a star just like them. Charlie had his favorite Jamaican piece of ass, Bev, with him. In between doing some blow, she blew him, standing him up against the wall. After she swallowed his load, she hummed, "Hmm, I love that vanilla cream."

The next morning Charlie met with his least favorite Cro-Magnon, Bruno, at the airport and they started going at each other as soon as they met.

"You better not fuck this deal up. I could have done this shit myself," Charlie said.

"Who gives a fuck. Tony wants me here, so take it up with him," he told Charlie.

"Now, hook me up with the head Rasta chimp and let me complete the deal and get the fuck out of here 'cause I hate this place and being among these animals," Bruno said.

Charlie hooked Bruno up with King and then he was on a flight home later that afternoon.

When Charlie got back, he was still fuming over turning the deal over to Bruno and ready for a face to face with Tony over it. Charlie was weighing his options. Since he was almost paid up with Tony, he was in a position to tell him to fuck off and he would just go back to his own businesses and not do any work for him in the future. He was tired of Tony treating him like shit and he wanted the respect he deserved.

Tony had sent a car to meet Charlie at the airport and had him driven directly to the club where Tony was. Charlie wasted no time in walking into the back office to talk with Tony. He looked like a man possessed and very angry as he entered Tony's office. Charlie immediately started in on Tony.

Tony cut him short. "YOU SHUT THE FUCK UP AND LISTEN! YOU'RE NOT TO NEGOTIATE DEALS LIKE THIS FOR ME!" Tony yelled. In a lower voice, he said, "Your fuckin' job is to whack people for me, make collections and enforce my deals." Tony reminded him, "And on this, you were on a working vacation just to see what these Rasta fucks had to offer."

"Hey, I thought..." Charlie started to say and, again, Tony interrupted.

"You thought wrong. You went ahead of my plans," Tony said.

Charlie was ready to tell him to fuck off, but he held off as Tony kept talking, "But we have another problem, which is why I wanted you back here so soon. Your spic friend José went out and got whacked the other night and it looks like it was either by his own or the Colombians. He had one of those necktie things done to him," Tony relayed to Charlie.

Charlie looked shocked to hear this and Tony watched closely at his reaction.

"How the fuck could this happen? José was too smart to get whacked."

"How do I know," Tony responded. "He either fucked with the wrong person or must have pissed someone off recently." Tony smiled a little as Charlie turned away from him. Tony started to let Charlie in on all the info he knew and said the only reason he found out was because it happened close to one of his downtown clubs and the cops at that precinct told him about it, hoping that he might be able to help.

"What the fuck was he doing downtown? He only comes downtown with me," Charlie said, thinking aloud and trying to figure out why it happened, while Tony offered no solutions.

"I have no fuckin' idea," Tony said and then told Charlie that maybe he should go home and get some rest.

Charlie left moments later and took a cab back uptown, but not home right away. He would visit a few spots José used to go to and see if he could find out what happened. Charlie had no luck though as Zapata's, José's main place to deal drugs, was closed down because of drug sales. Four other places José controlled were also shut down.

"These cops don't waste no fuckin' time if they ain't getting paid off," Charlie thought aloud, and he remembered how José had been running his businesses there for a good fifteen years too. It all bothered Charlie.

Charlie did catch up with Jackie Dee in an Irish bar at 210th Street. He informed Charlie that a lot of the people he dealt with also were getting locked up and were getting squeezed. Jackie was a little drunk and slow getting all the details out so Charlie went over to the precinct and had a talk with the sergeant who ended up warning him, "You better get out of the neighborhood, too, or you'll be next."

Charlie went with Jackie Dee over to his bar and they were having drinks, talking over their situation. As Charlie entertained some ideas aloud of what to do, Jackie Dee mentioned to him, "We can work for Tony."

Charlie looked at him as if he was nuts. "You don't even know the prick and you want to work for him?" Charlie asked him.

Jackie realized he made a little slip because Tony told him not to talk about what happened with José because he would talk to Charlie about it.

Charlie picked up on it and prodded him a bit. "Or, do you know him?" Charlie asked.

Jackie hedged a bit before answering. "Well, after José was killed, he had me come in and offered me a job with him," Jackie said.

"Oh, he did?" Charlie said aloud. "And how the fuck did he know about you?" Charlie asked Jackie as he felt he wasn't being too up front about everything.

"I don't know," Jackie replied and looked guilty.

Charlie sensed something wasn't right as Jackie got more uncomfortable and left the bar telling Charlie he was tired.

When Charlie got back to his apartment that night, he found a message from Tony on his answering machine that Bruno didn't close the deal with Jaba and had some trouble with King too. He warned Charlie that he shouldn't deal with the Rastas again 'cause King was under the impression that Bruno was going to buy direct from Jaba and cut King out of his end of the deal.

Charlie tried to talk with some of King's men the next day, but they told Charlie to lose their number and never come to see them again and to feel lucky that he was still alive.

Charlie was getting the screws to him from every direction now and he was without his major source of income and had tons of bills that would be piling up soon. Charlie thought his only solution was to work full-time again for Tony. Charlie thought about everything when he got drunk in his apartment that night and had suspicions that Tony engineered all this so-called bad luck he was experiencing. He wondered, Why would that fuck do this? What was the point? Was Tony that worried about me being on my own? Did he really fear me that much?

"If that fuck had anything to do with all this fuckin' shit, I'll make him pay *SOME DAY*," Charlie said and took a drink from his bottle of Finlandia. "*SOME DAY*," Charlie repeated, thinking that Tony will find out just how evil Good Time Charlie can be. Charlie kept thinking that he was tired of being pushed around by these so-called goodfellas, and that he made his bones and that, if he had to, he'll take them all out.

The next day, Charlie cut a deal with Tony as he resolved to work for Tony full-time again. He was Tony's number one strong arm man again, his main enforcer for his crew. Tony paired him with a new gorilla, named Vito, who was fresh off the boat from Italy and spoke about ten words of English. Vito had the most sullen dead-filled eyes you ever wanted to see. Vito wouldn't blink an eye when told to break someone's arms or legs, if he wasn't paying his debts. Vito had little sympathy for anyone who didn't pay. If he returned next week looking for a payment from a guy whose legs he broke the week before and couldn't work and he couldn't pay again, he would find something else to break. Vito was plain ruthless; he had no heart or soul to speak of. Charlie and Vito got all the hard jobs and got into a few brawls with some construction workers who could deliver a punch or two themselves. Tony enjoyed seeing Charlie come back with a black-eye or a broken rib once in a while, but they always collected what they went out for as Charlie and Vito never lost a fight. Charlie wondered why these fuckin' dummies would challenge their resolve, because they had the rep of always collecting and fucking up anyone who didn't pay.

Charlie owed Tony less than twenty thousand now. He thought about this last debt. The money was repayment for the Long Island house, but he considered all the interest he paid was like paying for a fuckin' castle. He accepted what happened because his daughter lived the way he wanted her to. Gia was talking divorce with Charlie now saying she wanted to be with someone else she loved. Charlie was agreeable to the idea, but was just buying time before he went through with it. He was worried at the divorce hearing she might say something about the type of work he did, but he didn't care that she wanted to be with that bald-headed doctor Donny fuck. Shit, they deserve each other, he thought. Since Charlie had been showing only fourteen thousand a year in earnings when he filed tax returns, he feared Gia might open her mouth in a divorce hearing and say he earned much more. Charlie didn't need Uncle Sam breaking his balls and probing up his ass with a microscope trying to ascertain his real earnings. Fuck, every wise guy since Al Capone never wanted to fuck with Uncle Sam. The IRS reps were like legalized Shylocks and would bleed you dry.

In the meantime, Charlie moved back downtown on Houston Street near the Mulberry Club again. Charlie was sad making the move because he had fond memories of his time uptown and his days hanging with José and Stevie who were both dead now.

CHAPTER 24

Times were not the same for Charlie. Even when he was in debt with Tony, he was striving for something, for his own freedom again and to get back to the days when he started out in this business. The old times he enjoyed were no more and no longer his; his situation seemed to be locked in with Tony's. Charlie sat in the dark, drinking a bottle of Finlandia, his first night in his new digs downtown pondering his life to this point in time. Was the life he wanted for himself a distant memory and no longer attainable? Money and power were what made his world go round. With Tony he still had that, but it wasn't his own. The lifestyle is what he enjoyed. People feared him, whether he was uptown or downtown, and he liked it when people would shit in their pants when he gave them his cold as ice stare. He liked the fact that he could bust up and disable someone for life with his bare hands and he liked killing people who he felt deserved killing. Some of his hits made him feel as bad as the people he whacked. Maybe they didn't deserve their fate, but they got in Tony's way and he had to enforce his boss's wishes. His position made him feel like a somebody—something he always wanted as a kid—and back then everyone didn't respect a nobody. For himself, he had a bad run of bad luck. He wasn't sure that it was Tony sabotaging his businesses so he could own him for life. He thought about just picking up and leaving New York altogether, but the life he became accustomed to was something he couldn't give up and he had to work for Tony and plot his next moves.

Charlie was looking for a score, something not connected with Tony and his crew. He owed Tony about twenty grand still. He did owe the IRS thirty grand and had to pay that off or they would have audited his ass for the last ten years; it was more of a payoff to keep them off his back. Charlie didn't have anyone right now he could trust to do a score with him. José and Stevie were gone and Jackie was a little bit of a weakling.

Charlie met up with an old customer, a guy named Randy, who was into selling nothing but designer clothes and owned a place on 59th Street near the bridge. Randy's clients consisted of rock stars, actors, actresses, musicians, all high-profile celebrities, and wannabes. Randy got invited to several parties with these celebrities where drugs were a constant. He told Charlie about how much coke would be circulating at these small elite parties and the cash that would be spent on them, too, and that the dealers at these parties would make on average maybe thirty or forty grand a night.

Charlie thought he might be able to take a few of these dealers down and make a quick easy score. One in particular happened to be a director, who lived in a ritzy apartment downtown and Charlie was able to sway Randy into telling him how much coke and cash he might have one night at a small party he was having. Randy didn't like the director anyway and thought he was a piece of shit because he screwed him out of money once. Randy found out how much the guy would have available and then beeped Charlie, who got entry into the building by using a phony badge with the doorman.

"Narcotics division working undercover," Charlie told the doorman.

The doorman just let Charlie in. Charlie told him to come with him because he needed him to knock on a door and announce that he had a package for the tenant. The doorman did exactly what Charlie said and Charlie bullied his way inside with a gun drawn, just as a narcotics cop would do and announced he was the police.

"GET THE FUCK ON THE FLOOR! FACE DOWN! EVERYONE!" Charlie yelled, telling them they were all under arrest.

Everyone was scared and did what he said. Charlie handcuffed them all, the doorman, too, and then put them all in the kitchen. Charlie then had the director fork over the drugs and cash he had telling him that, if he didn't, he was going to make it very rough on him and some of his celebrity friends. The guy cooperated without a fuss except that he asked Charlie for his warrant, but Charlie told him that his warrant was in his hands, showing the man his gun.

"You want this warrant up your ass and for me to pull the trigger, scumbag?" Charlie asked him?

The guy was scared shitless. After he handed Charlie the drugs and cash, Charlie put the guy in the bathroom with his head in the toilet telling him to wait there until his backup arrived.

Charlie was gone from the apartment for twenty minutes before the director realized that no backup was coming and that Charlie was no narcotics cop and that he had been robbed. The man couldn't report the crime because of a few high-profile celebrities he had there and because he didn't want any cops poking around his apartment.

Charlie got away clean with eighty-thousand in drugs and cash and split it down the middle with Randy. "Here's your half Randy, thirty thousand," Charlie said, giving Randy his cut in drugs and cash, but keeping fifty thousand.

Charlie paid off Tony and the IRS and was free of any debt.

Tony was pissed that he was out of debt with Charlie again.

Charlie thought, Now, any scores I make with Tony I don't have to kickback any cash to him since I'm all paid up.

Tony liked keeping Charlie in debt, which had made every job he gave him pretty much done for free, but now Charlie would have to be paid the full amount on each job given to him. Tony then decided to keep Charlie by not giving him as much work as before, telling him business was slow. This would keep Charlie from making any real cash and from branching out on his own again. Tony knew you needed money to make any moves.

"What the hell is going on?" Charlie asked Tony. "Where's my usual runs and how come I'm not getting any side jobs?"

"What can I tell you, Good Time? Business is slow and everyone is paying up lately," Tony stated.

Charlie knew that was a lie and Tony told Charlie that maybe he should take a vacation, without pay, of course, and come back and maybe things will have picked up by then. Tony then told Charlie that, if he needed any extra cash, his credit was good with him and he would lend him some.

Charlie was fighting with his so-called wife over money again. She was busting his balls about a trip she wanted to take with Alison, but he simply told her to get the money from her doctor friend. They still weren't divorced yet, so she felt Charlie was obligated to give her money when she wanted it. "You're still my fuckin' husband and we're still your responsibility," she would tell Charlie.

"Look, Alison is going to school now and your mother is living with you, you fuckin' lazy bitch. Get off your ass and go back to work," Charlie would respond.

She would threaten to file for divorce now and take him to court and reveal to the courts the money he makes that the IRS doesn't know about. "You promised me I would never have to work again!" Gia would throw up in his face.

"Well, I lied just like you lied to me about a lot of things," Charlie said.

Charlie called Gia on the phone one day when they both had cooler heads. He told her he would give her ten thousand now and two thousand a month to live on which he thought was generous.

"How do you expect me to live on that?" she asked.

"Look, that's all you get! The bank is closed and you'll get no more. Just get your ass back to work full time," Charlie told her. "And if you don't take this offer and take me to court, Alison will be in the market for a new mother," Charlie informed her.

Gia let him know that he was an animal for even thinking that and that she looked forward to the day he would be out of her life for good.

Charlie just let her know that it will happen the day his daughter is married and out of her house and to stop fuckin' breakin' his balls anymore 'cause he wasn't taking any more crap from her. With that, Charlie hung up the phone on her. Charlie sat there thinking. "Fuck, when I met her, I thought I'd be getting laid every night. Instead, I just got fucked," Charlie said aloud. He thought that he should shoot Gino for having won that fifty dollar bet which in the long run cost him over half a million. "I can't pick my fuckin' nose when it comes to bets, but that fuckin' bet I had to win," Charlie said aloud.

Charlie went back to work for Tony a few weeks later, working with Vito doing collections again. Vito a man of few English words finally started speaking sentences Charlie could understand and he started to get to know his partner a bit. Even though he butchered the language, Vito let Charlie know that he was from Sicily, that his father was killed when he was a baby and that he and his brother had to flee the country 'cause people were looking to kill them also so they couldn't take revenge for their father's murder.

Charlie would think and say to Vito, "Yeah sure, they snuck you out of Italy on a donkey cart. I saw that in a movie."

Vito had no idea what Charlie was talking about, but Vito said that at eleven years old he returned to Sicily and killed the three men who had killed his father, one by one with a stiletto knife and with the guns he took from them he then shot their kids so they couldn't take revenge on him and his brother. Charlie then learned that Vito came to America at age twelve and lived with an uncle who beat the shit out of him on a daily basis until one day he choked him to death. As he heard more and more, Charlie felt himself bonding with this psycho who would probably wind up being the next Charles Manson. Vito called Charlie his "good buddy" and Charlie would just smile when he said that. Vito would ask Charlie about his life as his English got better and could understand more and Charlie told him his story also. Charlie figured, so what. It was something to do between drives to collecting the cash and breaking heads. One time Vito patted Charlie on his back after Charlie told him a story about the orphanage and he nearly put Charlie's head through the windshield. Vito just didn't know his own strength.

Charlie decided to visit old St. Patrick's Orphanage one day that he had free as his reminiscing with Vito the day before prompted him to go and see the old place he grew up in. Charlie stood outside, just staring at the place for about ten minutes, thinking about his times growing up there and it seemed like it was another lifetime ago, but in reality it was about thirty years ago, Charlie now being thirty-nine. He thought it wasn't that bad as he stared at a hole in one of the fences that he was sure he made when he was a kid. Charlie looked in the cement and saw his name inscribed in it, something else he did when he was there. Charlie looked and saw a window that he would sneak out of and, as he looked at it, someone was sneaking out and he laughed to himself as he watched a boy scoot around the corner. Then, Charlie heard a voice.

"Charlie Luzzi is that you? You're still not that big for me to put you over my knee," she said. It was Mother Superior. As Charlie looked at her, he thought about that old bird still alive: she was so old that she must have been a waitress for Jesus Christ at the Last Supper; she must be like two-hundred years old. Charlie didn't notice her at first, but she was sitting in a chair in the garden near a statue of the Virgin Mother.

Charlie went over to her, smiling.

"So, one of my chicks has come back to roost," she joked with Charlie.

"Excuse me," Charlie said.

"Never mind," she said.

"How did you know it was me?" Charlie asked.

"I may be old, but I still can recognize a familiar face even though it's been years," she said. "You look good," she added and went on after Charlie kissed her hand. "I thought someday I would read about you in the papers, going to jail or the electric chair."

"Not me, Mother Superior," Charlie said, smiling.

"Well, I'm glad you proved me wrong and you turned into such a handsome young man," she said. "So, how have you been my son? What brings you around?"

"I just happen to be in the area. Thought I'd stop by, say hello," Charlie said. He told her he was married, had a daughter, and working in sales.

She could tell Charlie was lying about the sales thing though because his eyebrow would go up just like when he was a kid and was in trouble. Without a comment about his work, she just told him that life is an opportunity and it was never too late to change. After chatting a bit, Mother Superior asked Charlie if he would like to see his favorite nun, Sister Teresa. Charlie, of course, agreed and she told him to go inside. She still had the same room and was just recovering from an illness.

Charlie went in, looking over the place that he roamed for so many years and went to Sister Teresa's room. He knocked on her door and he heard her say, "Come in!" When Charlie entered, she stared at him a moment and then knew by looking into his eyes that it was Charlie. Her eyes filled up as she got up from her bed and Charlie went over and hugged her.

"My baby! My baby!" she cried out and Charlie began crying too.

"You don't know how good it is to see you, Sister," Charlie told her as they hugged each other for about five minutes. Finally, they both sat down and began to talk about everything. Charlie looked at Sister Teresa's angelic face as she talked and thought to himself for the first time what a pretty lady she was and years ago if she wasn't wearing that nun's outfit, what a classy woman she would have been. She was a beautiful woman inside and out. After talking a few hours, Charlie then took Sister Teresa and Mother Superior for lunch to a restaurant bar they frequented with Father O'Malley around the block. Charlie was surprised and smiled when the bartender knew them and served them their regular drinks, which were Rob Roys, and before lunch was over they had three apiece with Charlie remarking to Sister Teresa, "Now, that's good medicine and will get you well in no time" And they both laughed. "I didn't realize you could drink like that," Charlie said.

They jokingly told him that he started them drinking the day he came to the orphanage. Charlie laughed till tears came into his eyes when they raised their glasses and saluted him. Mother Superior then told Charlie they owed a lot to him, their gray hair, their wrinkles, too, on top of their drinking and Charlie laughed again. They sat for about two hours chatting over old times. When they asked Charlie about things in his life, they could tell that Charlie was sugar-coating things for them so not to worry them. Sister Teresa talked about visiting the Vatican one day and that she was saving for a trip so she could see the Pope one day before she died.

"Sister, you'll be around a long time," Charlie assured her and then Charlie told her that he actually was driven once in a Pope-mobile down in Jamaica.

Charlie enjoyed his lunch with the Mother Superior and Sister Teresa and really didn't expect to have as much as a good time as he did, but the two penguins he thought were fun. He paid the lunch tab and left a sizable tip for the bartender and waitress. Back at the orphanage, they were saying their goodbyes and Sister Teresa offered to walk with Charlie a bit down the block after Mother Superior went back inside. Sister Teresa really just wanted to talk to Charlie in private a few moments before he left so they sat on a bench outside the orphanage.

Sister Teresa got serious with Charlie letting him know that she knew he was lying about some things in his life.

"I raised you, my son, don't you think I know you better?" she asked him.

Charlie didn't have to answer. He just smiled at her.

"I've always kept tabs on you, my son. I know what you do for a living, I've always known," she told Charlie and then went on to tell him that she had a brother who was in the same business. He knew him and that his name was Bruno.

Charlie couldn't believe that it was Bruno, Tony's right hand man.

"It's too late for my brother. God save his soul, but you can walk away from it Charlie. I pray for you every day, my son," Sister Teresa said, smiling. "It's never too late to walk with God, Mr. Good Time Charlie."

Charlie looked at her, surprised to hear her use that name. He assured her that some day he will walk with God and kissed her on her forehead, handing her an envelope. "You just take that trip to the Vatican, Sister Teresa," Charlie told her, smiling at her. She insisted she couldn't take his money, but Charlie was more insisting and she did as they said their goodbyes.

As he walked away, she said, "God bless you, Good Time Charlie. You'll always be in my prayers." Her eyes filled up once again as she watched him walk away. Sister Teresa walked back into the orphanage. When she looked inside the envelope, she was stunned when she saw five thousand dollars inside.

Charlie walked down the block feeling happy about his good deed. It made him feel good to know he had fulfilled a dream of someone so close to him. The only other times he felt this good was when he did things for his daughter that brought a smile to her face. Charlie thought for a second that maybe the two old nuns set him up like his aunt had done. He laughed, but thought what the fuck? It was only five-thousand and it came from money he skimmed off Tony while doing his job.

CHAPTER 25

Charlie started to get into a rut. He would go smack people around day after day and, sometimes, do worse. He would come home after a day's work and get drunk. He was getting too depressed lately, especially after whacking someone, but the money and power he craved were still there, so he stayed with the job. It was doing the jobs for Tony that bothered him so much and resented it that Tony had more power than him, though that was one main reason people feared Tony so much. He couldn't blame Tony for keeping him around because there was no debt, but he couldn't make the break from him. Charlie's depression worried him endlessly. He really shouldn't be depressed; he was a man of power, respect, was making a good living, partying at night, and fucking beautiful women. Charlie would be depressed, in a bar drinking and looking at all those nine-to-fivers and think, I got it better than them. Sometimes, that would cure his depression for a short time, as he would go pick up some slut and do the town. Other times, Charlie would get out of his depression by looking at what his life was at one time and how he made something out of himself—a kid out of the ghetto who grew up in an orphanage and became a big time hood.

Charlie started to think about his options as he realized the source of his depression was working for Tony. He seriously started thinking about making a move and getting back on his own or even working for another boss who might treat him better and with more respect. Charlie was a free agent and could do anything he pleased. He just had to choose another path, telling himself that he would very soon, but it would be nice to make a score before making the move.

Charlie and Vito were getting along pretty good for two guys who didn't have much in common. When they collected they had everything set between them on what they would do if someone came up light on a payment. One day, Vito let Charlie know that they could make a score outside Tony's crew and keep all the cash and split about a hundred grand. Vito was looking to make some cash for himself, too. Vito told Charlie about the job: it would be in Staten Island and it was Vito's old boss who sold drugs. It had been five years since Vito worked for them, but he knew they were still operating there. Most important, he knew where they kept the drugs and cash. Vito told Charlie that they would have to be killed, because he didn't want it coming back to him.

Charlie thought about it when Vito told him. "Are they connected with anyone?" Charlie asked Vito.

Vito said that they were independent dealers, but did pay off some people to operate there, where they had been dealing right out of their house for twenty-five years. He told Charlie that they were linked to a biker gang and started dealing to support their own junkie habits and dealt with all the bikers in New York. Vito told Charlie the job would be easy because they lived in a bungalow off the water in a small community where everyone did drugs. They could go in on a Saturday night after all the dealing was done and catch them when they were stoned. Charlie told Vito that he would think about the job.

Meantime, Charlie gave Tony a shot of doing the right thing by him when he saw Tony at the club one day. "I would like you to move me up out of collections and the side jobs, so I can start my own crew."

Tony wasn't too receptive to Charlie's request. "No fuckin' way. You just keep doing what you're doing. What? You think you're a boss. I'm not giving you any more chances after that fiasco in Jamaica," Tony stated with Charlie getting angry.

"That wasn't me who blew that fuckin' deal. That was your boy Bruno who fucked that up," Charlie told him.

Tony let him know that he should have never discussed prices with Jaba and let Bruno do the talking and dealing. Tony was just making excuses because he never wanted to do business with those Jamaicans. He just wanted to get Charlie out of the way a few days to ice José. Tony wanted to keep Charlie under his wing longer, but Charlie had his suspicions all along.

"You're the boss and there's no fuckin' talking to you!" Charlie said angrily as he got up and walked out of the office.

"That's right, I am the fuckin' boss, and so don't you forget it!" Tony was steaming thinking that Charlie was an ungrateful fuck, didn't appreciate a fuckin' thing, and was a somebody only because he worked for him. Tony thought he could take that away if he wanted. But Charlie was a killer and Tony feared that. If he was to take Charlie out, he had to do it right because, if he didn't, Charlie would come after him and maybe whack his ass. Charlie wasn't a slouch like his father, Tony thought, but I am The Hammer and Charlie really should fear me.

The next day Charlie told Vito he would do the Staten Island job with him and a week from this coming Saturday they would go. Charlie scouted the area the week before on Saturday night. He noticed that it was everything that Vito said it was. People were going in and out of the bungalow all day long, but as Vito told him; everything stopped after ten at night and the bungalow looked like an easy mark. Charlie figured he would do the job after eleven.

That Saturday night, a little past eleven, Charlie walked up to the door of the biker drug dealer. The door was slightly ajar, so Charlie just pushed it open and walked in with a gun drawn and showing a badge yelling, "POLICE!"

He startled one guy sitting down on the couch just finishing a hit of coke and looked up at him. "FUCK YOU, MAN!" the biker said as he stood up. He stood about six feet one inch tall and weighed about two hundred and thirty pounds, with long hair and a beard. He wasn't wearing a shirt and he had tattoos all over his body.

Vito followed up behind Charlie with a gun and he was wearing a hat trying to conceal his identity. Charlie just thought it was dumb and wasn't doing anything, but what could he expect from his Guinea partner when Vito thought Moby Dick was a venereal disease.

The biker grabbed a large knife from the table and went for Charlie, wailing the knife at him and cutting his arm. Charlie kneed him in the groin, sending him down to his knees. Then, grabbing the biker's arm, he broke it over the arm of a nearby chair, making him scream with pain. The bedroom door then opened and a woman with a shotgun came in, pointing it at Charlie ready to shoot, but Vito wasted her right away with two shots to her head and chest. Her blood splattered against the walls.

The biker got up and went for Vito screaming at him, "YOU FUCK!" But Charlie's gun butted him, and he went down again. Charlie thought that this fuckin' biker was one strong prick. He picked up the unconscious biker and put him on the couch, telling Vito, "HURRY! GET THE DRUGS AND MONEY! LET'S GET THE FUCK OUT OF HERE!" He checked his wound, which stung like a bastard, but wasn't bleeding too badly and wasn't that deep.

Vito returned minutes later with about twenty-five thousand and some coke and a scared six-year-old girl under one of his arms who had just awakened.

The biker regained consciousness and looked at Vito. "YOU FUCKIN' ITALIAN SCUMBAG. YOU'RE NOT GETTING AWAY WITH THIS!" said the biker and Charlie couldn't believe the balls on this guy.

"WHERE'S THE REST OF THE FUCKIN' MONEY!" Vito demanded in his inept English and heavy Italian accent with the gun to the little girl's head.

The biker wouldn't tell him, "UP YOUR ASS, GUIDO!" replied the biker.

Charlie hit him with the gun, cutting a gash open in his head.

"YOU PUSSIES ARE REAL TOUGH WITH THOSE GUNS!" the biker shouted.

Charlie cracked him again with the gun. This time the biker was silent as Vito threatened to kill the girl if he didn't say where the money was.

"KILL THE FUCKIN' BRAT. I DON'T GIVE A FUCK!" the biker challenged, saying the mother is dead and he didn't want her anyway.

Vito, instead of shooting the girl, grabbed the knife on the floor and put it to the girl's throat. Charlie thought Vito was bluffing, but he saw that look in Vito's eyes that he was going to slice her throat.

"PUT HER DOWN!" Charlie yelled at him, telling him that wasn't part of the deal, that she was just a baby, and they weren't animals who killed kids.

Vito said if he couldn't take it to go outside.

"PUT HER DOWN OR I'LL BLOW YOUR FUCKIN' HEAD OFF! I SWEAR TO GOD!" Charlie commanded, pointing his gun at his head and cocking the gun. Vito let the girl drop to the floor. As Charlie was asking her if she was all right, she crawled over to the couch. Charlie saw Vito going for his gun and Charlie without hesitation just fired three bullets into his chest. Vito fell backwards to the floor dead. The biker then jumped up and Charlie shot him twice also sending him sprawling back on the couch and then to the floor, also dead,

"Enough with you already, you prick. You would have let that fuckin' animal kill that girl," Charlie said looking around the room. "Yeah, it would be easy...what a fuckin' mess," he said as he looked at the girl who looked to be in shock, but not physically harmed. Charlie grabbed the money, drugs, and dragged Vito back to the car, putting him in the trunk. Then he got in and drove off. Charlie saw a few people as he left, but they were stoned and listening to loud rock music, so he casually drove away through the small community.

Charlie found a desolate spot to dump Vito's body after he crossed the bridge into Brooklyn. It was along the river in a parking lot near Chuck E. Cheese's, a nice place to leave a rat fuck, Charlie thought. Charlie for the hell of it went through Vito's pockets and found another forty grand on the prick that he probably pocketed before coming out of the bedroom. "I hope you fuckin' rot in hell, you fuck, holding out on me and then going to kill a kid," Charlie said and then got out of there.

The next day, Tony was yelling at Charlie, asking him where Vito was, that he was never late.

Charlie gave Tony one of his own great answers, "How the fuck should I know, boss? I'm not his fuckin' babysitter."

Tony complained about the fact that he better show up. He owed Tony sixty grand.

Charlie couldn't hope but smile to himself. "I'll go find him and collect it for half," Charlie jokingly volunteered.

"Fuck you, asshole!" Tony told him, not thinking it was funny.

Charlie thinking that, if he were Tony he wouldn't hold his breath for the sixty large. Charlie then settled a gambling tab with Tony that he had for thirty grand that he lost recently.

Tony looked at him. "You were holding out on me. Where'd you get that money?" Tony asked.

Charlie just told him he had a run of luck in Atlantic City.

Tony knew he was lying, but he took the cash anyway. He hated it when Charlie was all paid up 'cause he was always leery of Charlie cutting out on him without notice. Tony always liked to have that edge on him, but he was running out of ideas of how to keep him in debt.

Tony had become tired of his long-time girlfriend, Gloria. He planned to unload her soon. On top of getting older and heavier, she was becoming a tired piece of ass he didn't want to fuck anymore. Tony had started screwing on a regular basis one of his waitresses, named Melissa, at one of his clubs. She was younger, prettier, well built, and could really suck his cock. Tony liked her young tight pussy. As for Gloria, he told her he needed to have her work at one of the companies he owned because he couldn't trust the people who were there. This kept Gloria a little busy during the week so he could have more free time for Melissa.

Gloria had not worked for a good twenty years since being Tony's steady girl so she really couldn't say no to Tony, plus it also made her feel useful. Tony always gave her an allowance for being his steady. She did ask him if her working for him would mean she would get more money.

"No fuckin' way. I give you enough money each week," Tony told her.

Gloria had sensed that her time with Tony might be wearing thin and that he was ready to dump her. She wasn't stupid though, so she let Tony know something in a nice way: being around him many years, she knew a lot about him and his businesses. Tony found out a long time ago that she had a few secret hiding spots where she kept track of some of his dealings and had it on paper. He would never take a chance on whacking her fearing that some of the documents she had would fall into the wrong hands, which meant he would be fucked. Tony really had no reason though to do anything to her. During the times when there were pending indictments against him, she was the only one he could rely on to hide money and drugs for him. Tony was just tired of fucking her and being with her as a girlfriend. Gloria felt it coming on because he used to go to her apartment every other night to get his rocks off and take her out to dinner, but those visits and dinner dates had dwindled down to once a week.

Gloria once had the idea that, if she was able to have a child with Tony, things might be different. The only time she got pregnant was right after she was with Charlie's father, Sal, many years ago and Tony made her get an abortion. Gloria never got pregnant after that and Tony always felt it was her fault. Maybe Sal knocked her up their night together and Tony had been shooting blanks all those years. Gloria was surprised how she managed being with Tony all these years and had prepared for the day when he got tired of her. She had been socking away money that he gave her all their years together. Tony had already paid off her apartment and the furniture in there, so she didn't have to worry about finding a place to live when he did dump her. Gloria often thought though that she would trade all her possessions right now for a husband and kids which she never had. She hooked up with Tony at such a young age and never knew any better until it was too late; she was then well into her forties. Now in her fifties, she felt a big hole in her life, a deep emptiness, that she had missed out on something better and that she had better plan for a life alone.

Charlie was still working steadily for Tony, but doing so was much harder now since he was working alone as Vito turned up dead in Brooklyn. His death had been a mystery to Tony who thought that maybe some other mafia head might be plotting a takeover on him. Charlie liked watching Tony sweat like this because when Tony got paranoid over someone trying to make a move on him he wouldn't pay as much attention to Charlie and the outside jobs Charlie did for him. That allowed Charlie to skim a little extra for himself, plus Charlie got enjoyment knowing that he had become the source of Tony's heartache and worries.

Jackie Dee, who used to work for Charlie, was now doing gofer work for Tony. He drove Tony around and worked in the club, swept up, and did errands. Charlie asked Tony to let him have Jackie to at least drive him around for the collections so that he could let him stay in the car on his Manhattan runs and wouldn't waste time looking for parking spaces. Tony let Charlie have Jackie, but told him he better not think of pulling any side jobs with Jackie. Charlie knew that Tony was still worried about him branching out again on his own and that Jackie could be part of his crew again. Tony also told him that he wanted to know about any new side jobs or deals so he could approve of them.

Charlie would say to himself: Yeah sure, like what you screwed up with the fuckin' Jamaica deal. You think I'm stupid enough to let you get involved again if I have the cash to score a deal like that for myself. But Charlie would just tell Tony what he wanted to hear, "Sure Boss."

Tony knew he would try again sometime soon to be on his own again. He finally thought he came up with a plan to put Charlie back in debt with him. It entailed Charlie working a job with Bruno where they were to whack a guy and cut out his heart and bring it back to Tony. In preparing the plan, Charlie never saw Tony as angry as he was now to have someone killed this way. Charlie didn't want to work a job with

Bruno though because he hated the prick's guts, especially after the way Bruno fucked up his Jamaican deal.

"How much does this guy owe you?" Charlie asked Tony, while they drank their espressos at the Mulberry Club.

"Over two-hundred thousand and he's unable to pay back right now 'cause he's just out of the hospital. But, he won't pay back when he gets out either, so he says," Tony told Charlie, calmer now.

"Why kill him then? Wait till he gets out and see if he does. You're not going to get anything out of him after he's dead," Charlie suggested.

Tony told him that he was through fucking around with this deadbeat and he wanted him dead so he can't spend the money either and that he had to make an example of him. "I just want him dead!" Tony emphatically told Charlie, letting him know that he would be paid well for the job.

Charlie told him that he didn't need the old man Bruno to do this job and he would also take Bruno's payday, too, for the job, but Tony insisted that Bruno was to go with him.

"How much is the job?" Charlie asked.

"Twenty grand," Tony replied.

Charlie knew it had to be somebody who was important because those types of paydays on hits went on people who had some sort of power. "Who's the mark?" Charlie asked.

Tony hedged and said that Bruno would tell him when they did the job.

Charlie then let Tony know that after this job he was going back on his own again and pulling out. He had enough cash to start his own business again and he had already scouted a few places uptown to open up a bar.

Tony felt this was coming and just let Charlie know that he needed him to do this job first. Then, he might even back Charlie on his move back uptown, which surprised Charlie and made him a little apprehensive, knowing Tony. Looking on the positive side, Charlie planned on his own crew to be in control of his life again. He felt he deserved it. Tony seemed to agree, but would it happen? Would Tony finally give Charlie his way? Charlie had paid back all his debts to Tony, had been loyal, and worked everything Tony had thrown at him.

CHAPTER 26

The next day, Bruno arrived in front of Charlie's apartment building to pick him up so they could do the job. Charlie emerged from his building and got into the car with Bruno who was busy chomping on a hero. Charlie gave him a scornful look thinking, all this fuck thinks about is eating. Every time he saw Bruno at the Mulberry Club or at Tony's gambling spots, Bruno was stuffing his face.

"Let's go," Charlie said.

Bruno just grunted as he chewed a mouthful of food. "No rush, let me finish my hero first," Bruno said with his mouth half-full.

Charlie looked at him, shaking his head.

Bruno shoved the last bite in his mouth and chewed as he asked, "Got your piece with you?"

"Yeah, I got my piece, but maybe I won't have to use it if I get the deadbeat to pay," Charlie told him. Bruno let Charlie know that he'll probably have to use it because he knows the prick won't pay.

"And if you don't use it, I will and after I waste the fuck, then I'll use it on you and really show you how it's done, boy," Bruno stated.

"What the fuck is your problem?" Charlie asked him. "I've done over a dozen hits. What do you think, I'm a fuckin' novice? This shit ain't new to me. If the dickhead doesn't pay, he's dead, end of story, and I don't need you telling me my job. Just drive the car and I'll do the rest," Charlie told Bruno in an angry tone. He wished that it was Bruno he had to shoot; he would love to empty his chambers in that baboon's head and he would do it for free.

Bruno drove Charlie into Harlem. Charlie asked where he was going and Bruno told him he would know soon enough. This was Charlie's old stomping ground where he first started out. Bruno pulled the car around a corner and stopped across the street from a candy store. It was Big Red's candy store.

Charlie stared at Bruno, knowing the mark was Big Red. "Is this some sort of fuckin' joke?" Charlie asked Bruno.

"You see me laughing, boy?" Bruno asked sarcastically. "Your old nigger friend is the mother fucker not making his payments, so go do your job or I'll do it for you," Bruno informed him.

"I'm handling this. You make one fuckin' move towards that store and I'll make your wife a widow," Charlie told him, staring at him with that cold stare.

"Watch who you're talking to, asshole. I'm a made man. You fuck with me, and you're one dead mother. Now, get the fuck out and do the job," Bruno ordered.

Charlie told him that he needed just ten minutes alone with him.

"For what, a fuckin' family reunion? Okay, you got ten minutes before I come in blasting," Bruno stated.

"No, you just wait here for me to come out, and I'm not fuckin' around, Bruno," Charlie stated coldly, looking him dead in the eyes. Charlie got out of the car and walked towards the candy store as Bruno opened a newspaper in the car, first checking his watch.

Charlie walked into the candy store and he immediately started for the back room, totally ignoring the young black kid at the counter who got in front of Charlie saying, "What do you want around here?"

"I'm here to see Big Red," Charlie told the kid.

"Haven't you guys done enough to him already?" the kid asked.

Charlie got annoyed with the kid, not in the mood to play games. "JUST TELL BIG RED HIS BROTHER IS HERE TO SEE HIM!" Charlie said in a loud voice as the kid stared at him.

The back door opened up and out came Big Red walking with a cane. "My little white brother, what's all the shouting about? Your eyes are all bugged out and this doesn't sound like a social call."

Charlie walked over to Big Red, gave him a quick hug, and pulled back as Big Red didn't hug back.

"You're right, this isn't a social call. I wish it was, but we got to talk, my brother," Charlie stated.

"Brother? So you are working here 'cause of that fuck Tony, The Hammer?' Red asked, knowing that Charlie was still working for him.

"He sent me as a worker, but I'm here as a brother for you, Big Red," Charlie told him.

Big Red then smiled and gave him a hug. "So, Good Time, it is good seeing you. Come in the back," Big Red told him and they went in the back to talk it over.

"How did you get into this mess with Tony? You're the one that told me about this prick years ago, so how?" Charlie asked Big Red, as they both sat down.

"Well, after I was shot, I was out of commission for about six months and during that time all my runners were getting busted by the cops and that fuck Tony took my bar for the back interest on the money I owed. Being out so long didn't help. I came out with no business and no money coming in. I've been able to keep on the vig payments, but I just don't have that cash flow I once had, brother. I just can't make the payments anymore, Good Time," Big Red informed him.

"I always thought you were loaded," Charlie said.

"No, Good Time, those days are long gone. Fast women, slow horses, and bad booze, that's my story and it cost me all my stash to pay the hospital bills. I never had no insurance," Red stated. "Guess that money I spent to stay alive went for nothing 'cause they're going to whack me anyway," Big Red said.

Suddenly Charlie was sure that it was Tony who shot Big Red years ago. That was Tony's way to get businesses he was missing out on and he couldn't stand to see other people make money he could make. Tony was nothing but a bloodsucker; he wanted it all and was envious of anyone who had something he wanted and that could increase his worth. As Charlie saw it, he was a fuckin' no good, greedy Sicilian cocksucker.

"You wouldn't happen to have two-hundred grand lying around that I could borrow?" Big Red jokingly asked, as Charlie shook his head no. Big Red went on saying he couldn't even afford a good apartment now as he was living in the back of the candy store and just waiting for Tony to off him because he would be better off dead anyway.

Charlie got tears in his eyes and thought that some of this was his fault for letting Big Red stand up for him years ago. Charlie got up saying, "Big Red, my brother, you just don't worry about a thing. I'll handle this and I'll talk to Tony." Charlie went over and hugged him, letting him know he will get in touch with him in a few days.

Charlie went back to the car where Bruno was and he got in saying, "Let's go."

Bruno looked at him. "So, what the fuck is going on here, either show me the money or his fuckin' heart," Bruno said.

Charlie in a fit of anger punched the windshield, breaking it. "DON'T FUCKIN' PUSH ME BRUNO! Just drive this fuckin' car now and take me to see Tony before something bad really happens!" Charlie demanded.

Bruno was about to say something, but he saw the fury in Charlie's eyes and a big vein popping out on his head. He remembered someone telling him that he saw Charlie like this once and heard that was when Charlie was the most dangerous because he could take you apart at times like this. Bruno lost his balls at that point and said nothing. He drove Charlie back to see Tony, and the ride back was dead silence.

At the club, Tony was nowhere to be found, a tactic on Tony's part to make Charlie sweat a bit. He knew that Charlie would not do the hit and would want to talk with him first. Charlie waited for Tony, but Bruno told him after a few hours that he called in and asked that Charlie come see him in a couple a days about Big Red's situation or he will send someone else to do the job. Before leaving though, Charlie warned Bruno that nothing better happen to Big Red until he speaks with Tony and he told Bruno to make sure that Tony knows that too.

Charlie spent the next few hours walking around the village in a daze. Tony was again plotting Charlie's future, knowing full well that he would have to bail Big Red out. Charlie felt like a used piece of luggage that Tony would pull out of the closet when he needed to. Charlie's visions of getting his Good Time Charlie life back were again put on hold, but Charlie knew that one day he would have to get back to those days if he was to survive. Tony was like a cancer that spread into his system, while little by little taking his heart and soul away until nothing was left but an empty shell. He saw it with Big Red, Tony's girlfriend Gloria, and just about anyone else who stayed in business with Tony over a long period of time. But Charlie wasn't about to let Tony do that to him. He knew one day he would have to ice Tony once and for all and get out from under him. For now, he had to wait, bide his time and, when the time was right, he would destroy Tony just as Tony had done to so many other people.

Charlie went to one of his old haunts, The Zoo, to get drunk and try to forget his problems for the night. While there, one of his past conquests, Dizzy, walked in. She walked over to him. Charlie thought: This isn't what I need right now. This fuckin' crazy broad bugging me about the night I belted her.

Dizzy smiled at him and asked, "Well?"

"Well what?" Charlie asked her in a defiant tone.

"Aren't you going to buy me a drink? After all, we had such a good time that night," she asked Charlie, referring to their night together as though it was yesterday when it was years ago. Charlie just shook his head and ordered her a drink.

"And get me some of what made her this way," Charlie mockingly said to Mona the bartender.

"She's that way 'cause she's brain dead from her parents dropping her on her head too much," Mona said, giving Dizzy her drink. They laughed as Dizzy took her drink and downed it in one gulp. Then, she raised her top and shook her tits at them, put her top down, turned around, and walked out, saying she would see them later. Charlie just shook his head and continued drinking.

A little while later, two Hells Angel bikers came into the joint and started pushing customers aside who were in their way, while they followed a transvestite into the place. They went to the bar and ordered drinks that Mona didn't know how to make and one of the biker's got angry.

"Listen, you fruit loop. Make our drinks or you can suck our cocks," the first biker said with them both laughing as they were drunk already. Then four large bouncers came over and forced the two bikers out the door and the bikers told them that they will be back. The Zoo was a club that was a mainstay in the Village as wise guys owned it and no one with any ounce of brains would cause trouble there.

About an hour later, Charlie was still at the bar drinking his drinks as other patrons were sitting around. Suddenly, an object shattered the front window and flew into the bar. About twenty Hells Angels entered the place and, at the head of the group, were the two that were thrown out.

"I told you we would be back," said the first biker.

"What are you fuckin' faggots gonna do now?" asked the second.

All the fags in the place looked at each other and the bouncers who were also fags looked at them.

Mona came out from behind the bar. "Why don't you boys leave peacefully. We really don't want any trouble here," Mona said in a quiet, calm voice staring at the bikers.

The bikers all started laughing as the first biker pushed Mona down hard onto the floor and the rest started smacking the patrons close to them. Other bikers were going along the bar punching other customers. One who looked like the leader got close to Charlie. Charlie had his hand under his jacket, ready for any personal attack on him.

The first biker who pushed Mona down on the floor stood over her. "Since you're down there, why don't you suck our cocks you fag fuck?" he demanded.

A large redheaded guy named Turk, about six foot seven inches tall weighing two-hundred and seventy pounds, came over, picking Mona up and then stared at the first biker. "You just insulted my wife," Turk stated, as he quickly cracked the first biker in the mouth with a hard closed fist sending him flying backwards and teeth flying out of his mouth. The biker came crashing down to the floor, out cold. The other bikers stopped and looked at Turk, as the second biker reacted and threw a punch square in Turk's face. He didn't budge an inch with the punch.

Turk just smiled, took off his pinky ring, and put it in his pocket. "There's only one thing I like more than sucking cock and that's kicking ass." And he grabbed the second biker by the back of his neck and rammed his two inch nail in his eye and took it out and showed it to the biker who was screaming, "MY EYE! MY EYE!"

"Nice eye, now you can see what you look like asshole," Turk stated, showing him his eyeball.

As fights were about to break out all over the place, each fag in the joint pulled a gun on all the bikers who were well covered with Charlie grabbing the lead biker by the head and shoving his pistol in his mouth yelling, "MAKE PEACE WITH YOUR GOD, IF YOU HAVE ONE, SCUMBAG!"

"DON'T SHOOT, PLEASE!" the biker managed to say to Charlie, begging for his life and Charlie noticed that he was peeing in his pants.

Charlie pulled the gun from his mouth and the lead biker started to plead for his life further. "We didn't want no trouble, really. We just wanted to party, that's all," the lead biker stated as the manager of the club came over, a large man named Sally, who had huge tits and she looked at the lead biker.

"Now listen, sweetheart, would you like a bunch of fags to kick and then fuck your asses here?" Sally coolly asked him and continued speaking. "If not, then you have sixty seconds to get out of here or you will all be known as the best rump riders in town." Sally gave him a smile as she gave Charlie the okay to release him. The lead biker and his cohorts left without saying a word as they rushed the fuck out of there with their tails between their legs. Sally also made sure later they wouldn't return by calling her boss who sent word over to the Angels that the place was off limits to them. After the bikers had left, Charlie decided he had had enough excitement for one day. He managed to stumble home for some rest in order to face the Big Red situation tomorrow.

CHAPTER 27

Charlie woke up early the next morning and headed out to do his collections for Tony and stopped by the club, hoping to finally resolve the problem with Big Red. But Tony seemingly took an impromptu trip to Atlantic City with a lady friend. Charlie knew he was with the waitress Melissa. Charlie was still surprised that the old fuck could still get it up and fuck that young cunt. Maybe, it was just for show, Charlie thought, but he knew Tony must still be able to do the deed, as he wouldn't spend money on anything unless he got something in return.

Since his job was done for the day, Charlie hopped a cab uptown to make the rounds in the old neighborhood. He went to his old place, Good Time Charlie's, and there were all new faces in there now as his old crowd left when he left the place again. His old customers were now going to another place in the neighborhood called Rose's. Charlie then went over to a Spanish bar not too far from where José's spot, Zapata's, used to be, and he saw a lot of José's old friends. They all came over to say hello to him. Charlie thought it was nice of them, but Charlie had always been well liked with José's people who always called him Good Time. They all remembered the good days when Charlie and José were around, along with buying Charlie drinks left and right and giving him some free blow. Charlie hung out with them longer than he wanted to, but he was having a good time. He then took a ride over to Fort Lee and a place on Main Street called the Bombay Bad Mitten Club, a small place. The regulars there also used to go to Charlie's bar when they were in his neighborhood. Charlie also used to deal coke to the owner there, a guy named Paco, and a good steady customer of Charlie's. When Charlie entered the place, they too were happy to see him yelling, "HEY, GOOD TIME IS HERE!"

Charlie stayed 'til closing time, enjoying himself so much. Paco wanted to party with Charlie. "So, where do we go now, Good Time?" Paco asked Charlie.

Charlie suggested the Zoo downtown, but Paco said he heard of a place uptown that was fairly new where there was gambling and it was a nice layout too, fancy like Atlantic City, and, as it turned out, it was run by Charlie's old partner Johnny Riff. So Charlie did a couple of hits of coke and went to Johnny's new place.

Once there, the doorman asked them for ten dollars each and Charlie informed that doorman to tell his boss, Johnny Riff, that Good Time Charlie was here and he never paid money to spend money before.

"I'm not supposed to bother the boss," the doorman said.

"Well, you better bother him because, if you don't I'll be bothering you, and then, after I'm done with you, I'll be bugging your boss personally. So, let him know I'm here and don't make me repeat myself," Charlie stated. Charlie felt upset that Johnny was doing so well without him, so he wasn't in the mood for any shit to get into his club. The doorman made a quick call and then let Charlie and Paco in. Charlie was thinking how Johnny got hooked up again as he entered the eye-catching casino-like club and mentioned to Paco how nice it looked. It actually had that Tony The Hammer gambling club look to it. Nevertheless, Charlie was impressed as he sat at the bar and thinking: That half-a-spic did okay for himself.

Johnny made his way through the crowded club over to Charlie and they said their hellos, hugging each other.

"Long time, Good Time my brother, you look good," Johnny said to him. "Hasn't been the same around here uptown without you since you hit the big time downtown."   "So, what's been going on with you, fuck? It looks like you're doing pretty good for yourself," Charlie asked, and answered himself. "No calls or a word from you in years and you get a nice place like this and I see your even using our old charter too." Charlie noticed the charter behind the bar and then asking again, "So, talk to me, partner. What's been going on?"

Johnny just smiled and suggested a drink first, as he told the bartender to buy a round of drinks for Charlie and Paco.

After a quick drink, Charlie excused himself with Paco as he went with Johnny to his office in the back, where Johnny buzzed the waitress to bring them a couple of more drinks as they rehashed some old times. After the cocktail waitress brought in their drinks and left, Johnny took out a vial of coke and he and Charlie did a few hits.

Then Charlie got down to business. "So, what's the deal here, Johnny? Why am I cut out of this place? I never fucked you before and it looks like you fucked me here," Charlie said.

"Wait a minute, Good Time. You're the one that went downtown and left me alone up here, so no way did I fuck you," Johnny firmly stated.

"Cut the shit, Johnny," Charlie told him. "You know damn well why I had to go downtown. Don't play stupid with me. It doesn't suit you, Johnny."

Johnny explained to Charlie his situation: after their club was closed for good, Tony came to him telling him that he couldn't open up another club for a while, that Tony gave him ten thousand dollars, and not to associate with you while you were working for him. Johnny then went on to say that, ten months later, Tony came to him with Bruno with an opportunity to open up this place and he took it, but he got into debt with them by doing drugs, drinking, womanizing, and gambling himself, thinking all along that he was partners with Tony and Bruno. Now, they pretty much owned him. He also let Charlie know that he thought Bruno and Tony were assholes, that they lied to him from the start, and now he owed them over seventy-five thousand.

The scenario sounded painfully familiar to Charlie who knew Tony's M.O. as Johnny relayed to Charlie he wished it was them together again, but now there was no chance as long as he was in debt to Tony. Charlie just shook his head and took out some coke for them to do as they bullshitted more about the times they had together and he told Johnny he could keep the rest of the coke that they had left over as Charlie went back out to the bar for a few drinks with Paco. They stayed around to gamble a bit with Charlie winning five hundred bucks. Charlie and Paco then went to the bar again and Charlie bought a round of drinks for the people there. "It's on Good Time Charlie." With that, Charlie heard someone say that they had heard that name before and that he was a big shot downtown and someone else said uptown too but not anymore since he left.

Charlie looked at the guy saying, "It's not over yet. I'll be back uptown again." Then he left and went home to his apartment.

The next day in the early afternoon, Charlie woke and was again ready to face Tony and that asshole Bruno. With each passing day, Charlie increased his contempt for them both and he didn't fear either one of them anymore, knowing he could take them both out if he wanted to. Charlie took a shower as he tried to shake the cobwebs out of his system from partying most of the day before. He then went to the Mulberry Club to see Tony, but, again, he was a no show. Charlie started thinking that maybe they just might whack Big Red since the two days were past, so Charlie called Big Red up and told him to lay low for a few days and to call him at home in a few days until he had a chance to talk to Tony. Charlie returned again that evening to the club, but, again, no Tony.

Charlie had grown tired of waiting for that prick Tony to show up, so he decided to try to find him. He hit a few spots and then thought he might catch him at Gloria's place on Eighty First Street and Broadway. At Gloria's apartment building, Charlie asked the doorman to ring Miss Gloria Joyce's apartment and let her know that Good Time Charlie was there. Gloria told the doorman to send him up and Charlie took the elevator up to her sixth floor apartment.

Gloria let Charlie into her apartment as she was already wearing a nightgown in the early evening. She was a little drunk, too, as she stumbled around her apartment asking Charlie if he wanted to have a drink with her, but Charlie wasn't there on a social visit.

"Where's Tony, The Hammer? Is he here?" Charlie asked.

"No, the fuck is not here," Gloria replied. "He's probably with that fuckin' whore of his."

Charlie really wasn't interested in hearing her bullshit problems with Tony, as she gently pushed Charlie into a seat and stood opposite him opening her gown, saying, "I mean, is there anything wrong with me?" She continued as Charlie looked at Gloria's naked body. He thought: she isn't that bad for a broad in her fifties. "Look at me, am I fat or ugly?" she asked him.

Charlie told her she was fine and asked her where he could find Tony, but Gloria was too self-absorbed at the moment as she pressed her tits against Charlie's face and caressed the back of his head, saying something that shocked Charlie, "I'd like to do to Tony what he did to your fath..." She stopped in mid-sentence, but Charlie knew she was going to say father. He picked up her train of thought which wandered off and then back to her body. Charlie played it cool and didn't immediately press her on what she had just said because she might clam up altogether and that would be it, so he played along with her.

"You like my breasts?" she asked. Charlie told her yes as she took his hands and placed them on her rear so he could feel it. "What about my ass? You like my ass?" she asked.

Charlie said yes and then went on to tell her that Tony was a fool. "A hot piece of tail like you and he doesn't want you?" Charlie said, buttering her up more. "I'd be pumping this hot body of yours day and night, if I was Tony." Charlie stood up and started to kiss her and feel her up all over.

Gloria was getting wet between her legs having this younger stud wanting her and she grabbed Charlie. "I want to suck it," she said seductively.

"Get on your knees baby. Suck me off. I know you want it," Charlie told her.

She did, going to her knees and taking Charlie in her mouth, while she started moaning with a pleasure like it was the first one she ever sucked.

Charlie watched as she sucked him, then asking, "You want me to fuck you, baby?"

She said yes looking up at him and Charlie bent her over the couch and fucked her liked she was never fucked before, plowing her hard and fast, making her scream with delight.

"FUCK ME BABY!" she exclaimed delightfully.

As Charlie was pumping her, he was pumping her with questions at the same time. "Tell me about my father baby, TELL ME!" he commanded her.

"I will. I will, just don't stop, please! Just don't stop doing me, baby, it feels so good, baby. Do me, baby!" she cooed.

"Tell me about my father and I won't stop," Charlie told her.

"Tony will kill me," Gloria said.

Charlie let her know he would stop having sex with her if she didn't and told her he wouldn't tell Tony it was her that told him. "TELL ME!" Charlie commanded again as he slowed up on his banging her and then stopped.

Gloria pleaded with him not to stop and then she finally gave in to Charlie as he started doing her again. She told Charlie everything about that night with his father and how Tony killed him. Charlie was fucking her with anger when he heard some things he didn't want to hear, but realized she was a weak, young girl at that time and Tony was a predator who used her just liked he used everyone else.

After Charlie made Gloria cum a few times, she was worried about what she revealed to Charlie. Charlie assured her Tony would never know how he found out, plus he liked her and would be back for more. Gloria liked hearing that. It made her feel good as she purred like a cat and began sucking him again.

Charlie told her he had things to do right now, but let her know, "Daddy will be back for more, baby. You just keep that wet for me."

She told him to hurry back 'cause mama needs his tool inside her.

Charlie thought that he really is a motherfucker because this old bitch was old enough to be his mother. He left, knowing he would need Gloria and maybe more dirt on Tony later. Charlie left the building thinking long and hard about Tony, that this prick was now responsible for his father's death on top of the other heartaches he brought to the people he knew in his life, like crippling Big Red, killing José, and owning Johnny Riff. Tony was a spreading disease that had to be stopped and Charlie wasn't exactly sure how he would do it, but he was going to stop him, even if it killed him. For now, he had to cool down and get his head clear to figure out just how he would make Tony pay; it was a matter of honor now. It took a while for Charlie to get his anger under control as he thought about how he grew up in the orphanage because of Tony killing his father and how his life might have been different if he hadn't. Charlie thought about his businesses and how he knew Tony was behind sabotaging them, like the Jamaican deal so that he would continue to work for him. Charlie's mind was racing as he thought about each and every time Tony buried him into another debt. All these thoughts went through Charlie's head and how Tony must have been laughing at him all this time too. Charlie couldn't make Tony suffer enough for the things he did to him and his friends, but Charlie was going to get his revenge. Charlie finally got his temper under control as he walked the streets of Manhattan. He simply thought: Revenge will be mine Mr. Tony, The Hammer, Squateri. Your day is coming soon, someday soon. And Charlie repeated, Someday.

Charlie wasn't going just to take Tony out with a few bullets to his head, that would be the easy way, plus you can't kill a guy like Tony and not have some mafia heads wanting your ass. He thought cool and calm now and decided it was going to be a long, slow, painful process that he would make Tony go through. Charlie thought it had to be something like the way he set up Bennie Sr. and Bennie Jr., too, where no suspicion would come back his way. Charlie figured the best way to bait Tony at first would be to let himself go into hock with Tony again and take over Big Red's debt and this would keep him close to Tony which is what he needed to do right now. Besides, if his plan went right, he wouldn't be paying Tony anything in the long run.

The next day Charlie went to the Mulberry Club looking for Tony. He met with Bruno first who was still riding Charlie about not killing Big Red. Charlie let Bruno get away with it, knowing that, when Tony's payday came, he was going to off Bruno too as a bonus and it didn't matter to Charlie that he was Sister Teresa's brother. Bruno was an animal just like Tony and he needed to die also because, if Tony was dead, Bruno was in line to take his place.

When Charlie finally met with Tony in his office with Bruno looking on, he had to ask him, "Why did you set me up like that Tony? You know Big Red is like a brother to me, that he gave me my start in this business?"

And Tony just stared at Charlie. "What are you, an Italian or a moolie?" Tony remarked to Charlie.

Charlie just reiterated that Big Red was close to him even more than a brother, but like a father. That comment seemed to bother Tony because Tony expected that Charlie would one day refer to him as a father figure, despite all their bullshit. "Look Tony, I don't want anything to happen to Big Red, nothing at all," Charlie said staring into Tony's eyes. It was Charlie's intention that this little sit down would go smoothly and that they wouldn't be shouting at each other like in the past.

But Tony was trying to incite Charlie. "So, are you threatening me, because if you are...?" Tony started to say, but Charlie cut him off. "No, boss, I'm just making a statement and I just want to know how we can avoid killing Big Red?" Charlie calmly asked.

Tony sat back in his chair. "That's easy. Come up with two-hundred grand and take over his note," Tony responded.

Charlie cut to the quick with, "Let's cut the shit, Tony. What will it take to call off the hit on Big Red?" Charlie flatly asked again.

"Your blood," Tony said coldly.

Charlie just leaned back thinking he could kill him right now without anyone getting to him first. "Is that the way you want it?" Charlie asked him, staring at him.

Tony stared back at him, saying, "You know I always liked you, Good Time, but you cannot give me the respect that is due me. You have a big mouth and a lot of balls and, if you don't start respecting me the way you should, sooner or later you're going to provoke me to do something I don't want to do, maybe sooner." Tony stated trying to put a scare into Charlie, but it wasn't working.

Charlie was still cool, saying, "Just tell me what I have to do to call off the hit boss and I will be in your debt."

Tony liked the humble way Charlie approached him as Bruno watched too. Tony was thinking that he finally tamed the beast and Tony pushed Charlie to the limits as they kept talking, Tony let Charlie know that it was he that tried to kill Big Red years ago. Charlie deliberately remained cool. He was letting Tony have his control to let him think he was superior. When the meeting finally was coming to an end, Tony let Charlie know that he had to assume Big Red's note at the same interest he was paying which came out to six grand a week and he would pay it off just like he did all his other debts with Tony. Charlie even called Tony Don Squateri, to further show Tony that he was the boss he now respected. Tony was eating it up as he felt that now this prick wouldn't be as hard to handle as before and that he had him buried in another debt that would last at least five years. Charlie even kissed Tony's ring before he left his office. Bruno wasn't happy at all the way this meet went. He wanted Big Red and Charlie dead, especially after the way Charlie spoke to him in the car and he being a made man too. Tony then dismissed both of them saying, "Go make me some money. This new cunt I'm supporting is putting a big dent in my pockets." And Charlie and Bruno left Tony's office with Bruno giving Charlie some dirty looks and suspicious of his motives.

Charlie left the club and was able to tell Big Red that night when he called that it was okay for him to go back to the store because he took care of his situation with Tony. Big Red apologized to Charlie about having to take over his debt, but Charlie assured him it was temporary, that he should sit tight for now, and in about six months things were about to change; they were going to have some fun.

CHAPTER 28

For the next few months, Charlie did his work quietly and efficiently, indicating that he was a model soldier for Tony and his crew. He didn't say much to people inside the crew as he distanced his relationship with everyone at the club and kept his mind on the work he did for Tony. Charlie didn't even confide in Jackie Dee who drove him around, well aware that he was always trying to get on Tony's good side. When Jackie always tried to pump him with questions, Charlie didn't engage him in any business talk about Tony. Charlie knew he would report back to Tony. Tony though couldn't be happier about the change in Charlie and how he did his work because it was one less thing he had to worry about.

Charlie even moderated his drugs and drinking, and limited his good times that he liked so much. In his spare time, Charlie sought other ways to occupy his time, finding, in fact, that he enjoyed going to the movies. He liked this one picture called *The Godfather* and how it was about his world. One line in the picture stuck with him: "Keep your friends close, but keep your enemies closer." It so indicated his situation with Tony as he was Charlie's life enemy that he would have to deal with *SOMEDAY SOON*.

Charlie began to set the wheels in motion to Tony's downfall. He figured he would start with Tony's bookmaking operations. First, he had to find himself a clean cop somewhere, which was as hard as screwing a virgin on her period because it seemed every cop in Manhattan was on the take. Charlie decided a federal agent would suffice. He went over and talked with Big Red, seeking his advice on the matter. Big Red led Charlie to his aunt's son who just graduated three years before from the FBI Academy, and who now worked in New York. He was clean as a whistle. "Hell, my aunt warned me to watch out for him 'cause he's working the illegal gambling and narcotics division and he wouldn't think twice about arresting his own relative," Big Red informed Charlie. "Shit, come to think of it. I did hear he arrested his own father."

Charlie told Red to set up a meeting with only him and the agent because he didn't want Big Red to get involved yet with what Charlie had in mind.

Big Red looked at Charlie who had this gleam in his eye and acting like the Charlie he knew. "Good Time, I do believe you are enjoying yourself again," Big Red observed.

"Big Red, if what I have planned works to perfection, Good Time Charlie will be back in full force as well as the good times."

"Well, let the good times roll, little brother," Big Red said with a smile.

Charlie got his meeting set up with Big Red's nephew, FBI agent Perkins, and met him at an obscure location in Manhattan at an early morning hour. Charlie introduced himself as Steve Smith. Perkins wasn't really concerned about his name. He wanted any information he could get out of him that was reliable and that would further his career.

The agent was perfect for Charlie's purposes as he was a go-getter and ambitious looking to move quickly up the FBI ladder. Perkins did, however, want to know why Charlie was giving up the information on these gambling locations. Charlie just let him know that he was just trying to get even with the person who ran them and who was responsible for hurting a lot of people he cared about. Charlie didn't give Agent Perkins all of Tony's locations, but told him that he would give more when the places started closing down. Perkins wanted to know more because, if Charlie's info was right and something happened to him, he would be out of a good source like Charlie.

But Charlie just let him know that nothing was going to happen to him. "Do we have a deal?" Charlie asked.

"You bet your ass we have a deal," Perkins replied.

The two men agreed and Charlie told Perkins he would contact him when those spots he gave him were shut down. It was up to Charlie to pick the location and time when they were to meet in the future. They shook hands and went their separate ways with Perkins thinking he might have found the pot of gold at the end of the rainbow. He dreamed ahead that he might be in charge of the New York FBI office much sooner then he thought.

Over the next three months, Tony's gambling spots were getting raided left and right by the Feds as Charlie kept feeding Perkins the information he needed. Tony was losing his mind as it was costing him a fortune to post bail and get lawyers for his people who worked those spots. The Feds had seized over a half a million dollars in raiding those locations and on collection day, too. The numerous raids led Tony to believe that there might be a rat within his crew or one of the rival family members was trying to sabotage his territory, so they could eventually take it over. Then too, maybe it was a cop on the take who got caught and was giving up info to save his ass. Tony was becoming paranoid as hell trying to figure out who the fuck was dogging his operations. He began ranting and raving on a daily basis at the Mulberry Club. "I'M GOING TO FIND OUT WHO THE FUCK IT IS AND I'M GOING TO CUT THAT FUCKIN' PRICK'S BALLS OFF AND SHOVE THEM DOWN HIS THROAT. THAT MOTHERFUCKER IS DEAD!" Tony yelled.

One day, Charlie was sitting there when he was yelling and he told Charlie that when he found out who the son of a bitch was he was personally going with Charlie to do the job. It was all Charlie could do to keep a straight face and Charlie would just say, "I'll make the cocksucker suffer. We'll cut out his fuckin' intestines and serve 'em up as tripe in the club, Boss."

"We'll teach this bastard that no one can fuck with a Sicilian's money," Tony told Charlie. Still, the raids never stopped. With each passing week, something else of Tony's was being shut down.

One day Charlie walked into the club as Tony was ripping Bruno and his crew, another asshole. Tony asked Charlie who he thought was doing this to him. He just let Tony know that it would usually be someone close to him and someone who had a lot to gain. As he said it, he was looking at Bruno who was staring back at him, but Charlie didn't say it was Bruno. Bruno knew what he meant and so did Tony. "And when you find out, I'll take care of him for you Boss," Charlie said. "Nothing I hate more than a fuckin' rat, Boss."

Bruno was getting furious at Tony for even asking Charlie's opinion and raising suspicions on him, questioning his loyalty and pretty much pointing a finger at him, but Bruno couldn't do anything about it because Charlie was Tony's favorite the last few months as he had become the model soldier. Bruno was thinking of taking Charlie out in the near future because he hated him so much. For now, he, too, wanted to get the louse who was giving up Tony's locations and to quiet any aspersions cast on him.

Charlie thought it would be a good idea to let things cool a while, so he didn't feed anything to Perkins for a few weeks, thinking it would further implicate Bruno. Then, Charlie gave Perkins double the dose of gambling spots to hit: over the next couple of months Tony's gambling operations were continuously being closed and Perkins was making quite a name for himself with the Bureau. The pressure was building for Tony and more money was being spent on lawyers and bail.

Perkins was now kicking back to Charlie six-thousand a week to keep the information coming in. Charlie used that money to keep paying Tony the vig on the money he owed for Big Red's debt.

Tony was also drawing attention from the other family heads as they were thinking that this might affect their gambling locations in the future, but for now they were getting the action from Tony's customers who didn't want to gamble with him because they were getting busted so much. Tony started having Charlie do hits on people he suspected were giving him up to the Feds and even wanted Charlie to take out a police captain who he thought turned on him.

Charlie knew a hit on any type of law enforcement person or a politician had to be okayed by the New York Mafia head himself. He would need to hear that first hand. It was his right since it would have usually been a hit man from outside the New York area to do the job.

Tony was angry with Charlie about him not taking out the cop on his word, but Charlie would not have shown good sense if he did. In the end, Tony knew Charlie was right to back off. Tony was in a tough spot, he couldn't ask the other families for help on this because, if he did, he was leaving the door open for other families to come in and run his businesses, and he wasn't about to do that. One other thing that developed out of all of this: Tony began to confide in Charlie more and more. Charlie became one of the few people Tony felt he could trust, making Charlie revel in the thought that this stupid fuck didn't even consider him as the one who was sabotaging his businesses.

Charlie began his next move on Tony to add further problems for him: go after his after-hours gambling clubs where drugs were often circulated among his patrons. Charlie knew one club had a young woman who frequented the place. She used to get wired on coke every time she went there and drank like a fish, but worst of all she was illegal, under twenty-one. This woman had just turned twenty. Also, she happened to be the daughter of a well known congressman.

When Charlie met with and clued Perkins in on this place, Perkins's first reaction was to pass up on an after-hours club since these clubs were usually spots they didn't like to raid. Perkins knew that high-ranking officials and people who had cash usually frequented those spots.

Charlie challenged his integrity on letting this one go by him. "Don't tell me the payoffs are too good to close it up," Charlie insinuated.

"Don't push me. You know I'm not on the payroll," Perkins told Charlie. As he thought it over, Perkins considered all the factors and decided it was too good to pass up, even if he would be implicating someone he might know. Perkins told Charlie he had to be sure that the congressman's daughter was there before he brought in his men on a raid.

"I'm going to make sure that, not only will she be there, but the owner of the club will be also," Charlie informed him.

Perkins let Charlie know that this raid would also have to be okayed by one of his superiors.

Charlie told Perkins that he didn't care who else he had to bring in on this bust because he was just dealing with him and him only. Charlie then told Perkins he would signal him when it was a go and he left Perkins.

Charlie was still seeing the old broad Gloria when he could. In exchange for sex each time, Charlie would get some more pieces of information on Tony that he might be able to use for his plans to bring Tony down. Charlie made sure to meet her when Tony was out of town with Melissa, which was at least once every two weeks. Even with all his problems Tony was still finding time to coddle the whims of this little spoiled bitch.

Charlie dropped by Gloria's the same night he had met with Perkins earlier in the day. Every time Charlie dropped by to see Gloria, the horny old bitch dropped to her knees within minutes, sucking Charlie off. This night Charlie was giving it to her good and pumping her with questions about the after-hours club Tony had in midtown and if there was a back way out of the place. Charlie had to know because there had been a few times Tony came in or left without Charlie seeing him, using the entrances or exits he knew about. After Charlie had made Gloria come a third time, she let Charlie know about a secret exit through Tony's office that he had installed years ago just in case they were raided. Gloria kept worrying about Tony finding out about the two of them seeing each other, but Charlie told her not to worry. Gloria wished that she and Charlie could go out in public. Charlie just told her maybe sometime they would. Gloria told Charlie that last time Tony came to the apartment she didn't let him do her because she was saving herself for him. Charlie knew it was bullshit because this horny broad would suck and do anyone that came her way, but he didn't tell her that. He actually felt bad for her. Charlie let Gloria suck him off one more time while she asked him to shoot his load on her big tits. Charlie did and then he left saying he would be back next week, sometime, to take care of her.

Charlie couldn't help feeling pity for Gloria and he felt bad that he had to use her to get the information he needed on Tony. Then again, he didn't mind screwing the old bitch. She wasn't that bad, plus she got satisfaction out of it too and soon she wouldn't have to worry about Tony because he was going to take care of The Hammer himself. Charlie thought it funny: she actually worried about Charlie when he knew Tony really had to worry about him. Charlie knew she likened him to his father whom Tony had killed, but he assured Gloria a couple of times that he was smarter than his father and that Tony had met his match with him. Charlie got angry with Tony every time he thought about what he did to the father he never knew. He believed now it was his destiny to take his revenge out on Tony for his father and he was going to show that motherfucker Tony, The Hammer just who Charlie Luzzi was. The time was coming *SOMEDAY SOON*.

Saturday night came and everyone was flocking to Tony's after-hours club in midtown. Charlie came in at his usual time at midnight and all the employees liked seeing him because he tipped so well and customers would be glad to see him also. Various patrons there would shout out, "Hi, Good Time!" as he walked through the crowded club. Charlie stopped as usual at the bar first. He started the night out with his Finlandia on the rocks. Charlie cased the place and he spotted the congressman's daughter hanging with five other young rich kids. Charlie walked by their table and said hello to the young girl whose name was Stacy and her five friends. As a waitress walked by, he said, "Please get my friends a drink on me!" They thanked Charlie for his generosity and Stacy winked at him. Stacy liked Charlie because he was cute and polite for a wise guy, plus he gave her drugs when she asked him for some and Charlie never charged her. "You have a good time and enjoy your evening," Charlie told Stacy and her group.

"You holding any candy for me tonight?" Stacy asked Charlie.

He told her to just sit tight and he would see her later. He could see she was drunk because she slurred her words a bit with her friends laughing at her.

"Okay, Mr. Good Time, hope it's soon 'cause Stacy needs a hit real bad," Stacy said to him, winking again.

Charlie smiled and walked away thinking: can't wait to see what your daddy says to you tomorrow after you get busted tonight for being in this place high as a kite.

Charlie then saw Bruno's daughter who came to the club once in a while to hang out, drink, and gamble a little. She was a nice girl Charlie thought, but her only drawback was that she looked like her baboon of a father and even had a mustache, the poor fat girl. Charlie said hello to Bruno's daughter whose name was Gabby, short for Gabrielle. She liked Charlie even though her father told her not to even speak to Charlie. Charlie talked with her a few minutes and then he asked her if she would get some coke from the drug supplier in the club and bring it to Stacy's table and she did. Charlie went to one of the crap tables and made a few bets which he won. Then he strolled back past Stacy's table again and saw that they were sneaking some hits of coke. "Everyone having a good time?" he asked them.

"Great, Mr. Good Time, thanks for the candy," Stacy said.

Charlie ordered them another round on him and went back to the bar to have another drink. He saw Tony making the rounds through the club as he would usually do a little after midnight to see how the action was. Charlie then pressed a button on a beeper that Perkins gave him to signal that the girl was there as well as the owner of the club. Charlie ordered another drink and waited for the fireworks to happen.

About twenty minutes later, Tony's after-hours club was being swarmed outside by FBI agents. Perkins was leading the charge as they bullied their way into Tony's club. Scared patrons tried scattering to get out, but all the known entrance and exits were covered by some thirty FBI Agents who were lining up all the patrons against the wall yelling, "FBI, STAY WHERE YOU ARE! YOU'RE ALL UNDER ARREST!" Those words resounded throughout the club as Agent Perkins was directing the other agents and the patrons, telling them what to do.

Charlie, who had waited until they came in, immediately headed into the back office to where Tony was calling out his name and pushed one of his bodyguards out of the way.

"GET THE FUCK OUT OF MY WAY YOU FUCKIN' APE!" Charlie yelled to the guard, now on the floor, as Tony emerged from his office into the hallway.

"WHAT THE FUCK IS GOING ON!" Tony shouted.

"BOSS, IT'S A FUCKIN' RAID. LOOKS LIKE THE FEDS!" Charlie yelled.

"WHAT THE FUCK ARE YOU TALKING ABOUT?" Tony yelled back.

"WHAT DO YOU WANT, ME TO SPELL IT OUT FOR YOU? THE FEDS ARE ALL OVER THE FUCKIN' PLACE. WE GOT TO GET OUT OF HERE NOW!" Charlie insisted.

"I'LL FUCKIN' BLOW ALL THEIR HEADS OFF, THOSE FUCKIN' FEDS!" Tony shouted.

Charlie grabbed him. "This is no time to be a tough guy, boss. You can't afford to be arrested," Charlie told him. "C'mon, we can get out through the fire escape. You go first and I'll watch your back." Charlie urged him towards the window in the hallway as Tony's bodyguards stood there waiting for an order.

"Forget the fire escape, Charlie! You come with me," Tony ordered, telling the guards to hold off the Feds at the steel hallway door as long as they could while Charlie and Tony went into the office where they met Bruno.

"What is it Tony?"

Tony pressed a button to open a back door hidden by a bookcase. "The fuckin' Feds are raiding the club. Go get the car, Bruno. We got to get the fuck out of here," Tony ordered.

"My fuckin' daughter is out there. I have to go get her!" Bruno said.

Tony grabbed him. "Fuck your daughter. We're getting out of here! It won't do no good you getting arrested with her you fuckin' meatball!" Tony shouted at him.

Bruno quickly ran out the secret passageway to get the car, knowing that Tony was right and that he had always told his wife not to let his daughter come to the club so they would not have the headache of getting their daughter out of jail.

Tony grabbed a few things from his desk and in less than two minutes he and Charlie were out the hidden exit themselves, closing it behind them and meeting up with Bruno in an alleyway a block away from the club where Tony's hidden exit led them to the other block next to the club.

Bruno drove off with Tony and Charlie in the car, while he mumbled things about his daughter. "I told my fuckin' daughter not to come to the club. That it was unsafe and a lot of riff raff hung out there and she's better than that."

"Oh, really?" Tony said, taking that remark as an insult.

Bruno was at a loss for words.

"You should only hope that one of those losers gets drunk one night and takes your daughter home with them and knocks her up so he has to marry her, you fuck," Tony told Bruno, looking to insult Bruno more. "Your daughter is a nice girl, but let's face it Bruno, she's cursed with your looks."

"Why you got to disrespect my daughter and me like that, Boss?" Bruno said, all pissed off now.

"Because I am the boss," Tony said. "Hey, I got a better idea. Let's fix your daughter up with Charlie here." Tony laughed.

Bruno grew angrier, but he was angrier at the fact that Charlie was getting closer to Tony than him. He also was also very suspicious of Charlie's getting closer to Tony and he was going to find out what was behind Charlie's change in attitude towards Tony. After all, Bruno knew that Charlie really should have hated Tony for all the crap Tony put him through over the years.

CHAPTER 29

The next day, the big raid on Tony's club made all the papers. All the shit hit the fan when it was revealed that Tony The Hammer Squateri was the owner of the illegal after-hours club and was being sought for questioning. Tony was fuckin' livid, trying to figure out how the hell the Feds got that information. The newspapers really scrutinized the illegal gambling operation there and the drugs, while reporting that the under-aged congressman's daughter was there, too, drunk as a skunk, and doing heavy amounts of cocaine too, all provided by a Mafia member's daughter identified as Bruno's daughter, Gabrielle Marino. Bruno's daughter, as revealed in the papers, was being held on twenty thousand dollars bail for dealing drugs and the FBI would launch a full investigation on Bruno Marino and his businesses with the mob as well as Tony The Hammer Squateri.

Tony started throwing things all over the place at the Mulberry Club after reading the paper. "I'M GOING TO KILL THE MOTHERFUCKERS WHO ARE DOING THIS TO ME AND THEIR FUCKIN' FAMILIES TOO!" Tony screamed. Everyone thought he was going to have a heart attack the way he was going. He was especially upset that the FBI seized up to three hundred grand in money and drugs at the club and made a mess of the club too, as newspaper pictures showed everything there busted up.

Charlie was in his apartment reading the papers and was busting a gut from laughing so hard knowing that he caused all these problems. He couldn't wait to get to the Mulberry Street Club and watch all of Tony's suffering.

At the club, Charlie saw the aftermath of Tony's fit of rage as things were broken all over the club, tables, chairs, and the espresso machine. Everyone kept their distance from Tony too; they were afraid to get near him. The only one that Tony didn't yell at was Charlie as he asked Charlie for some advice. That made Bruno mad all over again as he kept a close eye on Charlie, who was being very smug and secure about everything. Bruno wanted to find out if it was Charlie who was the rat they were looking for. Tony had a big problem: he had fucked so many people in the past it could have been anyone who was waging this silent war on him.

Charlie, being the model soldier for Tony for about a year now, was one of Tony's main men. Bruno, unbeknownst to Charlie, was having a couple of his men keeping an eye on Charlie as Bruno looked to get something on him and then report back to Tony so he could get back into Tony's good graces.

Charlie, however, was smarter than Bruno and sensed that Bruno would try to expose him, so Charlie took precautions to stay one step ahead of him. Charlie could recognize that he was being tailed, so he just went about his Good Time image in his spare time and cooled it with meeting Perkins for a while. Charlie found a bug on his phone and he knew Bruno had it done, so he left the bug there and gave Bruno absolutely nothing he could use against him. Charlie was countering Bruno's every move. Charlie did however bust Bruno's balls a bit in a phone conversation with the ex-cop Frank to whom he talked about Bruno's daughter and her situation. Charlie told Frank on the phone that the he thinks the girl likes him and he didn't know if he should fuck her or not because she was a wise guy's daughter. Charlie only said this because he knew it would make Bruno see red. The day after the conversation on the phone with Frank, Bruno came over to Charlie at the club saying nothing more than, "YOU STAY AWAY FROM MY FUCKIN' DAUGHTER!" Then he walked away, while Charlie laughed to himself knowing his phone conversation got back to him.

Since Bruno was keeping the heat on Charlie, Charlie decided to have some of Bruno's men who were tailing him get set up. Charlie was able to get a message to Perkins to let him know that there was a big buy going down at a crack house at ten o'clock sharp that night. Charlie led his tail, one of Bruno's men into the crack house about ten minutes before and was able to ambush him. He then knocked him out, planted some drugs in his pocket as well as a gun he used in a hit in Newark, making sure to put the tail's prints on the gun first, and then scooted out the back into an alley that led back around to the front. Charlie stood outside as he watched about twenty Feds storm the crack house taking out all the inhabitants, which were mostly crack addicts. Charlie watched as his tail was being led out by an agent and screaming to them to let him go. His tail caught Charlie observing the goings on from across the street and Charlie was waving bye to the tail, grinning from ear to ear.

While the bust didn't turn up a big drug buy going down, the tail that Charlie set up was charged with the murder in Newark and possession of drugs with intent to deal. It made the bust another success for Perkins who was getting accolades from everyone, including the head of the FBI himself who gave him a medal for his work.

Perkins was now pressuring Charlie to give him his boss Tony The Hammer as they met at another obscure location on the west side of Manhattan. Nailing Tony The Hammer, a made man and Mafia boss dead to rights, would be the icing on the cake for Perkins's short career to date. Perkins, through his dealings with Charlie, had ascertained Charlie's true identity and knew all about his past, but didn't reveal this to Charlie since now he needed Charlie to help nail Tony The Hammer. Charlie saw that Perkins was getting hungry with power by asking Charlie all sorts of questions about Tony's businesses.

Charlie just told him that he was a "buffer" for the family and that's it, remembering another line from *The Godfather* that indicated that he was a soldier for the family. Perkins started getting a little too pushy with Charlie as he pried him for answers.

"Don't play with me, Good Time Charlie. I want this Tony The Hammer and you're going to give him to me, or I'll..." Perkins started to say.

Charlie interrupted him. "Listen to me, motherfucker, if it wasn't for me, no one would still know your name at headquarters. I give you what I want to give you and that's it. We do things according to my timetable, not yours and, if you don't like it, then find yourself another meal ticket, because I can disappear like fuckin' Houdini tomorrow and you'll be left with nothing more," Charlie vehemently told him.

"But you know more than you're telling," Perkins said.

"That's right, I do, so just go back to your office and exhibit a little patience and I'll make you more of a star than you already are. You have it good with me. Don't blow it and be like everyone else who wants more than they get," Charlie told him.

Perkins knew Charlie was right, but he wasn't about to back down and let Charlie dictate policy. After all, he was a top FBI agent now. "You listen to me, Good Time Charlie. You're just a hood and a murderer and, if I want I can take you down any fuckin' time I want. I don't give a shit what you did for me in the past. I'll take you down if I have to," Perkins stated.

Charlie would have liked to waste this ungrateful prick right now. Charlie thought Perkins was no better than Tony, another user and abuser, except Perkins wore a badge and hid behind what he thought was right. Charlie just left Perkins standing there saying, "Take me down, big shot, anytime you want and see what it gets you." Charlie walked away.

Perkins could see that Charlie was one tough hood who had his own set of rules and was not like the others.

That night Charlie was out drinking with Jackie Dee at a bar downtown after they did their collections. Tony's spots were changing all the time now with all the busts coming down on him, so Charlie had some crazy runs to do. They were at the bar drinking when they spotted two sultry blondes dressed in tight skirts, displaying all their assets. Charlie and Jackie bought them drinks and they got a little friendly, so they decided to party at a nearby motel where they had a Jacuzzi and mirrored rooms. Charlie and Jackie got adjoining rooms and they went to town on the two blondes who were making good use of their coke. The blonde with Charlie was named Debbie. Charlie did her right in the Jacuzzi. After they were lying in bed, she sucked Charlie off. Jackie's girl had him do the same, and it turned out these girls were bi-sexual. Charlie and Jackie then watched the two girls do each other and then fucked them one more time before they went on their merry way.

Jackie was wasted and talking too freely as he and Charlie talked about the old days and how this reminded him of those days. They talked about José and Stevie. Then, Jackie made a slip about being in the hotel room next to José the night he was whacked. Charlie never knew this and asked Jackie about it. Jackie all coked up and drunk told Charlie the whole story about how Tony had them come to the club that night and he set them up with two blondes and the hotel rooms. Charlie had his suspicions that Tony had been behind it, but now it was confirmed. What Charlie didn't know was that Jackie helped set it up.

Charlie left Jackie there as he passed out and went home to ponder these latest revelations. Charlie then went to meet with Tony as he had an idea he wanted to put into motion. He told Tony that he had an idea who was setting up his spots to be busted and Tony was all ears.

"Who the fuck is it?" Tony shouted.

Charlie told him he had to be patient as he wasn't totally sure, but he would know tonight for sure. He was going out to investigate it further and that he would have his answers the next day.

"I'm going with you, me and Bruno," Tony stated.

Charlie hedged a bit, but it could work out well for him this way. "If you have to come, boss, then just you. I don't trust Bruno and I'm not sure that Bruno should be involved with this either," Charlie said with Tony thinking it over and agreeing. Before leaving, Charlie told him he would contact him later.

Charlie then called Agent Perkins from a phone booth, telling him that he was going to give up all the information he was looking for that would land Tony The Hammer in jail for good. Then he told him to be at a bar-restaurant called The Dew Drop Inn at ten o'clock sharp that night. Charlie then called Jackie about eight o'clock that night, telling him he had to make a special pickup for him at this bar-restaurant called The Dew Drop Inn, and that he could keep half. Charlie told him that he would do it himself, but Tony had a job for him that suddenly came up and he couldn't make it. Jackie agreed when Charlie sweetened the pot for him telling him he had to pick up ten grand, knowing Jackie wouldn't pass up making five thousand dollars. Charlie told him that he had to be there at nine-forty-five sharp and look for a black man named Perkins. Charlie told Jackie to bring along a gun and to make sure that he just flashes it when he meets Perkins and that he wouldn't have to use it. Right after Charlie called Jackie, he called Tony and said he would pick him up at the Mulberry Club at nine.

Charlie picked up Tony at nine o'clock at the club and he drove Tony over to The Dew Drop Inn. They just sat in the car across the street and waited with Tony asking many questions. Charlie told him they'd have to wait and see. Jackie drove up about nine-forty and walked into an almost empty Dew Drop Inn and sat in a booth by the window.

"What the fuck is Jackie doing here?" Tony asked Charlie when they saw Jackie.

Charlie told him he wasn't sure yet.

But Tony was insistent on knowing what Charlie knew.

"Look boss, I was with Jackie the other night and he got a little too drunk and wired up on coke. I just heard him say a few things about this big meet he had and I heard him say something about The Dew Drop and I thought I heard something about a G-Man and something about working for a new boss," Charlie informed Tony.

Tony sat quiet for a little while thinking. "You sure about this shit?" Tony asked.

"I heard what I heard boss, but with Jackie you never know. He has a loose tongue when he drinks and, sometimes, he talks shit, but let's sit and wait," Charlie said.

Tony became silent as the two sat in the car and waited. A couple of minutes before ten, Perkins pulled up in his government car and got out. "Get down, Boss!" Charlie exclaimed, crouching down.

"What, what for?" Tony asked, crouching down too

"The plates on that car look like a government issue," Charlie stated.

"FBI?" Tony declared.

"Could be," Charlie said.

Perkins walked into The Dew Drop, observing the surroundings, but not seeing Charlie and Tony across the street as they crouched down in the car. Once Perkins was inside, Charlie and Tony sat up a little to see what was going on. Charlie was looking around to see whether Perkins had brought a back up this time, though he never did before and Charlie never gave him reason to. Charlie also knew that Perkins was never wired either because it would have been a waste of money, plus Charlie always warned him against it and patted Perkins down on a few occasions to make sure. Charlie saw it was clear as he and Tony watched what happened inside The Dew Drop. Charlie said he was going in for a closer look and told Tony to stay there as Charlie went across the street, but Tony got out of the car and followed.

Inside, Jackie was looking over Perkins who had walked in. Perkins was just looking at the bartender who asked him if he wanted a drink.

"Give me a bottle of spring water," Perkins said.

Jackie got up. "You Perkins?" Jackie asked, walking towards him and checking the two lovebird customers who weren't paying any attention to them. The bartender had his back turned to them while reaching down and getting a bottle of water for Perkins.

"Who are you?" Perkins said, expecting Charlie and looking at Jackie strangely.

"I'm here to collect for a friend," Jackie said as he opened his jacket to show his gun.

Perkins started to draw his gun, thinking this guy was here to kill him, as Jackie reacted by reaching for his. Just then, Charlie hit the doorway with his .45 drawn and Tony not too far behind him. Charlie opened the door and started firing his gun with both Perkins and Jackie turning towards the doorway with their guns, each getting off an errant shot. Charlie fired at both, hitting them both twice each in the chest, and then going over and firing once in their heads. "Fuck you, you fuckin' rat bastards!" Charlie yelled as Tony looked on. The two lovebirds were cowering underneath the booth as the bartender hid on the floor behind the bar.

"What the fuck, are you crazy?" Tony exclaimed to Charlie.

"Hey, they were ready to shoot us. And what did you come in for? They could have shot you," Charlie told Tony.

"Let's get the fuck out of here, now!" Tony yelled. They ran to the car and drove off as quickly as possible.

In the car, Charlie started going over what just happened. "Jackie must have spotted me. That's why he drew his gun. I had to go in and whack them 'cause they might have got to you, boss."

"I wanted to confront that fuck Jackie and find out who he's working with," Tony told Charlie.

"No talking to a guy who has a gun in his hand and ready to shoot and that black guy looked like he was ready to shoot also. Why didn't you stay in the car, boss? You could have caught a stray bullet," Charlie said, pretending to be concerned for his health.

"You did good, Good Time," Tony said, patting him on his shoulder. "One day I will take care of you, Good Time" You've showed me the past year how loyal you can be and what you can do. I think I owe you now and, as soon as this whole mess is cleared up, I will," Tony told him

"Thanks, boss. I just wish I knew who Jackie might be referring to as his new boss though," Charlie said, trying to create suspicion in Tony that it might be Bruno. Charlie then drove Tony back to the club and then planned to head home. Tony told him to lay low until the shooting blows over. With that, Tony gave him five-thousand, telling him go to Atlantic City a few days and then come back and see him because he may have some other loose ends to clean up.

Charlie went back to his apartment and opened the bottle of Finlandia he bought. He was having a private little party by himself, knowing he half-avenged José's death; he was on a mission and it wouldn't end until Tony got his. Charlie was thinking about how he set up both Perkins and Jackie and that they got what they deserved and in time Tony's day was coming *SOMEDAY SOON.*

Back in his office at the club, Tony reflected on what Charlie did for him and he knew he promised Charlie that he would get what he always wanted. He thought Charlie was a jerk for believing him because he had done this before and promised him the world, but it was always to get Charlie to do his job better. Tony needed Charlie on his side right now, even though he didn't trust him, but he showed in this instance tonight that he was someone he could rely on until he caught all the traitors within his camp and then it was back to business as usual.

CHAPTER 30

The next day, the papers reported the shooting at The Dew Drop Inn. Fortunately for Charlie and Tony, no witnesses were able to identify the shooters and it was obvious that the bartender and the lovebirds there were too scared for their lives to look at what went down. The FBI investigated as much as it could, but had nothing but dead ends. Perkins had all along kept Charlie a secret among his people at the Bureau as Charlie was his number one informant who was making Perkins a household name and you never let anyone else on the inside know who your informers are, especially if you are prospering from them. They actually blamed the shooting on the Chinese since Chinatown wasn't too far away and Perkins had made some recent busts there, plus Jackie had prior drug arrests too.

Tony was pleased with the results and no repercussions came his way. After all, he didn't need any more problems. It all seems to fit for him—Jackie working together with Perkins. But one thing stuck in his mind: Charlie saying he had overheard Jackie talking about a new boss, so it was obvious someone was telling Jackie what to do all along because he didn't think Jackie was smart enough to do this alone. Charlie was playing Tony just right. With every move he made to this point, Tony was on edge all the time now and losing sight of his businesses.

Bruno, meanwhile, was getting frustrated not turning up anything on Charlie. He lost one good man that Charlie had set up in the crack house, including spending a lot of money bugging his apartment and having his men trying to keep up with him.

Charlie was looking to make the big move on Tony now, but he wanted to get Bruno out of the way first and then leave Tony for last. He figured the best time would be on a Sunday night at the after-hours club that Johnny Riff ran for Bruno. Bruno always hung out there on Sundays and this would be the best opportunity to eliminate him. Bruno usually was with his nephew whose name was Tomas. Bruno was training Tomas to make collections for him and to do some other jobs Bruno wanted him to do. Before Charlie went over to the after-hours club, he called Big Red and asked him to lay low for about three weeks as he would need him very soon. Big Red dropped out of town and would call Charlie to let him know where he could be reached.

Outside Bruno's club, Charlie pulled up and didn't see his car there yet, so he just sat and waited. Bruno showed up with Tomas about a half hour later and it was just the two of them. Charlie thought: Great, they're alone and I wouldn't have to kill anyone else. Charlie watched as they entered the club. Ten minutes later, he went in, paying the cover charge too.

The place was pretty crowded and Charlie saw a lot of new faces in the club since the last time he was there with Paco. This was better for Charlie because not too many people knew him and, when the cops showed up later, his name wouldn't be brought up. Charlie headed to the bar and had a few drinks as he looked over the club. He figured that Bruno would be in the back office with Johnny Riff, while his nephew Tomas probably counted the receipts from the night before which would take them a couple of hours at least. Charlie made one trip to the bathroom to have a few hits of coke, too, to loosen up a bit before he did what he came there to do.

Charlie then went back to the bar and he saw Johnny come out from the back office, his face looking really strained. Charlie figured that Bruno was probably working him over about the receipts from the past few days. Charlie called out to Johnny who then walked over to him at the bar. "You're looking a little pale, Johnny. How's it going?" Charlie asked him.

"This fuckin' place sucks," Johnny said to him in disgust. "I bust my fuckin' balls all week and these fuckin' bloodsuckers take it all."

Charlie showed little sympathy and told him he should have stayed with him.

Johnny asked Charlie if he could help him out because he wasn't making enough with them and that maybe he could talk with Bruno.

"Sure, as soon as you pay me that five-thousand you owe me from the time you took ten thousand to lose me as a partner," Charlie told him.

"Good Time, you have to be kidding me. I don't have it," Johnny said.

Charlie just told him that wasn't his problem and that he better get the cash because it was due him.

"What, you going to kill me if I don't give it to you? Like you killed Stevie," Johnny said.

"Don't push me tonight. I'm not in the fuckin' mood," Charlie told him. He told Johnny he would go with him right now to speak to Bruno in the back room to ask him for his money. Then they left to talk with Bruno.

Charlie walked into the office with Johnny. Bruno never bothered looking up as he kept counting the money in front of him.

"Bruno, I have to talk to you about a problem I have," Johnny started saying.

Bruno blurted out, "I don't give a fuck about you or your problem, so get the fuck out while I count!"

"You don't understand. I owe my old partner five-thousand and he's come to collect tonight. He's right here," Johnny informed him.

Bruno looked up to see Charlie standing there with Johnny. Tomas looked on and said nothing. "I don't give a fuck what you owe this asshole. Fuck you and him. You're not getting a fuckin' nickel of this money," Bruno firmly stated. Then he pointed his finger at Charlie saying, "And you, you fuckin' loser, get the fuck out of my face. Do you hear me, or I'll fuckin' throw you out myself and you got three seconds and your ass is mine."

Charlie stared at him and said calmly, "Listen, you old fuck, you don't scare me. I'll put you in the ground and piss on your fuckin' grave. I'm here for my money and I'm not leaving 'til I get it, so hand it the fuck over or I'll just take it. It's your call, old man." As Charlie and Bruno stared at each other, Tomas looked at the two men, expecting something to happen. "I'll fuck you up Charlie," Tomas said, trying to be a tough guy.

Charlie paid him no mind and stared at Bruno, but used his peripheral view to see if Tomas made any sudden stupid moves. But Tomas did, reaching for his gun. Bruno saw the move and yelled to him not to, but it was too late.

Charlie pulled his forty-five out and shot Tomas three times in the chest before Tomas could get his nine-millimeter out of his holster. Bruno got up and lunged for Charlie, but Charlie quickly stepped aside and knocked Bruno to the floor, unconscious, with the butt of his gun.

Charlie looked at Bruno lying on the floor and pointed his forty-five at his head as Johnny looked at him. Charlie was poised to pull the trigger, but couldn't and didn't. For some reason, he wanted to take Bruno out another way and this wasn't how he wanted to do it. Charlie withdrew his gun knowing it was probably a mistake and then he took his five thousand off the desk that Johnny owed him. Charlie noticed Johnny in the corner of the room frozen not saying a word. Charlie also noticed that Bruno must have pressed the trip alarm under the desk while he was sitting there, which went directly to the nearest precinct where Bruno had several cops on the take.

"See you later partner. We're all even," Charlie said to a shocked Johnny, leaving him and Bruno to explain to the cops how Tomas got shot. Charlie left the club quite calmly, but quickly and drove away thinking that now there was no turning back. He wanted to kill Bruno but he didn't. Tomas got in between the confrontation he always wanted with Bruno. Whether it was in a blazing gunfight or in a hand-to-hand struggle to the death, he wanted that battle. Maybe it was the fact that Bruno was the brother of Sister Teresa that kept him from pulling the trigger. Sister Teresa had been the only other woman in his life other than his daughter he had any compassion for and who had compassion for him.

Charlie went to his apartment and quickly cleaned out all the necessary stuff he would need. In twenty minutes, he was gone from the apartment never to return. He knew he had to go into hiding for a while. Charlie went up to the Bronx to hide out. Everyone knew he never liked the Bronx, so Charlie felt it would be a good enough location to hide out. He chose a dilapidated motel to stay in, too, in an impoverished neighborhood. As Charlie checked in at the desk, he noticed all the roaches running across the floor. "Is this the roach motel?" Charlie sarcastically asked the desk clerk. The clerk didn't bother answering and just gave Charlie a room in the front where he could see the street.

This room is like something out of the *Twilight Zone* TV show, Charlie thought. The door was a solid steel door and the windows had bars as if anyone would actually want to climb up into these rooms. Charlie had a good view of the street where he could see any cars that came into the lot and those parked on the street. Charlie just remained in his room for most of the next week, checking the papers for anything about the Tomas killing. Charlie knew he was a marked man now, knocking out a made man and taking five-thousand of his money and then killing his nephew to boot. Tony would have to side with Bruno on this, so Charlie had to let things cool a bit before he could take his revenge on Tony.

Charlie had to figure how he could meet with Tony first before he whacked him. Charlie remembered that every Saturday afternoon he would leave his bodyguards at the club and meet with Melissa alone at some secluded spot that no one knew about. Afterwards, he would stop at a candy store on the Upper East Side of Manhattan and play lotto numbers. Charlie tried remembering the name because Tony had mentioned it once or twice to him. He knew it started with a "D" so he went through the yellow pages directory for Manhattan's Upper East Side and found it was Danny's candy store on Second Avenue.

So, Charlie would be waiting there this coming Saturday to meet Tony.

Charlie then contacted Big Red and told him that the day was coming this Saturday for them to move on Tony and asked him to come back to New York on Friday and recruit three of his best men to do the job. They were to meet him at the broken down motel where Charlie had been staying, where he would go over the plan with them. Charlie also told Big Red to make sure that, when he comes in on Friday, not to be visible and to lie low the day and night before the move on Tony. Also, Big Red and his men were to come to Charlie after midnight.

That Friday, Big Red met with and brought his three most reliable, trusted men. Charlie went over the plans for Saturday.

On Saturday, Charlie got to the candy store early in the afternoon to case it out. It was not such a big place, and cozy enough to allow him a private conversation with Tony when he got there. Charlie figured Tony would probably arrive anytime after six, so Charlie went in and hung out while pretending to read a few magazines. The owner of the store, Danny, an old man about a hundred years old went over and asked Charlie if he wanted something. Charlie just told the old man to keep cool because he was just waiting to meet someone. Then he gave the old man a ten dollar bill for the magazine he was reading and told him to keep the change. The old man was cool with that. Charlie noticed that the store didn't get a lot of traffic.

Charlie didn't have to wait long. He heard Tony enter, saying hello to Danny and started to ask the old man for fifty dollars in quick picks. "How much is the lotto this week?"

"Thirteen million," said the old man.

"Unlucky thirteen? That's my lucky number. Make it a hundred in quick picks, Danny boy," Tony said, throwing a hundred dollar bill on the counter.

As Danny was punching out the tickets, Charlie came up behind Tony with his hand in his pocket, holding a gun. "Hey, boss!" Charlie said.

Tony turned around. "What the fuck are you doing here?" Tony asked.

"Just wanted to have a little chat with you. That's all," Charlie said with Tony noticing Charlie's hand in his pocket and knowing he had his hand on a gun.

"With a pop gun in your pocket?" Tony asked.

Charlie told him it was like his American Express card and "that he never left home without it."

Tony told the old man he'd be right back as he went with Charlie to the back of the store to talk. "You're in lots of fuckin' trouble this time. You're a dead man, hitting a made man, and killing his blood relative," Tony informed him.

"They moved on me first, boss. I was only defending myself and, if I wanted, Bruno would be dead too now, but I only knocked him out when he came for me," Charlie told him.

"Yeah, I believe you. You're just a born fuckin' loser, that's all. Everything you touch turns to shit, sooner or later," Tony stated as Danny the old man came over to the counter where they were talking to hand Tony his lotto tickets. One came loose from the pile and fell on the counter with Charlie picking it up and handing it to Tony, who took it saying, "I don't want this after you touched it. It's a fuckin' loser, just like you," Tony said. Looking at the ticket and then to Danny, he said, "Hey, Danny, if you're playing lotto tonight don't use these numbers, 3, 10, 14, 30, 41, and 52. They're losing fuckin' numbers." Tony laughed reading the numbers on the ticket and then stuffing it in Charlie's shirt pocket.

Charlie was staring at Tony for mocking him and making light of his situation with Bruno, but Charlie then smiled saying, "This loser will keep the ticket in memory of the late Tony The Hammer."

Tony's mood changed quickly. He never liked being threatened by someone he thought was beneath him. "You ain't got the fuckin' balls and, if you do, pull the fuckin' trigger now tough guy or get the fuck out of my face or..."

"Or what Tony, kill me?" Charlie said, finishing his sentence.

"You got ten seconds to get out," Tony said.

Charlie wasn't scared one bit from Tony's threats saying, "How much time did you give my father Tony?"

Tony's jaw dropped.

"Surprised that I knew, Tony?" Charlie asked him.

Tony was still shocked to hear that Charlie knew.

Tony was scared now as Charlie had that cold stare in his eyes again.

"I don't know who told you that, Charlie, but someone is feeding you some false information. I didn't even know Sal," Tony stated.

"The next time we meet Tony, it will be the last time. Not now, it's not the time or the place," Charlie said.

Tony was relieved that Charlie wasn't going to whack him right there. "Why don't I try to square things with Bruno for you, Good Time? Give me a few days and call me at the club," Tony offered, telling him that he does believe his side of the story and that Tomas was a hothead and tried to move on him. He still believed that Bruno was behind all his gambling spots being closed.

"Do what you want, Boss. I'll be seeing you, *SOMEDAY SOON*," Charlie told Tony, while making him think that he was open to suggestions. Charlie slipped out the back door just in case Tony had someone with him in the car he came in.

Tony was fuming after Charlie left. He left the store, got in his car, and went back to the Mulberry Street Club. Once back at the club, Tony put out a fifty thousand dollar hit on Charlie and ordered all the spots where Charlie hung out staked out 24/7 so that he would get Charlie before he got him.

CHAPTER 31

Charlie got back to his dilapidated motel room within the hour and made calls to make sure his family was safe from Tony, just in case Tony or Bruno tried to use them for leverage. He called Gia to take Alison and stay at her boyfriend's summerhouse for a while until he called her. Gia wasn't too happy about Charlie dictating to her about what she should do, but Charlie told her it was absolutely necessary. The gloves were off now and Charlie knew that Tony was going to pull out all the stops to get him before Charlie got him. He didn't know how long the heat would be on him after he went through with his plans that night.

Charlie had a few drinks of some cheap vodka he had bought up the block. He thought about his life up to this point and about his final dance with Tony that was coming soon enough. Charlie felt a little drained and worn out. He always lived his life in the fast lane. Looking at his surroundings, he thought that everything he did and strove for was now in the toilet. He had hit bottom. He lost everything he always valued—his house, family, and his businesses. The one thing he still had was respect and power; he knew people still feared him. After he made his move on Tony tonight, he would get back to the Good Time Charlie he used to be.

Big Red and his crew met Charlie at his motel room in the Bronx at about nine o'clock at night. They were ready to go. The plan was to catch Tony after making his late night runs and picking up the cash from his after-hours businesses and large gambling spots. Tony always made this run personally and brought along a few of his bodyguards, including one of his crew. Charlie hoped that Bruno would be one of them this night so he could kill two birds with one stone. Charlie was banking on the lack of time factor, which would make Tony react and not call for some more of his men to back him up when it went down.

If Charlie was right and Tony did react without getting back up, then the maximum number of people they faced would be four. Charlie let Big Red know beforehand that, after this score, he and his men and Charlie would not be able to show their faces in New York ever again. They were all okay with that. Charlie was okay with it too, since he went through with his divorce with Gia. She was marrying her boyfriend soon. He was very well off, and Charlie knew that his daughter would be well taken care of. He would miss her, but Charlie resolved that it would be better this way for everyone involved. He looked forward to the day he would see her again and explain everything to her when she was older. Charlie mailed a letter to Gia letting her know that he was going on a long vacation and would contact her in the future, sometime, when it was safe. He also mailed her all the insurance policies he had taken out naming his daughter as his heir.

Charlie and Big Red with his men pulled up outside Gloria's apartment building in a rented car that one of Big Red's men got with a phony license. Charlie had called Gloria earlier, telling her to keep her phone off the hook so that, if Tony called her that night, he would get a busy signal. They looked over the building a few minutes making sure it was safe to start their plan as three of Big Red's men got out of the car. Two were wearing the same uniforms that Gloria's apartment building required the doorman to wear and the other had an Airborne Express uniform on and he was holding a package. They went around the back and the man in the Airborne Express uniform knocked on the door. As the freight elevator doorman inquired about the package he had, Big Red's man knocked him out and tied him up, allowing the rest of Big Red's men to take their places. They got the front doorman to come down to the freight elevator entrance where they were able to knock him out and tie him up also. Then they put the two unconscious doormen in a laundry cart in the laundry room which they locked up.

The second of Big Red's men, dressed like a doorman, hurried to take his position in the front door of the building. Charlie got out of the car and walked over to the front door, waiting for Big Red's man to let him in. Charlie was waiting when an old lady came up to the door holding a shopping bag and rang the bell for the doorman. "These idiot doormen always have to go to the bathroom when I want to come back in," she griped to Charlie.

Charlie got a little antsy thinking maybe something went wrong, but then one of Big Red's men, Denny, appeared in uniform and opened the door.

The old lady asked him, "Where's Toby?"

"He got sick, Mama and went home. I just got here to take his place," Denny told her.

Charlie butted in so she wouldn't ask him any more questions. "Can you please tell Miss Downs I'm here to see her?" Charlie said, using a phony name so the old lady would not know whom he was really seeing.

"Yes sir, let me look that up for you," Denny said as the old lady walked away and went on the elevator.

"You did good. You'll be okay here," Charlie said with Denny agreeing and then Charlie got on the elevator to go see Gloria.

Charlie knocked on Gloria's door and when she opened it, he saw that she was wearing some frilly nightgown. Charlie came in with his gun drawn just in case.

"What's the matter?" she asked

"Not that I don't trust you, honey. It's just that I don't trust Tony," Charlie said, looking around her apartment.

"Well, don't worry. He's not here," she said.

Charlie saw she was right, noticing her phone was still off the hook. "Phone is still off the hook, Good Girl," Charlie said to her with her saying that Tony gets pissed when he calls her on Saturday nights and her phone is busy. Charlie told her not to worry because Tony will be getting a lot angrier before the night is over.

"If I'm such a good girl, why don't you come over and show me," she offered.

Charlie thought this broad never let him make the first move; she's so hungry for him. He watched as she opened her nightgown and started playing with herself, letting the nightgown fall to the floor.

"First, we have to talk," Charlie told her.

"We can talk later. Let's fool around now," she said as she went over to him.

Charlie figured he should bang the bitch one quick one then it would be easier to talk to her once she got off. He then put her on the floor on all fours and did her doggy style while pumping her with questions about Tony. As usual, she was giving Charlie the answers he needed, but she got worried when Charlie asked her what she had that would make Tony come over that night and in a hurry. She just told

Charlie that it would be suicide and he'd kill them both. As Charlie kept plunging into her, he kept talking to her, "Don't worry about him. I'm the killer. I'm the one he should worry about, so tell me how I can get him here or I stop screwing you." He stopped ramming her, leaving her dripping wet.

"No, no keep doing me! I'll tell you, baby, just do me, baby!" she begged.

Charlie started pumping her again. She couldn't get enough of Charlie. She loved it so much she would do anything for it. She then let Charlie know that a few years ago, Tony trusted her with these papers he gave her and this black book, which she had hidden in her wall safe. It seemed those documents Tony had and the black book contained a lot of information on politicians and cops he owned. It also had all the payoffs that were made to him and names of the dealings he had with other Mafia bosses in the New York area. Charlie now had the ammunition he needed to bait Tony. Tony kept this as leverage and also told Gloria, if anything happened to him and was rubbed out by someone in the family that she was to mail it to the Feds. Then Charlie let her know how pleased he was with her. He let her suck him because she loved doing that, ending with his cum all over her.

After they finished, Charlie told Gloria he wanted her to call Tony and then told her what he wanted her to say to get him over. She was scared to make the call. Charlie told her again to do it, but she said she couldn't. Then Charlie smacked her and got her on the ground again and banged her up the rear. She was now starting to come across to Charlie's way of thinking as she never had a guy do that to her before. He ended by telling her not to worry because he would take care of Tony, then she wouldn't have to worry about him anymore, and that they could be together all the time. Charlie was telling her anything to get her to make that call, even saying that they will be together forever and married too as he rammed. When he pulled out, he shot his load all over her. Finally, Gloria said she would make the call if Charlie would do her up her rear again while she made the call because she would be less nervous. Charlie told her he would when the time came. Charlie knew Tony's Saturday night timetable and had to wait a little while before he had Gloria make the call. He made her a drink, too, to calm her nerves a bit first. Then it was time for Gloria to call Tony on his car phone. Gloria again got cold feet. "I don't want the same thing to happen to you that happened to your father," she said.

Charlie just told her not to worry and fuck what happened to his father and just make the call. He then grabbed Gloria by her hair and rammed his tool inside her again, giving her the phone to make the call. She started dialing the phone. As she heard the phone ringing, Charlie was pumping her pussy and then she heard Tony answer the phone.

"WHAT!" Tony answered loudly. That's how Tony always answered the phone, not caring who was on the other end, as if the person calling was bothering him.

Gloria started going into her act. "Tony, help me! It's Gloria! A nigger is here with red hair and OH GOD!" Gloria exclaimed, as Charlie was pumping her hard. "He made me open the safe and said he was going to rape me, OH GOD!" Gloria exclaimed again, as Charlie and she came at the same time. "He's saying he's going to fuck the white bitch real good and not like that old Italian fuck." Charlie smacked her and she screamed, "NO! DON'T HURT ME! PLEASE, DON'T HIT ME AGAIN!" she pleaded.

Tony was asking questions, but Gloria kept up with her act saying that he would kill her in ten minutes after he fucks her and then burn the apartment with her in it and then send the black book to the Feds if Tony didn't pay them what they want. "OH, NO! NOT AGAIN!" Gloria exclaimed over the phone as Charlie rammed her again. "TONY, PLEASE HELP!"

Tony was telling her to tell him that he will give him what he wants and to wait. He'll be over as soon as he can. Tony was trying to find out some things from Gloria, but wasn't getting any answers, except that the nigger was by himself and with that she hung up the phone. Tony was throwing a fit inside his car. "THAT FUCKIN' NIGGER FROM HARLEM, HE'S MAKING A FUCKIN' MOVE ON ME! I'LL KILL THAT NIGGER MYSELF!" Tony ranted. "TAKE ME TO GLORIA'S!" Tony ordered and ranted all the way to her apartment saying, "How did that nigger get into her apartment? Where was the doorman? Why didn't I get that stuff out of her apartment a long time ago? After all, I wasn't seeing much of her anymore." Tony was thinking it was a setup because he didn't think Big Red would be there alone. Tony had three of his men with him so he felt they should be able to take care of the situation.

At Gloria's place, Gloria was saying that Tony didn't give a fuck about her and that all he cared about was the book. Charlie was going over it in his head, what Tony might be doing right now. Gloria just gave an Academy Award performance and sounded too convincing for Tony not to come right away, especially thinking that he wasn't up against much, just one person.

Charlie would only wait a half hour at the most, the time it would take Tony to get his men from downtown to uptown to back him up, just in case it was a trap. But knowing the black book was at risk, Tony couldn't take any chances, not after hearing the desperation in Gloria's voice. Charlie expected Tony to be showing up soon. He had purposely met with Tony earlier in the afternoon to set up his play tonight. He had planned it this way to throw off Tony's thinking and make him more prone to react rather than see a real trap at this moment.

CHAPTER 32

As Tony's Lincoln Town Car raced through the Manhattan streets to get to Gloria's, Tony was actually thinking that maybe he should let Gloria get killed by that nigger Big Red. It would serve her right for opening the safe and he would deal with Big Red at a later date about the black book, but instead he wanted to kill that nigger right now. One of his men was trying to tell Tony to let them handle it and let them go in first and make sure it wasn't a trap, but Tony just told his men to shut the fuck up and he would do the thinking. Whenever Tony got this enraged, it was best to just let him be and let him give the orders. Finally, in a ride that seemed forever to get to Gloria's building, the Town Car pulled up in front. Tony took a moment to look at the entrance of the building. He looked up and down the block, but saw nothing unusual. Tony noticed the usual doorman sitting in his chair and it looked like he was asleep. Denny and Big Red's other man, named Tito, brought up one of the knocked out doormen from before and propped him in his seat, knowing that Tony was on his way.

Tony got out and told all his men to come with him. Then all four men went into the building and Tony looked at the doorman who he thought was sleeping. "Look at this rat fuck. He's sleepin'!" Tony said and told his men to stand him up. Tony punched the knocked out doorman in his face bloodying his nose and the two men let him go and he fell to the floor. As Tony and his men watched the doorman fall to the floor, the maintenance door swung open and out came Denny and Tito with silenced machine guns and fired at Tony's men, killing them all instantly as Big Red came up behind Tony pointing a gun to his head with his other man named Bugsy. They made Tony drop the gun he was pulling out. Denny and Tito then pulled a large laundry cart out and quickly loaded Tony's men in there and Tito wheeled them into the maintenance room out of sight with the doorman too. Then they covered up their blood on the floor with a large rug and tied Tony's hands behind him.

"You fuckin' niggers are dead!" Tony stated.

"You better reassess the situation you dumb fuckin' guinea wop bastard. We're the ones with the guns," Big Red said. Bugsy and Denny started pushing Tony towards the elevator with Big Red telling him to move and Tito following.

Once in the elevator, Big Red was sticking it to Tony as his men held Tony at bay. "You don't look so tough now, Mr. Big shit and you're not as big with the mouth either like you were on the phone a few months ago asking me for your money," Big Red said.

Tony told him to have his gorillas let him go and lose the gun and he'll talk with him man to man, "BOY."

Big Red told him that boy lived in the jungle with Tarzan.

"What the fuck are you doin' here?" Tony asked angrily.

"Didn't you hear? We blacks are moving on up, to the East Side, to get a little piece of the pie, scumbag," Big Red told him as the elevator opened up. Big Red's men muscled Tony out the door. He was trying to fight them off saying, "I'll kill you niggers." They just punched him a few times in the gut and face and dragged him to Gloria's apartment where they knocked on the door.

Charlie let in Big Red with Denny and told Tito and Bugsy to stay outside, just in case Tony had some of his other men coming. "How did it go?" Charlie asked Red.

"Smooth as silk, Good Time," Big Red said with Tony looking up at Charlie.

"I should have known you were behind this," Tony said to Charlie.

"You expecting the Pillsbury Doughboy, you dumb shit?" Charlie said to Tony.

"You fuckin' piece of shit," Tony said to him and Charlie cut him off.

"Oh, stop your fuckin' whining. I've been hearing your bullshit for over twenty years now and I'm tired of it," Charlie told him.

"Where's Gloria?" Tony asked.

"She's tied up in the kitchen," Charlie informed him. He wanted to keep her away from the action, just to be on the safe side. Then he asked Tony if he finished his runs for the night with Tony asking him what the fuck did he care. Charlie then told Big Red to have Tito and Bugsy go downstairs to Tony's Town Car and go over it with a fine tooth comb, telling him all the little hiding places in the car. They were to take everything inside the car and trunk that was green or white over to their car. They were then to take Tony's car to the river and burn it. Big Red did that as Tony stared at Charlie who in turn stared back at him. Charlie could see in his eyes that Tony's car was full of money he picked up and that this was going to be a healthy score. Big Red then came back into the apartment and Tony looked at him.

"I should have killed you a long time ago, you black fuck!" Tony said.

Red told him he never had the balls to kill him, that he sent fools out that day to do his work. "You're finished, old man. You're nothing," Big Red told him.

"Untie me, you chimp, and we'll go at it right now. I'll take you and your little white brother on and kill you both like I killed his father" Tony said to Red as Charlie stared at him. Big Red just gave Tony a punch in his side making him cringe.

"Knowing you, Tony, you could never have killed my father by yourself. You always needed someone to do your dirty work," Charlie stated. He was just guessing, but somehow he knew he was right because it was like he felt his father's presence with him, feeling no fear on what he was doing. Charlie then told Tony he was going to give him a chance to go one on one with him, that is, if he had the balls for it. Tony knew this was the only chance he had. Charlie didn't care at this point. He had Tony defeated and he wanted to see if Tony was the tough guy he said he once was. In his sixties now, Tony was still in shape, though heavier than he once was, but still had that power build. Tony The Hammer got his nickname from being able to hit you so hard that it was like being hit by a hammer, but Charlie didn't care. He wanted to kill Tony with his bare hands.

"Come on, tough guy, untie me. You think I'm afraid to take you on. Untie me and, after I kill you, I'll kill your fuckin' chimp friend too. You both will die tonight 'cause I'm Tony The Hammer. I made my bones when your scumbag father was pissing you out," Tony told Charlie.

Charlie put his pistol down as he asked Big Red to untie the prick. Big Red was reluctant, but he did as Charlie asked. After all, if Charlie lost, he would just shoot the fuck anyway. It was Charlie's show and he was going to let him play it his way. After all, Tony did kill his father Sal.

After he was untied, Tony got up, getting the feeling back in his hands first as he stared at Charlie and Charlie stared at him. Both men were filled with anger and the years between them had come to this.

"Ready to die?" Tony asked Charlie.

"I'm standin' right here. Come and get some," Charlie said.

He was about to say something else when Tony suddenly lunged at Charlie, catching him with a hard right to the face, but Charlie stood his ground, even though he was staggered by the surprise punch. Charlie cracked Tony with a hard right to the side of his head, making Tony stumble backwards and the two men began to stalk each other with their fists clenched, cocked and ready like two heavyweights circling the room.

"You got balls. You're not like your father. He would have been begging for mercy right now," Tony stated, trying to bait Charlie into a stupid move.

Charlie came in too close and Tony nailed Charlie with a hard right into his ribs, breaking one or two. Charlie felt it as Tony followed with another punch to his kidneys. Charlie was hurt, but it also made him madder. He started unleashing punch after punch to Tony's face and body pounding him with hard smashes that were hurting Tony, while covering up as he backed up. Charlie was relentless. With each devastating punch to Tony's face and body, Charlie was breaking something or drawing blood. Charlie pounded him for two minutes as the punches came fast and furious, releasing all the years of frustration, anger, and hate Charlie felt towards Tony. Big Red watched as Charlie made Tony's face look like hamburger. Tony was hurting bad and thinking that Charlie was like a rampaging bull coming at him, but Tony managed to get a thundering right to Charlie's chin as Charlie tired from releasing all those punches. Charlie was stunned that this fuck could actually come back with a punch like that after beating him so badly. Tony managed a few more hammer like punches to Charlie's face and ribs, breaking a few more ribs and cutting a big gash over

Charlie's cheek that squirted blood. Charlie then got a second wind of strength after Tony doubled him up momentarily with a hard punch to his stomach. That's when Charlie started pounding Tony again with some deadly blows to Tony's gut. Just when he thought Tony was done, Tony pulled out a pair of rosary beads made out of steel wire from his pocket and put it around Charlie's neck and summoned all his remaining strength to choke the life out of Charlie. Charlie had wedged one of his hands under the beads. Big Red saw what Tony had done and realized he could choke Charlie in seconds with the beads and was looking to get off a shot at Tony, but they were struggling so intensely that Red couldn't get a clear shot, plus Charlie put his hand up for him not to shoot. As he put his hand down to his side, Tony said, "You fuckin' punk. You're dead like your father."

Charlie made a short lunging motion with his hand and suddenly Tony's eyes bulged. His hands went numb, letting the beads fall to the floor and his arms falling to his side like lead. Charlie fell forward to the floor, gasping for air, blood trickling down his neck from the beads. He had a bloodied knife in his hand, a knife from his pocket that he had just stuck into Tony. Tony's stomach was bleeding and he had a stunned look on his face as he fell back and sat on the floor looking at and holding the knife wound in his stomach.

Big Red went over to Charlie. "You okay, Good Time?" Big Red asked him.

"I'm okay, I'll be fine," Charlie told him

Big Red kicked Tony in the face. "Let me finish him. You said I could kill him," pointing his gun at Tony's head and Tony looking up at him.

"No, Big Red, not yet and I said you would be the last person he would see alive and you will be," Charlie said, slowly getting to his feet and staring at Tony.

Tony gave him a half sardonic smile. "What are you goin' to do? Just stand there and watch me die?" Tony asked them. "I won't give you the pleasure of bleedin' to death that quick," Tony said, laughing between coughs.

"You won't have to Tony. I won't let you die here, not after all you've done for me," Charlie stated and then he told Red that they were taking him to the elevator.

Big Red asked him what for; that they should just finish him and go.

But Charlie told Big Red to come with him as they took Tony to the roof of the building. Tony knew what was going to happen and still had enough fight in him to put up a struggle with them, until they tied his hands again and Big Red jabbed him a few times with his gun butt.

On the roof, they got Tony towards the edge and Charlie began. "You know Tony, it seems fittin' to be up here with you. Is this where it happened?" Charlie asked, referring to his father being pushed off the roof some forty years ago.

Charlie stared at Tony and Tony stared back. "Your father was a deadbeat, you asshole, a loser just like you. I was more a father to you then he would have ever been and I could have made it good for you, eventually it would have been all yours, you dumb fuck," Tony told him.

"Bullshit, Tony, you're too fuckin' greedy to let anyone share in your empire. You kept me down all these years, took away any chance I had at a family life, and sabotaged every little success I had goin' for me," Charlie said.

"I did you a favor. What kind of family do you think you could have had with that scumbag father of yours? You were too stupid and having too much of a good time with the drinking and drugs to keep what you had goin' for you. I just took away what you would have lost anyway, you fuckin' loser," Tony said, coughing up some blood.

"Oh yeah, I'm the loser, the guy who touches everything and it turns to shit. But you Tony, you're a fuckin' bloodsuckin' cancer. Everything you touch, you drain every bit of life out of them and, when you're done suckin' the life out of someone, you just leave them to dry up and die. You're no better than me, you fuckin' lowlife and I'm not mad Tony with what you did to me because I got so much satisfaction out of watchin' you suffer these past six months with me little by little taking everything you valued away and bringin' you down," Charlie stated, looking at Tony's surprised face and relishing the fact that he could tell Tony what he did to him. "Yeah Tony, it was me all along and now it's over. You're done, end of story," Charlie said. "You know, it might be better that I let you live. That black book would bring a lot more hardship to you than just simply wastin' you here now, but I'm a fair man. I'm goin' to give you a chance at redemption, a chance you never gave to my father, Big Red here, Gloria, and myself," Charlie said. He walked over to Tony with Big Red nearby and Charlie signaled to Big Red. They got Tony up and on the edge of the roof, lifting his legs so he would be dangling off with only them preventing him from going over.

"C'mon Good Time, we've both done enough to each other. Let's call it even, no hard feelings, kid," Tony said to him. "What's all this talk about redemption and a chance?"

"You can live Tony, but you have to ask my father for forgiveness," Charlie said, as Tony was dangling from the side of the roof. Charlie had one leg and Big Red had the other.

"What?" Tony said in disbelief. "How can I ask your father for forgiveness? He's dead."

"I guess that's the whole point," Charlie said, letting one of his legs go, leaving Big Red holding the other,

"And I guess I'll have to put you in touch with Sal," Big Red said, smiling.

Tony began screaming, "NO! NO! DON'T DO IT! DON'T!"

Big Red spit into Tony's face as Tony wiggled his body and head. "DIE YOU FUCK!" Big Red said and let Tony go.

Charlie and Big Red watched as Tony's body spiraled downwards with Tony desperately trying to get his tied hands apart, while screaming at the top of his lungs. It was like slow motion to Charlie and Big Red watching Tony's body fall and then come to a crashing halt when he hit the pavement head first with his head opening up and blood gushing out in five different directions. Charlie and Big Red stared at Tony's lifeless body.

"Looks like he's a big hit on Broadway too," Big Red said. He and Charlie looked at each other with Charlie saying, "Let's go."

On the elevator going down, Charlie told Red to go ahead and get the men together and meet him in his Bronx motel in about two hours, while he saw Gloria one last time and knowing he had about twenty minutes tops before Tony's body was found and the police came.

Charlie went into Gloria's apartment and untied her. He told her, "Remember, you were tied up, so you won't be held accountable."

"What happened to Tony?" she wondered.

"He went to meet my father," Charlie said.

She asked Charlie if he was okay, seeing some of the blood on his neck and Charlie just stared at her. "What's wrong baby?" she asked.

Then Charlie started in on her. "So, what really happened that night with my father?" he asked her.

She played innocent and dumb.

Charlie started giving her a going over, telling her he was sending all the documents to the Feds, even though Tony was dead and that her life wouldn't be worth much staying in New York as a lot of suspicion would be cast on her and the Mafia heads would be wanting to talk to her, as well as the FBI who would seize all her assets and property.

Gloria got scared. "Why you doing this to me, baby. What about us?" she asked.

"There is no us. You're just a cunt that used my father once and that I used back to carry out my revenge," Charlie told her.

"What will I do?" Gloria asked Charlie.

"I don't give a fuck what you do. You can start suckin' cock again for all I care 'cause that's about all you're good for you ugly freakin' fat bitch," Charlie told her with her breaking down in tears and wishing Charlie was dead like his father. Then Charlie cracked her in the face, knocking her across the room telling her he was not fuckin' with her anymore and not to fuck with him because he was her worst fuckin' nightmare now and then Charlie left.

Gloria cried for a while and her tears turned to anger. "That fuck used me. I'll fuckin' fix him," Gloria said aloud to herself. She called Bruno up at the club, telling him what happened: Charlie whacked Tony; he had all of Tony's documents; and the black book with information about all the Mafia heads and dealings and territories.

Bruno couldn't believe what he heard and knew that his name would be implicated in Tony's black book. He knew he had to stop Charlie before it was too late. Gloria hung up with Bruno after telling him as much as she knew. Then she made herself a drink and sat in her chair. "Fuck them all. They're all fuckin' scumbags, all of them, they should all fuckin' die," she said aloud. She started thinking about Tony's dead body lying outside her building somewhere and she was thinking about calling the cops, but thought Tony should rot out there.

After all, he left her for another bitch. Then she started thinking that it wasn't that bad and that maybe she could hook up with Bruno.

CHAPTER 33

Charlie got back to his motel room. Big Red was there with all his men and they were drinking beers and eating some pizza that they had picked up at some all-night place. Big Red gave Charlie a big smile, as did the others when he came in.

"Good to see you, my brother. I got some pizza and beer for us. Your business all done?" Big Red asked.

"All done. What's all the smiles about? How did we make out with the car? How are we as far as any witnesses?" Charlie asked Red.

"No one saw us. We got away clean. We burnt the car up with Tony's men in it and left the doorman unconscious and still tied up," Big Red informed him with Charlie asking how much money they got away with. Big Red smiled at Charlie saying, "You know, Good Time, they say crime doesn't pay."

"C'mon Red, don't leave me danglin'. What did we get fifty, seventy-five thousand?" Charlie asked.

Big Red's face went sour. "Five or six," Big Red told Charlie.

Charlie's jaw dropped. "Only six fuckin' grand? We broke our asses for only six fuckin' grand!" Charlie exclaimed, sitting down in the chair. "I'm sorry, guys; I thought there would be a lot more in the Town Car. I guess I've done a lot more damage to Tony's businesses than I thought and there was nothin' left," Charlie said, apologizing to them.

"Oh, don't sweat it, Good Time," Big Red told him. "After all, five or six hundred grand is enough to go around, I think," Big Red stated smugly.

Charlie just looked at him.

Big Red got a big fuckin' grin across his face as the other guys started laughing.

Charlie realized that Big Red was breaking his balls and that they scored a lot more than he thought they would. "You son of a bitch!" Charlie exclaimed to Big Red. He got up and hugged Big Red as they laughed.

"You did it, Good Time," Big Red told him.

"We did it. We did it, man," Charlie said, putting his hands on Big Red's shoulders. He held him at arm's length, hugged him again, laughing, then giving the other guys high fives, and hugs.

"That fuckin' chump Tony got so fuckin' paranoid about his places being raided that he took all the cash with him," Big Red said.

Charlie laughed, agreeing with him. Charlie and Big Red made the cuts, giving Big Red's three men seventy thousand a piece, leaving Charlie and Big Red two-hundred grand apiece.

Big Red's three men left, saying that New York wore out its welcome and they were island bound, somewhere exotic where there were a lot of naked women around. They left right away.

Charlie spoke with Big Red and told him just to leave him ten thousand. He would hook up with him for the rest of his cut later when he meets with him down south.

"I just have a couple of loose ends to tie up," Charlie informed him.

"Hey, Good Time, it's not worth it. Our work is done here. There's going to be a lot of heat once this black book and these documents are mailed to the Feds. Plus, you think that old white cunt you left alive didn't call some of Tony's friends right now and who knows who's lookin' for you now," Big Red told him.

"I just want to see my daughter before I go," Charlie told him.

"Bullshit, you know they'll be watchin' her," Red stated firmly.

"They don't know where she is right now."

"You can't take that chance, brother. You put her life in danger as well as yours, so let's get the fuck out of here," Big Red suggested. He suddenly realized why Charlie really wanted to stay. "It's not your daughter. It's Bruno. You want to whack him before you go. You have nothin' to gain," Big Red told him.

"Yes, I do—satisfaction. I want the satisfaction," Charlie told him with that look of determination in his eyes.

Big Red, knowing there was no convincing him otherwise when Charlie got this way.

"Look, you get down to Virginia, brother. I won't be far behind you and we'll laugh about this over a drink," Charlie told him.

With that, both with tears in their eyes, Big Red gave him a big hug.

Charlie said, "I thank God you were always there for me, brother. You're the only family I've ever really had, other than my daughter."

Big Red left, telling him not to keep him waiting too long. One hour later, Big Red caught the first flight out of New York to his destination.

In the meantime, Charlie relaxed a bit in his motel room. He enjoyed a slice of cold pizza, a beer, and drank his cheap vodka. Charlie knew that Bruno was going to be acting boss. He felt that Bruno was an animal and might go after his daughter and that's why he wanted to take Bruno out. He kicked himself for not killing Bruno that night he killed Tomas. Charlie was thinking about many things and looked forward to going down south with Big Red. Maybe they would open up a bar somewhere. Hell, with the cash they had between them, they could do that on one of the tropical islands. Charlie was also thinking that first thing on Monday he would mail out that black book and those documents to the Feds. When that shit hit the fan, they all would be scurrying for their lives, not knowing who ratted them out. If he killed Bruno, he would be the last link to him that would let them know. He thought Bruno wouldn't do that 'cause then there would be questions to him about why this book was kept in the first place by Tony and they would kill Bruno just through guilt by association. Charlie knew Bruno would be desperate to have that black book now, if indeed Gloria told him about it, so Charlie had to make sure his daughter would be safe before he left New York. The other side of the coin was that Charlie could make a deal with one of the other family members giving them the black book letting them know it was Bruno and Tony who kept the book on all the families. They would sure as shit band together and kill Bruno and take over his territory too. It was another way to leave without Charlie ratting out the other family members, because Charlie didn't really have a vendetta against them. He had killed Tony and all he wanted was Bruno. So, Charlie was thinking that maybe he would go that route instead of sending it to the Feds, but time was a factor too. Each day Bruno was loose on the streets was another day his daughter could be in danger and it might take a little time in having a meeting with one of the other family bosses. Charlie thought that might be the best way to go and he was going to look into meeting with the Big Boss in New York.

Charlie needed someone he could trust to be a go between. The next night, he went looking for his ex-cop friend Frank, checking the places where he might find him hanging out. Word was on the streets about Tony being killed in Manhattan, so Charlie had to be careful where he went. He chose places that he knew people wouldn't know him with Tony's crew and where he could find Frank. Charlie also waited until after midnight to begin his search.

Charlie caught up with Frank at a bar called Doubleday's on Two Hundred and Sixth Street, an Irish hangout. Frank was drinking at the bar with some of his Irish buddies, just shooting the shit, telling his pals that the department fucked him over. Charlie didn't recognize anyone except Frank, which was good. He went over and said hello to him.

"Hey, what the fuck are you doin' here? Slummin'?" Frank asked. He asked Charlie if he was buying.

Charlie just thought to himself that these Irish fucks are always looking for a free drink. He bought Frank and his friends rounds anyway and made some small talk with Frank.

Frank was drunk and talking a lot of shit about how Charlie was too big for him now, that he was a downtown man, and Charlie never called or came around anymore.

Charlie just let him talk because he needed him right now and he let him look big among his buddies. He kept buying the rounds, but told the bartender to say it was on Frank. Charlie didn't want anyone hearing or recognizing his name right now, not knowing if he was hot or not. Charlie was wondering if it was a good idea to contact Frank, but then, under his breath, Frank asked Charlie if he had any work for him.

Charlie got him to sit at a table so they could speak in private. He thought about having Frank deliver a package for him, wait for an answer, return to him, and pay him two thousand for the job, but he had to make sure he wasn't followed. He presented the idea. Frank said it was a cakewalk for him and he would do it. Charlie then gave him an address where to meet him the next day, the time to meet, and to make sure he was sober.

The next day Frank showed up on time and sober. They were on a Bronx corner about a mile from where he was staying. Charlie gave Frank a thin package with a proposal inside for the head Mafia boss, telling him that he had this black book and documents, in exchange for his family's guaranteed safety, he would hand it over to him. Charlie included copies of what was in the black book and the documents, so they would know it was for real and also that he would inform them who kept this information on them. Charlie instructed Frank where to go, to wait for an answer, and to make sure he wasn't followed. He then gave Frank fifty dollars for expenses and told him he would get the two thousand when Frank came back with an answer.

Frank went downtown to the address Charlie gave him. It was a very private club called The Sons of Italy Social Club and Frank knocked on the door. A huge Italian answered the door. "What do you want?"

"I'm here on behalf of Good Time Charlie who asked me to give this to your boss and wait on an answer," Frank informed the big Italian who looked Frank over. He took the package from him, telling Frank to wait there. About twenty minutes later, the big Italian returned. "YES!" he said to Frank and closed the door in his face.

Frank stood there thinking that was it, but then the big Italian opened the door as Frank began to walk away. "I was supposed to give you this too," he said, handing Frank a note. Frank stared at him as he closed the door again.

"Big dumb fuckin' guinea," Frank muttered as he walked away thinking that he could have given it to him in the first place, and that he couldn't chew gum and walk at the same time. Frank then walked up the block occasionally checking his back to see if he was followed, but he wasn't. Frank was back uptown about two in the afternoon and had a few hours before he met Charlie, so he decided to hang out at the bar where he got off the train, but not drinking and staying sober as per Charlie's instructions.

Frank then went to meet Charlie at the restaurant where he would be, and Charlie made him wait a good half hour before he went in to speak to him. Charlie was just being cautious as to make sure Frank wasn't followed. Charlie then went in and sat with Frank.

"You're late. I thought something happened to you," Frank said to him.

Charlie told him he was fine and inquired about how it went.

Frank just told him they sent out one of their men with a "yes" and gave him this note, which Frank handed to Charlie.

Charlie gave Frank an envelope with the two grand inside and he told Frank he threw in an extra hundred saying, "You can have some drinks on me tonight." And with that Frank thanked him and they both left.

Charlie took a cab back to the motel and read the note on his way back. He was happy that he could make the deal with the head man. Charlie had the cab stop at a nearby liquor store near his motel and then noticed a black Caddy that he hadn't seen before. He knew then that he might have been followed, so he walked into a building a few blocks away from the motel he was staying at and went down through the basement and out the back. Charlie made his way through an alleyway and checked where he last saw the Caddy, but it was gone. Charlie managed to get to his motel room without anyone else noticing him.

Charlie went over the note and it was signed by the Don himself. He had seen his handwriting once before. The instructions to him were that he could get the black book and documents to him anyway he wanted. He didn't have to deliver it himself as he knew about a contract that was out on him from Bruno and he was not going to interfere with any internal differences in the families. That was their private war and not his affair. The Don promised Charlie no harm would come to his family. He told him twice in the note that he would make sure of that. Charlie knew it would be okay now for him to leave New York after he got the black book and documents to The Don himself. It was also a good business move on The Don's part because with the information he had in that black book he could little by little take over all of Tony's territory personally, using the black book as leverage against Bruno, knowing he was so close to Tony and might have been in on this information with him. Bruno could become a target from the other Mafia bosses thinking that he might be doing the same as Tony did. So, no matter how he looked at it, The Don stood to benefit the most.

It was Wednesday and Charlie had Frank once again make a trip for him to The Don's club. This time Frank delivered a package containing the documents and the black book. Charlie only paid him five-hundred dollars this time, since Frank had been complaining about going through the two-thousand and that it wasn't enough money. Frank went anyway with the same set of instructions as the last time and Frank was to return with some type of confirmation that it was delivered.

Frank fucked up though. While downtown, he stopped for a few drinks at a topless club after getting the note of confirmation from The Don's big Italian friend. Frank came back uptown and met with Charlie.

Charlie was fuming seeing that Frank had gotten drunk before he came back uptown. Charlie took the note from Frank and then threw the five hundred cash in his face.

"You stupid drunken fuckin' Irishman," Charlie told him and stormed out of the restaurant where they had met. Outside, Charlie saw two men walking quickly across the street towards him and they looked like soldiers to him. He quickly went back into the restaurant and out through a back exit and hid behind the smallest dumpster among a few there in the back alleyway. He waited with his gun drawn. Two men came out the back exit and looked around. Not seeing anything, they began cautiously walking towards one of the big dumpsters. Charlie came out from the small dumpster he was hiding behind and fired at the two men who had their backs to him. He killed them both, shooting them twice each. He then put them both in the big dumpster, closing the lid on them and went out the alley, catching a cab back to the motel.

Charlie had the cab drop him off a few blocks away from the motel. He walked to a spot where he could observe the motel a while, scout it for any suspicious characters that didn't fit that area, and also maybe see if he could spot a black Caddy or another big car in the area. Charlie waited about an hour and, after seeing nothing, he went in the back way of the motel.

Charlie had a few drinks and decided to call Gia to let her know she and Alison would be safe. She immediately started busting his balls about six thousand that he owed her and that she wanted the money as soon as possible. Charlie then got into it with her: he told her she was a selfish bitch, while he had been making sure that she and his daughter would be safe and well off, and all she could think about is six thousand that he owed her from a while back. "If you want your fuckin' cash so bad, then you'll have to come see me to get it, you fuckin' bitch," Charlie told her. "'Cause, after tomorrow, I'm gone from here, you hear me!" Charlie told her. She said she would come by, despite the fact that she had to go to such a depleted area of the Bronx.

She did tell Charlie he would have to come down to her because she wasn't going to leave her new Lexus parked anywhere in that neighborhood. Charlie was furious with Gia, but he wanted to give her this six grand because she really needed it for Alison and he never wanted to hold back money that was due his daughter.

Charlie spent the rest of the night drinking and looking forward now to getting out of New York. Shit, if he didn't have to wait until tomorrow for his wife, he could just pick up and leave tonight, but one more night wouldn't hurt him. Charlie kept his guns easily accessible just in case, too, as he lay there thinking maybe he should go after Bruno tonight. He was willing to wait until the heat died down.

CHAPTER 34

The following morning, Bruno was able to find the motel where Charlie had been staying. The second time Charlie met with Frank, Bruno was able to get a tail on Frank. Although Charlie took out two of Bruno's men in the back alley of the restaurant, there was a third in a car that spotted Charlie coming out of the alley and watched as he took a cab close to the motel. Bruno's man got the license of the cab Charlie caught and they tracked the fare and the area. Bruno had a few men work the area and they pinpointed the motel.

I'm going to shoot that fuck myself. He's had it coming a long time now. I will get my revenge as well, for Tony and my nephew Tomas, Bruno thought as he sat in Tony's old office at the Mulberry Street Club. Bruno got a few of his reliable men together that afternoon so he could go to whack Charlie. Once his men had him under control, it would be Bruno's kill. He didn't want to wait for nighttime when it would be easier. Besides, this was a pretty desolate area, filled with junkies and crack heads, and he wasn't worried about witnesses. He just wanted Charlie's blood right away.

Charlie just finished showering and thought better about catching any flights out of New York, since the airports might be staked out with some of Bruno's men. He planned on having Gia drive him to the bus terminal in the north part of the Bronx, take a bus to Atlantic City, and then catch a flight or train down there to meet up with Big Red. Charlie knew he had to keep the lowest profile to get out of New York. In the meantime, he just waited, having a few drinks of cheap vodka and watching television to pass the time. Charlie was leaving everything behind and traveling light. As he looked around the room, there were his unwashed clothes that he had been wearing the past few days. The room was a fuckin' mess.

Three o'clock came around and there was no Gia. She was late and Charlie was checking the window to see if her car was there yet. There was no Gia, so Charlie just sat down and watched some more television, keeping an eye on the clock. He had the windows wide open, waiting to hear a horn honking. Three-thirty came and still no Gia. Charlie became antsy, so he turned down the sound on the TV set and turned on the radio to the news station to get an update on the traffic report, thinking she might be stuck in traffic. He got the report a few minutes later: there were no major jams along the routes she would be taking to get to him and he checked the clock again.

Where is that fuckin' stupid bitch? She's never on time, Charlie thought. You've got fifteen more minutes Gia and then I'm gone and you're out six grand. As they announced the winning lottery numbers from the night before, the announcer read: "And Saturday's thirteen million dollar jackpot has still gone unclaimed. There's one lucky winner out there walking around with a winning ticket. For those who have not yet checked those numbers, they are 3, 10, 14, 30, 41, and 52."

Charlie thought back to Saturday with Tony and recounted the numbers that Tony called out for Danny, the storeowner, not to play. Charlie wrote the numbers down when the announcer repeated them again. Charlie turned off the radio and thought: The shirt, one of these shirts. He started going through the various shirts lying around the room and found the shirt he was wearing Saturday night. He found the lottery ticket that Tony had shoved in there and he looked at the numbers. Charlie stared at the ticket. "In memory of the late Tony The Hammer Squateri. I'll be a son of a fuckin' bitch," Charlie exclaimed as he looked at his winning numbers on the ticket. He started laughing as he fell on the bed and kept laughing. Charlie stopped laughing, thinking how things had changed, and smiling.

There was a knock on his door. Charlie got up from the bed and checked outside to look for Gia's car. He saw nothing. He grabbed his forty-five out of his holster on the back of his belt and then grabbed his Glock-9 mm off the table nearby. He slowly approached the door as another knock was heard.

"Who is it?" Charlie asked aloud. He heard Frank, the ex-cop's voice, saying it was him. Charlie looked and backed away from the door. It seemed Bruno had recruited Frank and paid him to help him get Charlie and help him get into his room easily, but Charlie knew Frank had no way of knowing he was there.

"What do you want?" Charlie asked.

"I'm here to help you, Charlie. I know you're in trouble. So, c'mon open up," Frank said.

Charlie went up to the door and quietly unlocked it. Then he backed up again behind the bed for a better shot in case it was a setup.

"The door is open. Come on in, pal," Charlie said loud and clear as he had both his guns pointed at the door.

With that, the door flung open and three men and Frank came barging in with their guns drawn and looking to shoot.

Charlie fired first, blasting Frank in the chest and head. At the same time, he got the second guy in the doorway, hitting him all three times. As Charlie fired away, they just got off errant shots as they fell to the floor. The third man fired and shot Charlie in his upper chest near his shoulder, causing Charlie to move away firing his gun and putting a bullet in the third man's eye and chest sending him back and downward. The fourth man took aim at Charlie, who pushed the bed up and then fired at him four times with the .45 jamming on him. "Fuckin' forty-fives!" Charlie exclaimed, throwing the gun down thinking it was over, but seeing another shadow by the door quickly raising a gun to Charlie.

Charlie raised his nine-millimeter and Charlie could see that it was Bruno. As Bruno was firing, he hit Charlie twice in the chest sending him backwards with blood spurting out of his chest.

"DIE YOU FUCK!" Bruno yelled at Charlie.

Charlie fired his gun as he was falling backwards and he caught Bruno three times, "FUCK YOU, YOU BASTARD! YOU DIE THAT'S FROM GOOD TIME CHARLIE!" Charlie yelled back as Bruno was falling backwards, but not falling down. He grabbed onto the dresser draw, firing two more times and striking Charlie in his shoulder and hip. Charlie was raising himself against the wall, firing two more times at Bruno. He struck Bruno in the stomach and in his cheek. Bruno fired twice again, hitting Charlie in the leg and stomach. Both men were falling to the floor, but they both maintained their ground as they looked up at each other, staring at each other, giving each other a faint tough guy smile as they both raised their guns one more time. Both fired simultaneously, but only Charlie's shots caught Bruno twice in the head and Bruno went down, falling to the floor dead.

Charlie slowly slid down the wall that was keeping him up. Charlie laughed a low laugh as he looked at Bruno as he rolled down to the floor and on his side. He was going in and out of consciousness looking to see if there was anyone else to shoot, but he got them all. He then caught sight of the winning lotto ticket next to the television. He laughed to himself thinking that he would have only pissed it away on coke, booze, and women. He had been there and done that before.

About five minutes later, Gia pulled up with her Lexus and honked her horn as three police cars pulled up. She saw another car with a nun in it waiting as another police car pulled up.

"What the fuck is going on here!" Gia exclaimed. "Look at the place the asshole makes me come to," she said as she waited for Charlie to come down, thinking that with all this commotion she might have to go in and get him. Then she thought that maybe the cops were there to arrest Charlie and they would lock him up before she could get her money.

Up in Charlie's motel room, Sister Teresa was cradling Charlie in her arms with tears in her eyes and Charlie was listening to her talk. Sister Teresa always seemed to soothe him. It seemed she found out through a relative that worked with Bruno that Bruno was coming for him and she went there to warn him before Bruno got there.

"I'm sorry, my son. I came as quickly as I could. Can you forgive me?" she asked Charlie.

Charlie was unable to speak and he just nodded his head as tears filled his eyes. He was trying to direct Sister Teresa with his eyes as he kept pointing his eyes towards the television.

She wasn't catching on at first. "What Charlie?" she asked.

Charlie again motioned her with his eyes to the television set.

She looked at the set, went over, spotted the ticket, picked it up, and looked at Charlie.

Charlie nodded to her.

Sister Teresa went back to Charlie's side and asked him, "Are you trying to tell me son this ticket is a winner?"

Charlie nodded yes.

"I'll make sure your family gets it," Sister Teresa said.

Charlie was shaking his head no.

Sister Teresa was at a loss, not knowing what Charlie wanted her to do with it.

He motioned to her with his head and she finally realized what Charlie was saying.

"You want me to keep it?" she asked Charlie.

With that, Charlie nodded yes. He slid his hand towards hers and shook it slightly as to say I want you to have it.

She tucked it away in one of her pockets. Some people staying at the motel were filtering into the room with two cops coming in behind them. One cop started yelling to the curious people to clear the room. The other looked around at all the dead bodies and then saw Charlie still alive, as another cop came to the door.

"He needs an ambulance quick!" Sister Teresa said.

The cop at the door told her it should be here soon. The other cop looked at Charlie, and then told the Sister that she should administer last rites.

She began to pray as Charlie held her hand.

As she prayed for Charlie, Gia entered the room. "Oh, my God!" she exclaimed with one cop asking her who she was. She let him know that she was his ex-wife as she looked at Charlie on the floor, his bullet-ridden body soaked with blood. She stared at Charlie as the cop told her he was sorry and then he looked over the dead bodies around him.

Gia noticed an envelope on the table and she went over as Charlie was receiving last rites from Sister Teresa. The cops were busy with the crowd assembling outside the crime scene. Gia scooped up the envelope and put it in her purse, knowing that the money was in there that Charlie was to give her. "Is he going to make it?" Gia asked the cop. The cop shook his head, that it didn't look good. She then slipped out the door and left. She wasn't about to deal with any questions about Charlie or hang around to see if he would make it. She had things to do that night and wasn't about to be detoured into anything that had to do with her ex-husband, besides she could call later to find out if he lived.

Sister Teresa kept saying prayers for Charlie as he was thinking, Unfuckin' real! Time for Good Time Charlie to meet his mom and dad, just keep Tony away from me when I get there, and let the good times roll...

Suddenly Sister Teresa stopped as Charlie's grip on her hand loosened up and dropped to the floor. Charlie was dead. Sister Teresa closed Charlie's eyes.

"I'm sorry, Sister," said the cop to her.

"It's okay, he's finally walking with God!" she said as the cop put his hand on her arm a second and smiled to agree with her. The cop then got up and walked towards the door.

Sister Teresa was saying to Charlie, "Remember, that day you left the orphanage and said that someday you would make me proud of you. Today is the day, my son. I will put this to good use, Good Time Charlie."

One year later at St. Patrick's orphanage: Mother Superior was standing with Sister Teresa at a new wing just completed at the orphanage, now a tri-level building that included a large new playroom with an indoor basketball court, swimming pool, and all the amenities. Plus, all the rooms were completely renovated with new beds and furniture, along with a renovated playground with new swings and monkey bars.

"It's like a brand new orphanage," Mother Superior said.

"But still with that old cozy feel to it," Sister Teresa added.

They closed the lights to the new addition and walked outside into a bright sunny day.

"So, don't drink that much before you see the Pope, Sister," the Mother Superior said, smiling.

"Just a little wine," Sister Teresa said smiling.

Mother Superior told her to have a good time as she went into the original St. Patrick's Orphanage building, though it looked new on the outside with the recent work done to it. Sister Teresa closed the doors to the new St. Patrick's wing and walked over to the plaque beside the door and rubbed it for luck. The plaque read: "IN LOVING MEMORY OF OUR SON CHARLES A. LUZZI. GOD BLESS AND PROTECT HIM FOR HE KNEW NOT WHAT HE HAD DONE, BUT IN THE END HE FOUND GOD. Sister Teresa then walked down the steps to the street where a cab was waiting for her and she got in. She kissed her beads as she spoke under her breath, "Thank you, Good Time Charlie for the trip." Her eyes teared up as the cab driver drove away saying,

"Everything okay, Sister?"

"Yes, everything is fine. I'm just thinking about a friend of mine and when I meet with the Pope in Italy I want to say a prayer for him," she told the cabbie.

"Must be a heck of a guy. What's his name?" the driver asked.

"His name is Good Time Charlie," she told him.

"Hey, I know Good Time. He's a good guy. Is he okay?" the cabbie asked.

"Yes, he's fine," the Sister said after a long pause.

"When you see him, tell him I said hi," the cabbie said.

Sister Teresa smiled at the cabbie. "When I see him? I will...someday... *SOMEDAY SOON.*"

THE END

CHARLES A. COZZUPOLI

ABOUT THE AUTHOR

Charles Anthony Cozzupoli was born on 116th Street in Harlem, New York and educated in the public school system in both New York and New Jersey. Growing up and working in an Italian neighborhood, he was educated in the ways of the Mafia. He along with his father owned and operated a bar (most times after hours) in the Washington Heights section of New York City. He now resides in the Hudson Valley with his wife, Roseann. They are the proud grandparents of eight beautiful grandchildren.